Praise for Dreaming Beauty

"Well-written and carefully plotted." – *Jim Doran, author of* Kingdom *series*

"Beyond Disney…Beyond Grimm…Beyond imagining!" – *Bonnie K.T. Dillabough, author of* The Dimensional Alliance *series*

"Fabulous fairytale retelling!" – *Julie, Editor's review*

"It had me hooked from the very first page" – *NaDell, book store manager*

Books by C. Rae D'Arc

Dreaming Princesses
Dreaming Beauty
Fairest and the Frog

Haunted Romance
Don't Date the Haunted
Don't Marry the Cursed
Don't Dance with Death

* * *

Oz's Haunting Survival Book

FAIREST

AND THE

FROG

DREAMING PRINCESSES, BOOK 2

ISBN: 978-1-961733-04-6 (paperback)

Cover design by: Arcane Covers

Published by Bursting Box Publishing
BurstingBoxPublishing.com

To the Pearls of this world:
Let your light shine.

Map of Somnus

and surrounding kingdoms

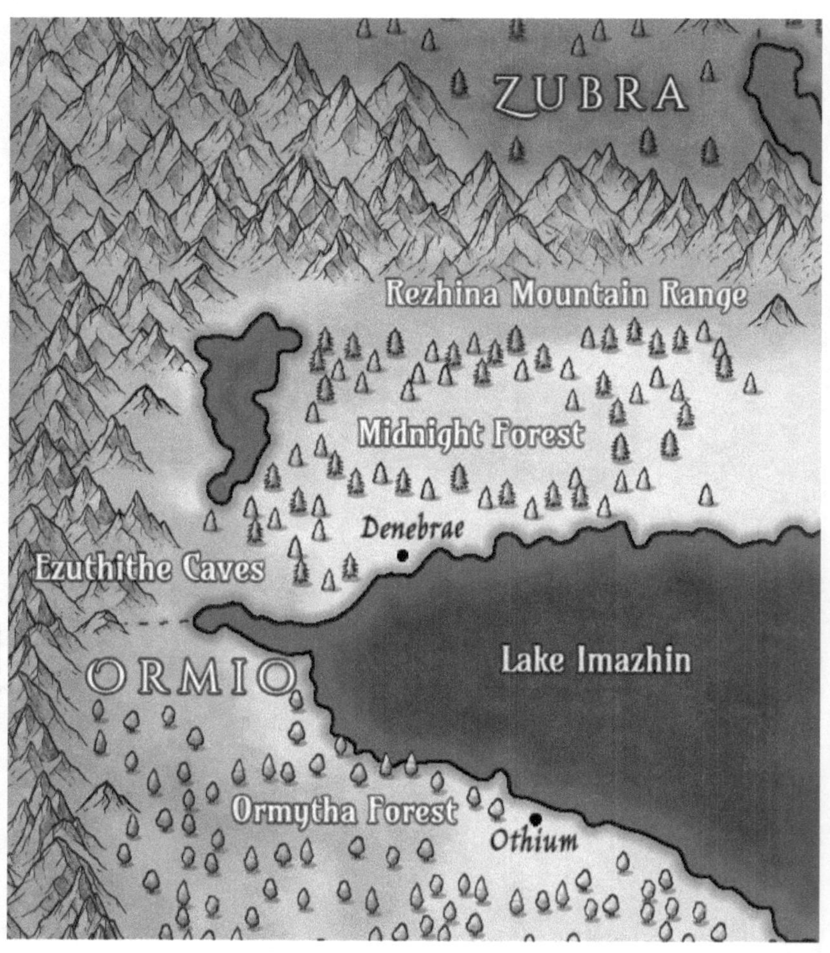

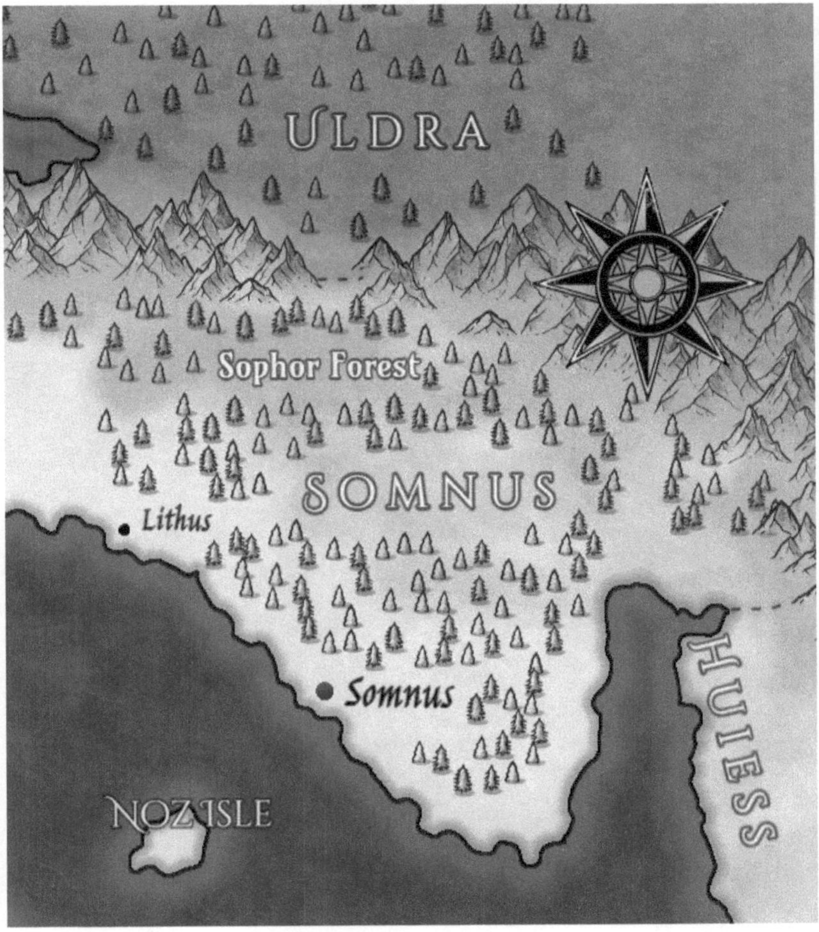

ULDRA
Sophor Forest
SOMNUS
Lithus
Somnus
NOZ ISLE
HUIESS

C. RAE D'ARC

PART 1

"And the princess…put [the frog] upon the pillow of her own little bed, where he slept all night long."
- *The Frog-Prince*, by Brothers Grimm

Chapter 1

MARIN

I loved everything about the water: the way it provided life for drinking, living places for fish, and livelihoods for sailors. I loved its moods, as calm as a still pool and as passionate as a storm. I loved it even as a butcher dumped his cartload of muck into the Imazhin Lake. Being downwind, I gagged on the scent of death. One day, soon, I would change the butchering practices. Perhaps today, if all went well.

"Marin," Ranae called to me. My husband's low ponytail slipped around his face as he bent over the dock to stare at something in the blue-green waters of Lake Imazhin. "Come look at this. I think this little guy needs help."

"What is it?" I asked, quickening my step to join him, grateful that I had worn my dock outfit and planned to change into my gown later. I wore a simple dark blue kirtle that opened wide under my arms and neck and was decorated with no more than a thick pink sash around my waist. My black hair was tied up with a matching ribbon. As much as I loved to dress up and glamorize, ball gowns and loose hair had no place on the docks. One never knew when a jump into the lake might be necessary.

I joined Ranae's side, enjoying the fresh water scent clinging to my husband's dark brown hair and admiral uniform. He pointed at the water with an arm that testified to his working experiences on warships. Only six months after our marriage, I still had to force my eyes away from his muscles to the object of interest. Something wriggled in the strands of sea leaves.

A frog.

I squealed and jumped back. Yes, I loved everything about the water...except the amphibians.

Ranae laughed. "Marin, he needs help. You saved eels before, yet you refuse to help a little frog?"

"I love all creatures of the sea," I said, "and would dive in head-first to save anything. Except a frog." Disgusting things, from their annoying and persistent croaks to their slippery squishy bodies, and from their nasty webbed feet to their bugged-out eyes. Please, remove them from my sight.

My husband stared hard at me, as though challenging me to do what I knew was the right despite the warts.

"Will you?" I asked.

Ranae rolled his eyes, then shucked off his red admiral tunic, black leather boots, and tan socks. He slid into the water as naturally as a merman. I stood on the other side of the dock, unwilling to watch Ranae struggle to free the little monster.

"There you go," he said softly. I smiled. As the Admiral of the Somnus Navy, Ranae Irving could be surprisingly tender when he wanted to be. He climbed back up to the dock, slumping across the wood to soak in the sun's rays.

"Thank you," I said, kneeling beside him and placing a quick kiss on his forehead. "You are my hero."

"Because I do your dirty work for you?"

I smirked back. "If saving a frog is my dirty work, that might make me a saint."

He sat up and teased me with one of his disarming smiles. "You might be. No one else refuses to eat meat for the sake of protecting our environment."

I shrugged. "I have no taste for things that once had beating hearts, and the butchery waste contaminates the lake."

Ranae's chuckle cut off as someone called his name. At last. *Liverthas* was fully docked and ready to be unloaded.

Ranae carried his tunic, boots, and socks over to the ship he had once captained.

After settling another skirmish between Ormio and Huiess, the great warship had docked at Ormio for some quick supplies. Transporting cargo was a menial job for the ship, though its timing had been convenient, and one could never be too careful when the cargo came from Ormio or Huiess.

Five men rolled three massive barrels down the dock to the loading bay. Ranae confirmed the reports with the captain while I tested the product. Three barrels of Ormio's finest wine.

"Excellent," I said, taking a sip from the third barrel. It was just as sweet as the first, with a touch of apple.

"Hold on." Ranae poked the ticklish spot in my side. "No samples. What if it was poisoned?"

I scoffed. "I highly doubt that these three barrels of wine sat on a ship full of sailors for an entire night without anyone sampling them."

Ranae laughed. "Good point. Should we get them up to the castle then?"

* * * * *

After delivering the wine barrels for Emer's party, Ranae and I went upstairs to change for the event. My sisters called me a chameleon (which were much better than frogs) for my tendency to change like the tides depending on the occasion. I smiled at the thought of my customized gown for Emer's birthday masquerade that evening. With royalty and dignitaries from all three kingdoms present, the gown would present me as a princess, someone with the influence and authority to create changes for the environment. I needed to appear as sane as possible when suggesting "insane" ideas such as hygienic and humane practices.

Ranae finished changing into his admiral's ceremonial uniform first. I slowed, distracted by how attractive he looked in his crisp red tabard with my father's crest of the Imazhin Lake Monster and Ezuthithe Cave Dragon. Ranae watched with a small smile as I removed my sash and kirtle.

"Will you just stand there, or do you plan to help?"

"I thought you would never ask."

Two long strides brought him to my side. His hands tickled me, and his mouth found mine.

"Ranae," I laughed and pushed him back. "We have no time for that."

He answered with a teasing grin.

Goddess above, I loved being married to him. He would make a wonderful father. Someday…

I turned away from him to pull out my customized green and blue bliaut. It was the same color as the Imazhin Lake and was decorated with silver threading that looked like waves around my neckline, the draping sleeves, and base. I kept my back to Ranae as I slipped it on and asked for his help on the laces. I released my hair from its updo, letting the wide curls drape around my shoulders. Then I turned around.

Ranae's eyes and mouth gaped. At the same time, a woman's voice cried.

"Help!"

We turned to the doorway. I was content to wait if someone else answered the woman's call first, though Ranae was at the door before the second call came.

"Help! Somebody!"

I followed Ranae out to the corridor. The castle seamstress stood at the corridor intersection, her grey hair frazzled from distress, her hand braced against the wall.

"Elisa," I called. "What is the matter?"

"Princess Emerald! She fainted and won't get up! Please, come!"

"Emer?" I panicked. Of course, she had fainted. She pushed herself too hard. I knew she should have let Garnet help. Garnet was only one person, except she knew how to delegate duties to all the right people. No, Emer just had to do everything herself.

Angry and frustrated with my first younger sister, I followed Elisa's hurried steps to the scent of stagnant soap water in the weaving room.

Emer lay on the stone floor, her brown gown ripped on the bottom, blonde hair loose and crumpled, and her right index finger bleeding.

"What happened?" I asked. "Why is she bleeding?"

"I asked her to grab the thread from the spinning wheel. She must have scraped herself."

I questioned her with my eyes. "And she fainted?" That made little sense.

Garnet entered the room, draped in flowing red and intricate golden embroidery. "Something happened to Emer?" she asked, slightly breathless.

Elisa repeated what little she knew, and Garnet went to inspect the spinning wheel. Frowning, she almost reached to touch the spindle, then pulled her hand away.

"Who else was in here?" she asked. "Nobody touch this spinning wheel until it has been examined. Ranae, go find a physician."

My husband gave a quick nod and sprinted away.

Elisa flustered. "What's wrong?"

Garnet pointed at the spinning wheel. "A strange slime coats the needle. It might be poisoned."

"Poisoned?" I cried. "How? By whom? For what purpose?" A hundred other questions raced through my mind, though I doubted anyone in the room knew the answers.

"Princess Tanzanite might have seen the culprit," Elisa offered. "She was in the room before Emer and I entered."

"Tanzi?" I asked. "If she was here not too long ago, where is she now?"

"I don't know," Elisa said, wringing sweaty hands in her wrinkled apron. Her aged voice shook a little more than usual with her unease. "I expected her to be the first to arrive."

Garnet knelt on the floor beside Emer and rotated her to lie flat on her back. She frowned. "I know of no such poison that acts this way. Where is that physician?"

I poked my head out to the corridor to check if my husband was on his way. Not yet.

Back to Garnet, I asked, "Is she still alive?"

Garnet broke a hair from her black strands and held it over Emer's mouth and nose. It wiggled ever so slightly.

"She still breathes," Garnet said, "though I cannot say for how much longer."

Heavy boots echoed down the corridor until Ranae arrived at the doorway, panting and sweating.

8

"In here," he said to the following physician.

The elderly physician looked over Emer, examining her finger, her hands, and the spindle of suspect.

"It's poison," he confirmed, "but what kind, I cannot say. I'll need to examine the substance in my laboratory."

"Is there a cure?" I asked.

He shook his head. "Unfortunately, I cannot know how to cure her until after I determine what's in the poison itself. All I can say for certain is that it's spreading quickly. If she was struck down instantaneously, I'm afraid we might lose her before nightfall."

I gasped, unable to bear the thought of losing Emer. On her birthday, of all days.

"What can we do for her?" Garnet asked.

The physician shrugged. "Let her sleep. Perhaps it's a blessing that she fell unconscious the moment the poison struck. I sense it would have spread even faster if she were awake."

"Unconscious," Garnet said, almost a whisper. If I knew Garnet any less than I did, I would have missed the hint of a plan in her quiet tone.

"Excuse me." She left the room with no explanation, though I had a guess.

As much as I wanted to follow her, I wanted to see to Emer's comfort first.

"Elisa, fetch two guards and a stretcher to carry Emer to her room."

"Of course, Your Highness." She bowed and exited.

With the physician bustling about the comatose Emer, I snuck into my husband's arms and buried my face in his chest. He was still a little damp from his quick run for the physician, though I needed his comforting strength. I barely managed to hold back my tears as my mind sank down a whirlpool.

How did this happen? Who would do such a thing?

Light footsteps clicked at the doorway. My youngest sister entered with an unreadable expression.

"Tanzi, there you are!" I said, stepping away from my husband. "Emer has been poisoned. All she did was scratch herself on the spinning wheel, then she collapsed."

My youngest sister gasped dramatically. If Garnet was the master of subtlety, Tanzi was the master of drama. She was in a phase where she treated life as a stage and she was the main player. There was no such thing as a small expression from her those days.

She fell to her knees beside Emer and sobbed without tears. "What tragedy has fallen on Emer?"

Considering my current emotions, it was nothing short of hypocritical to scold her passion, though Tanzi's over-performance irritated me. "She was

10

poisoned," I said. "The physician is working on her right now." I tried to sound hopeful.

I failed.

"Oh, the horror!" Tanzi cried with her hands to her cheeks. "What about the masquerade? It must continue as planned! Guests have already arrived."

Guests… Oh no. How could we celebrate at a time like this? How could we honor Emer's birth when she lay dying? On the other hand, how could we postpone the celebrations when Emer worked so hard to make everything perfect? How could we turn away guests who traveled across the valley to attend—who may take offense from our cancellation?

Overachieving Emer had invited dignitaries from all across Rezhina Valley, even the warring Huiess and Ormio Kingdoms. Somnus was fairly neutral through the skirmishes, though my worst worries had involved the others mocking my attempts to clean the lake or starting an all-out brawl in the ballroom. I never considered worse options, such as leaving them unentertained or turning them away.

"Tanzi," I asked, "did you see anyone else in the weaving room before you left?"

She squished her eyebrows and lips in a thoughtful pose. "Now that I think about it, yes. I saw someone in a hooded black cloak dodging around the corner before I came looking for Elisa."

"A black cloak?" I asked. With black cloaks never out of style, it could have been anyone. "Did you notice anything else? Whether they were a man or woman, how tall they were, or what kind of shoes they wore?"

Tanzi nodded. "I think it was a man. Was it the soul reaper, come to take away Emer?"

"Doubtful." I shuddered and pushed away thoughts of childish stories. "Anything else?"

She shook her head. "No."

"Great," I muttered. A man in a black cloak hardly narrowed our suspects, especially with guests arriving from all across the valley.

"Actually," she added, "I think there was an Ormio crest on his cloak. Why would the soul reaper wear an Ormio crest?"

"No reason at all, so rest your worries." Except the alternative was equally unnerving. Someone from Ormio had poisoned the spinning wheel? I frowned at that thought. Why? It was such a random little thing that was more likely to affect a servant. How did they know Emer would be the one to fall? Had Emer been poisoned by accident?

Until we knew for sure…"Tanzi, go tell Father and Mother what has happened. They will take care of the guests."

My youngest sister rolled rebellious eyes, yet headed off. Guards with a stretcher entered a moment later. I instructed them to be careful as they situated Emer onto the stretcher, then followed as they carried her upstairs to the bedchamber that she shared with our younger sisters, Pearl and Tanzi. Her complexion was pale as a ghost, though her index finger and right hand had turned an unnerving dark purple.

Pearl was in the bedchamber, still preparing for the ball and completely oblivious to recent events. As soon as we entered with Emer on the stretcher, she worried herself into tears. I explained everything I knew to her. Pearl wiped her large brown eyes and helped me to lift Emer to her fleece-stuffed mattress.

Garnet arrived and excused the guards before removing a small vial from her dress.

"Is that one of your sleeping potions?" Pearl asked.

"She is already asleep," I said. "Your potions are enough to knock out hardened soldiers until past sunrise. Do you know how it will affect someone who is already comatose?"

Our eldest sister clenched her teeth. "The physician said the poison is spreading quickly, though sleep has delayed it. We need time to identify the poison before we can determine the antidote. Putting Emer in a deeper sleep will give us time."

Pearl burst into a fresh load of tears.

I disliked the plan, yet saw no alternative. I nodded and helped Garnet to pour the potion down Emer's throat. We watched for a moment after, ensuring it worked. Emer's color slowly returned even while her breathing nearly disappeared.

Sniffling back her tears, Pearl drew Emer's woolen blankets around her shoulders. "Please wake up soon. Until then, sweet dreams, dear sister."

Chapter 2

EMER

Princess Emerald Reo woke to the sounds of Somnus, which were remarkably quiet compared to her bustling and confusing dreams of London. There was no constant hum of electric fans, no gurgles from plumbing within the walls, and no automobiles rushing down cobble streets.

There were also no sounds of pedestrians in the city markets nor fairy wings fluttering outside her window. No mermaids laughed from the Imazhin Lake as its calm waves lapped on the pebbled shore.

Instead, there was a distant clattering of pots and dishes as friends prepared breakfast in the castle kitchen below.

A hundred years had passed since Emer's sixteenth birthday, when she had pricked herself on a spindle poisoned by Tanzi, then put to sleep by Garnet. After all that time, she found it difficult to believe she was awake. Everything that happened after Caden had found her in her wildlife bedchamber felt surreal.

Not only had the castle been abandoned by her family, but the entire city had been abandoned by its citizens. The kingdoms of Somnus, Ormio, and even Huiess had fallen to the tyrannical clutches of her youngest sister, Tanzanite.

Of all people, Emer wondered, *little Tanzi?*

This strange alternate future of Somnus almost felt more dream-like than her dreams in England. In England, nothing had felt familiar. From the clothes to the buildings, from the lack of magic to the surplus of technology, and from the people's mannerisms to the mountainless landscape, everything had been foreign and beyond her imagination. The state of Somnus, however, was everything she remembered… in ruins.

Much had changed during Emer's hundred-year slumber. Since then, chaos reigned. Every heir of Somnus, Ormio, and Huiess was killed or put to sleep, leaving Tanzi alone to take the throne of the whole Rezhina Valley. Her mother, her father, and all who were most loyal to the true heirs of the valley were dead.

Emer slipped her hands across her linen blanket, soaking in the soft smooth fibers and the simple feel of it. She sat up and stretched, twisting her muscles, still

16

healing from her recent beating from Charlotte the ogress princess. Emer slouched to her bedchamber window overlooking the front courtyard. Quiet fog crept across the land, but she could pick out the pyre where Charlotte had tried to kill her…where Emer had pushed Charlotte to her death instead.

She stepped around the door the ogress had broken from its hinges and down the winding staircase. Continuing through the corridors, she followed the sounds of breakfast preparations, leading her to the smells of freshly baked bread and butter. She could almost taste the salted butter on warm wheat.

One corridor away, she heard a masculine voice roar.

"Are you mad?"

Emer smirked to herself, thinking the accused might be crazy, but the speaker was the one who sounded angry.

The angry voice continued, "We don't have time to chase after legends. Our people are dying today, and it will only get worse when the ogres find out what happened to Charlotte."

"That's exactly why we need to wake them," a calmer voice responded. Emer smiled as she recognized Caden's baritone voice. Despite his reluctance to rule, the Prince of Uldra had a way of speaking with authority when he wanted to. "We need allies in this valley, so the more princesses we wake, the more allies we'll have."

The first voice growled. "With princesses who've been dead for the past century? That wasn't the plan. We were supposed to—"

"Who do you think will be more likely to help us?" Caden interrupted. "A large number of princesses whom we save from poisonous sleep or a tyrant who wanted nothing to do with our kingdoms for the past century? Did you really think we'd convince Queen Tanzanite to help us?"

Emer stepped into the kitchen that was already crowded with Caden's entourage. Prince Caden Seaver wore a short tunic that matched his sky-blue eyes and thick riding trousers. Despite his travels, his black hair was groomed to a short cut above his ears and his full beard was maintained at a two-week trim. He jutted his chiseled chin at Prince Leo Bahr of the lost Braeder Kingdom, whose thick brown hair and thick beard had been left to the whims of sleeping positions. Caden was tall enough to look over Emer while slouching, but Leo was even taller, head and shoulders over Emer.

With Caden too busy shoving his face into Leo's, Mica noticed Emer's entrance first. Prince Mica Wright of the fallen Zubra Kingdom wore his usual padded joupon that disguised his muscled figure but matched his round face. His pre-maturely receding dark brown hair and dimples only added to the rounded effect. In typical Mica fashion, his finger poked Caden like a woodpecker for his attention.

"Did you really think Queen Tanzanite would fall for—what, Mica? Oh, good morning, Emer." Caden followed Mica's nudging and gestures to Emer's entrance. His face transformed from determined diplomat to welcoming lover as he stepped away from Leo and greeted her.

"We weren't finished yet, Seavers," Leo growled. "The question isn't who might be easier to persuade, but who do you think the people will follow? Princesses alone can't win a war. We need their people and resources."

Caden frowned and folded his arms over his chest. What Emer used to think was a doubtful expression, she learned was actually his manner of thinking things over.

"Emer already explained that we don't need to wake all of her sisters," Caden said. "Mostly Princesses Pearl and Garnet."

Leo shoved a pointed finger at Caden. "But you said no one knows where Garnet is. She could be dead, for all we know."

"Not probable," Emer said. "She was in my dream and more aware of my situation than I was. I believe she is alive."

"But do we have any idea where she is?" Leo argued.

"No," Emer admitted, "though Pearl or Marin might, and we know their general whereabouts."

Leo grumbled. "Pearl *or* Marin *might*. And we only know their *general* whereabouts?"

"We know Princess Pearl's in the Midnight Forest," Caden said. "So, we find and wake Princess Pearl. With her influence, we may gather some aid and strength to return north against the ogres. Is that satisfactory, Leo?"

The large man huffed. When his back turned, Caden whispered to Emer, "What he doesn't know is that on our way to Princess Pearl, we'll pass the general location of your sister, Princess Aquamarine." He winked.

Emer warmed at his tease and their shared hope to find her sisters. She wanted to find her sisters more than anything, except, "What about the ogres and the treaty with your kingdoms?"

Missing Emer's comment, Leo asked, "What are we supposed to do with the ogres attacking our kingdoms and coming after us for revenge on Charlotte while we wander through the forest?"

Caden grunted. "My father said he can postpone the treaty for one more month. Charlotte's parents knew she followed me into Rezhina Valley, but were worried when I returned without her. They think I'm searching to bring her home. I don't plan on telling them that she's dead until we return with our allies in force."

Prince Shinópu chose that moment to speak. Emer hadn't even noticed him sitting against the wall, cleaning his two curved swords. The former dwarf prince who'd been enslaved by Charlotte rarely spoke, making his two words all the more condemning. "Gother escaped."

"Oh." Emer cursed, "Beshrews."

"Beshrews is right," Leo growled. "Despite being her human slave, he was Charlotte's most devoted servant and a fighter too. You can bet he'll run straight to Uldra and survive to tell the ogres exactly what happened."

It was Caden's turn to grumble. "Then we'll have to move quickly. How soon will you be ready to leave, Emer?"

Emer raised her empty arms. "This is all I have." She remembered a similar scenario in England before Caden and Mica had whisked her away from Boscastle.

Caden squinted as if he also recollected the moment, and Emer smiled at the shared memory. Even if Prince Caden of Uldra was a different man from The Honorable Caden from England, he shared the same dreams. They were different men, yet so similar. Most importantly, they valued Emer the same.

Looking over her tattered attire, he muttered, "We'll find a proper gown to present you as a princess worth listening to."

A stout woman with dark features but a bright attitude stepped forward. Jesse was one of the finest servants Emer knew because she was also a friend. She added, "If Emer doesn't mind, I can alter some of Charlotte's gowns to fit her."

Emer cringed to think of wearing the dead ogress's clothes. At least they would be fashionable and the ogress's size gave Jesse a lot of material to trim and reuse.

"Thank you, Jesse," Emer said. "As disgusting as Charlotte was, I would be honored to wear anything of your handiwork."

Leo growled. "We don't have time to make dresses."

"Give me some credit," Jesse scoffed. "I can make alterations while we rest the horses."

"Speaking of horses," Mica said, "I believe Charlotte left us a full coach with four horses. The storage space and extra horses should make our travels quicker."

Caden nodded to the others. "Pack the coach. We'll start westward at noon."

With that settled, Emer joined the others for breakfast provided by Thachuma—a dwarf refugee who stood a couple of hand-spans shorter than Emer and sported a thin black goatee and a ponytail down to his waist. Most notably, he was a fantastic cook who could make a feast from the most meager of supplies. His wife, Jesse, helped with cleaning and serving. Emer spared a special smile for Jesse, partially for her fond memories of interacting with her in England.

Emer caught her arm as she passed with a bowl of fresh water from the pump. "How are you doing?" she asked. "Charlotte spared you no mercy."

Jesse shrugged. "It wasn't the first time the ogress princess threatened to eat us, but it was the closest she got. Thank you for saving us."

Emer didn't feel like a hero. She felt gross whenever she thought of Charlotte's horrible ending. Instead, she analyzed the wounds around Jesse's wrists, comparing them to her own. The evidence of Charlotte's brutal bindings were nearly healed away.

Still, Emer asked the nearby plants, "Healing moss, will you flourish and grow while we eat, that by the time our plates are empty, we may harvest a section of you to spread across our wounds?"

The moss between the crevices of the stone walls wiggled in response and began to spread itself. Jesse stared in awe. "No matter how many times I see your magical influence over plants, it always amazes me."

Emer grinned. "Me too."

Thachuma took the duty of personally serving breakfast to Shinópu, the only living heir to the lost kingdom of Zhafan. The quiet dwarf prince responded to the service with a silent nod.

As soon as breakfast was cleaned, Jesse and Emer slid moss around their wounds, then went to pack Charlotte's belongings. Emer wrestled with the idea of stealing from the ogress princess. She mostly wanted to remove any evidence of her presence from her father's castle. There was also the benefit of having more options for clothes, and the ogres had likely stolen the fabrics and possessions from the kingdoms they conquered, and there was the fact that Charlotte had tried to kill Emer... At least one of those justified the repossession in Emer's mind.

Thachuma had small finger foods prepared for lunch as everything was packed into the carriage. Between Charlotte's luggage and the princes' packs, there was only space for one person to sit in the carriage. The men suggested Emer sit inside, but she was too anxious to sit behind windows.

"Give the seat to Jesse," Emer said. "If Thachuma stands on the back, Caden and I may drive the carriage."

For some reason, Caden frowned at her suggestion. "That would put Shinópu on my horse, who doesn't like anyone else handling him."

Despite her efforts to remain stoic, Emer's countenance fell. "Oh. I had hoped to discuss more with you about finding my sisters."

"Er…" Caden squirmed. "Would you, er, like to join me on my horse?"

Emer blushed a little at the thought of sitting behind Caden on the same horse. She expected driving the carriage to be like a casual discussion in a sitting room. Sitting directly behind Caden—wrapping her arms around him for support—was more intimate and less conducive for casual theorizing. Still, she pinched her lips to hide her emotions and nodded.

She tried to restrain her nerves as everyone prepared their horses. Shinópu and Thachuma sat on top of the carriage while Jesse took the seat inside. She gathered one of Charlotte's dresses and some supplies, saying she'd work on the alterations during the drive. Leo and Mica saddled their own horses. Caden took his seat first, then reached down to help Emer up. She took his hand, disappointed he wore riding gloves already. She swung her leg over, stretching her dress to make sure it appropriately covered her ankles. Despite the problems caused by her lost sense of touch while dreaming, she almost wished for her hypoesthesia to return as she became too aware of her legs against Caden and the heat emanating off of him. She accidentally rocked her heel against the horse's flanks, jolting it forward.

Emer's hands impulsively braced herself, tightening around Caden's waist and pressing herself into his back.

Caden calmed his horse with some words and patting before twisting toward Emer. "Performing your own stunts, are you?" he asked with a wink.

Emer's blush exploded. The quote from their English dreams referred to a time Caden had caught her from one of her many falls. Losing the ability to feel anything had made her quite clumsy in England. She consciously loosened her arms around his waist and cleared her throat.

"How are we supposed to find my sisters?" she asked. "Even if we have the hints that they sleep somewhere along the northern shores of Lake Imazhin, it would take months to search every room in every building in Somnus alone, not to mention the cities of Lithus and Denebrae and the forests surrounding. My sisters went into hiding. I know them better than anyone, but even I have no idea where they might have gone."

"We shouldn't need to search every room in every building," Caden said. "There's a theory that each of you is surrounded by a curse. Thorns surrounded your castle, centered around your location. I believe that the forest near the town of Denebrae was renamed the Midnight Forest because it's where Princess Pearl resides. I'm confident that if we do a broad search through the city streets, we'll find some unnatural phenomenon where the other princesses lay."

"Oh," Emer said. "I wish I had known that when searching for my sisters while you were gone. I would have been less meticulous and wasted less time."

Caden shrugged. "It's only a theory."

Emer looked back towards the lake. "Is the mist one of these unnatural phenomenons? Perhaps Marin is somewhere in the lake." That actually made the most sense to Emer.

Caden slid his hand across the back of his head. "I don't think so. I found some more records during our last visit in Uldra. The mist is supposedly centered around Noz Isle and has some sleeping spell on it. Anyone who tries to sail to the island finds themselves falling asleep. It's one of Queen Tanzanite's defenses to keep anyone from sneaking up on her, allowing her to capture visitors in their sleep."

"Interesting," Emer said, "and terrifying. How close to the island do we need to go until the spell takes over?"

Caden shrugged again. "Not sure, but I'm not volunteering to experiment."

Emer agreed. "I had a lot of time to think and search on my own while you were gone. My sisters might have rested in my father's favorite inn, but it was destroyed. I think their next place to seek refuge would have been at the lake, on the ship *Liverthas*."

Caden twisted in his seat to look back at her for confirmation. "The lake? Are you sure?"

"It was like any other body of water before my hundred-year slumber." Well, not every other body of water, Emer mentally corrected. She reflected on the ocean from her dream, the great grey waters with a never-ending horizon. She wished Marin could have seen it.

Chapter 3

MARIN

My least favorite dreams were those where I lost my teeth. Each night after I lost a baby tooth, I dreamt of my teeth coming loose and falling out. I always tried to keep them in place with my tongue, allowing spit to gather in my mouth as I became too scared to swallow and choke on my own teeth.

Imagine my disgust and horror when consciousness returned to me for the day, only to find a loose tooth in my mouth.

I sat up quickly and spat it out. It bounced off of the wooden floor with a clink-clunk. I stared at it and felt at the new hole in my mouth. It was one of my front teeth.

How had that happened? How does one lose an adult tooth in their sleep?

I reflected on my dream. It was easy to remember. Nightmares usually were. I had been on the run with my sisters, though Emer had been missing. Tanzi

29

asked me to fetch some water, tossing me a pail. It had hit my face—my tooth. Then I had fallen into darkness without end.

I stretched my eyes awake, blinking a couple more times, struggling to remember… Where was I?

Instead of my bedchambers, I sat up in a small cottage room with a stone fireplace of dying embers, a rocking chair in the corner, and a deep green rug across the wooden flooring.

The other objects in the room were even less familiar. A black and shiny rectangular object covered most of the stone wall above the fireplace. A strange round device sat on the nightstand beside me, showcasing the numbers "7:13" with an odd blue glow. There was also a flat black box with a long string attached to one end, leading to the wall. A similar string connected another object to the wall. The second object looked like someone had put a cone hat on a vase.

I wondered again where I was and how I arrived there. Pulling back my covers, I screamed.

Croak.

I scrambled out of the bed, screaming all the more.

"Marin!" the frog croaked, somehow speaking coherent words while his oversized mouth croaked again. "What is the matter?"

"What is the matter?" I screeched. "Help! Guards! A *talking frog* is in my bed and it knows my name!"

"We have a frog in the bed?" The frog jumped and searched about.

No guards came to my aid. Where were they? My father had posted guards outside our chambers ever since he noticed our tattered shoes from escaping to the midnight masquerades. We always had guards to sneak past, especially when traveling.

"Guards!" I called again, hoping they were merely delayed. I backed away from the bed, nearly stumbling on the rug in my hurry. The nasty little creature hopped on the bed I had recently vacated. I made it to the door and shut myself out. The guards would take care of it. Wherever they were…

I passed no one in the hallway, even as it opened up to a small seating area with another large black rectangle on the wall. Just beyond that was a decent sized kitchen with multiple metallic appliances.

Forget the guards. Where was I? Never before had I seen a kitchen so clean despite the dishes in the sink. No smoke-stained walls, no blood or flour spotting the counters, not even grime on the floor. Only fingerprints smudged the smooth surfaces. A window on my right announced the outside world, encouraging me to go through the door beside it.

The world outside greeted me with one of the most captivating and beautiful sights of my life. I stood on a wide stepping stone before a fresh green lawn. It broke away below my sight as the land dropped off. Then…

Water. So much of it that it stretched far beyond my sight to my right, to my left, and all before me. Unlike Imazhin Lake, this water smelled strongly of salt and brought a chilly breeze with its curling waves. A scattering of clouds caught the sun's rays from the opposite horizon, blocked by the cottage.

The nightmare of loose teeth and frogs in the bed had turned into paradise. I had died and gone to heaven. It all fit except for the tooth and frog.

Where else could I find such a blue horizon without a single jagged mountain in sight? Surely nowhere in the Rezhina Valley.

Forcing my eyes to break away from the view of perfection, I started around the cottage to the front. Everything about the home was quaint: the small wooden door, the flower vines crawling up the edges, and the miniature windmill. The only piece that stood out was the strange carriage resting on a section of loose rocks. The carriage was made entirely of shiny blue metal—no wood, even for the wheels. I felt at the black wheels, unable to determine its material. I tried the door handle, though it refused to open. Locked?

A low hum entered my ear. I stepped farther from the front entry of the cottage towards the sound. It grew in volume and in pitch. The pathway of rocks extended to a black path with white stripes. A road? How was it so smooth?

A black version of the metal carriage rounded the bend in the road, entering my view between the bushes. It had no horses, yet it moved faster than any carriage.

I yelped as its hum increased and it raced by. Another one—a grey one—followed close behind.

Whatever they were, I did not want to wait for them to come back. I went back to the house through the front door, creeping my way through the little rooms. I found a broom and wielded it like a weapon as I checked for the frog. If it was still in the cottage, I had scared it into silence. I shut the back door and locked the bolt.

What was this place I voluntarily locked myself into?

I explored the house, intrigued by the metallic devices in the kitchen. The large box in the corner caught my eye the most. Its double doors on top and bottom drawer looked like the shiniest wardrobe. Why would a wardrobe be in the kitchen? I opened one of the top doors, surprised to find cool air and food inside. Was that milk in a glass bottle? There were several more glass containers with varieties of fruits and vegetables. All of them had "organic" on their labels. I smiled when I found no meat. Whoever stocked this cold storage knew my tastes. Closing the door to keep the cold inside, I noticed a little quote attached to the side.

I read, "'The time will come when men such as I will look upon the murder of animals as they now look upon the murder of men.' - Leonardo Da Vinci." Whoever he was, I hoped he was right.

If I had my way, I would ban butcheries from within city boundaries. Not only did they stink something awful, scar children with the sight of slaughter, and create waste second only to sewage, they also openly carted their bloody entrails and carcasses through the town to dispose of them in the lake. This was an improvement to leaving them in the alleys, though I worried about the lasting effects on the lake. Not to mention the pieces that often fell off the carts, and their traveling stench. I found the whole process disgusting and uncivilized.

I pondered on the words of Mr. Da Vinci a moment longer before moving to the next object. On the counter were several smaller metallic devices. One called itself a compost bin. Another was a toastmaster. At least the knives were familiar, even if these were particularly shiny like they came straight from the blacksmith. They also hung directly on the wall without any support. I grabbed one and pulled it away with a little tug. Magnets? I set the knife back, amazed that it stuck to the wall as before, then continued down the counters to the sink. Even the sink was metallic. Next to it was yet another metal object of crisscrossing wires. A single plate, cup, and four-pronged fork rested on top. What kind of place was this, with seemingly unlimited metals they used even for drying their dishes?

Nestled between the cabinets was a device that made absolutely no sense to me; another metal box with a door and numbers. It had a simple glass plate inside. Curious, I pressed on the word "start."

The thing came to life with light and a humming sound!

I jumped back and yelped, staring at the numbers that counted down from thirty.

What was it doing? What was it counting down to? What would happen when it was over?

I stepped to the back door, keeping my eyes on the humming box. I reached for the door handle in case I needed to run when it reached zero.

3…2…1… It announced "END" and beeped with a high pitch. Nothing else happened. Cautiously, I stepped closer. Two steps away, it repeated its beeping. I jumped, shocked and heart pulsing. It seemed to do nothing else. I hit the word "Stop," and the "END" announcement was replaced with static numbers. Was it a timer then? After another five minutes of staring at the timer box and nothing happening, I decided it was safe to resume my exploration through the kitchen.

A pile of papers sat in a small alcove of counter space. Underneath was a small box labeled "Recycling" with several papers tossed inside. I picked apart the unfamiliar word, intrigued by the concept. Yes, if we simply reused our waste, then less of it would end up in our lake.

Examining a few of the discarded envelopes, I noticed some similarities. They listed "Current Resident" or the name "Maureen Irving" as the recipient. Irving was Ranae's last name, though who was Maureen? A confusing address of numbers and letters followed, almost like a code. The easiest part to decipher, "Ellenborough, Maryport, UK," gave me no clues to where I was.

Behind the pile of papers sat a little picture in a simple frame. For something no bigger than my hand, it was remarkably detailed. What artist had painted such realistic visions?

I picked it up and studied it, confused. It was a picture of me perhaps a couple years ago. I was grinning widely, standing in front of a boat named

Liberation. The boat was unlike anything that sailed the Imazhin Lake. It was white without the seams of wood and had metal for its railing. Surprise, surprise. More metal.

I studied myself in the picture. How was it possible? Some incredibly talented artist painted me as a younger woman in front of some fantasy boat?

Nothing made sense.

Where was I, and how did I get here?

I returned to my explorations, finding a complicated lavatory. What was with this place and its white metals? Was there a mine nearby to make the materials? There were also several bottles made of a translucent and flexible material. One labeled as "antibacterial hand soap" gave the most complicated descriptions of soap. Having never used liquid soap before, the concept intrigued me.

Still, my mind kept returning to the sight of the great water beyond. I set down the bottle called "Conditioner" and went to the window. Peering between odd curtains of white slats confirmed my expectations. That great blue was still there.

Stepping back outside, my attention became captured by the waterscape. I needed to see it in person. I needed to know it was real.

I walked towards it, passing the defined line between trimmed grass and wild grass. Emer might have stopped to analyze the differences, though my eyes stayed on the blue horizon. At least until I almost tripped over the square poles on the ground. Two of them laid parallel, lined with wooden planks below. Nothing happened as I stepped over it, so I allowed my focus to return to the sea.

The grasses cliffed for a meter down to a beach made of more rocks than sand. Despite the evening sun, the breeze was cool. Squinting, I could barely pick out mountains and land on the other side of the water. Was this Imazhin Lake? No. It was saltier and greyer than the blue-green tones of the Imazhin.

I sat on the stony ground, content to stare the day away with the one thing that was familiar: the water.

Time slipped away between the calming breaths of the waves. In…out…in…out.

The sun began to land on the horizon when a sound of cacophony grew from the distance. It came from behind me and grew louder. I searched for the source of the noise, finding only a single object coming closer. It was massive. A tube of blue and purple rolled on the parallel poles that I stumbled on earlier.

Worry rumbled through my heart as the beast roared closer. Was I allowed to be there? What would happen if it caught me?

I crouched against the little cliff where the grass dropped to the beach. The beastly noisemaker zipped past with the speed of our fastest horses—maybe faster. It had three compartments tagged with the single word "Northern."

Although Somnus was on the northern side of Imazhin Lake, nowhere in Rezhina Valley was there a beast like that.

Troubled, I waited until the beast was far from sight and sound, then ran back to the house, crouching in case anyone was around. The house was lit in red. Before sneaking back inside, I turned around to catch the glory of a red sun reflecting off the water and clouds. It was absolutely beautiful. A thought crept into the corner of my mind wishing to share the experience with someone…someone special…someone I loved.

"Ugh, this is a nightmare."

I turned towards the voice, finding the same brown frog that stole into my bed that morning. It crawled, too tired to jump up the patio edge within kicking distance of my feet. I screamed.

"Wait, Marin! Wait!"

"How do you speak? How do you know my name?" I screamed, grabbing the back door and swinging myself inside. "Get away from me!"

"Marin, wait! It is me, Ranae!"

Ranae? That name slammed into me like a gust of wind.

One motion away from shoving the door closed, I slowly widened it, unable to connect the nasty little creature to the man I loved.

"Ranae?" I asked, half terrified for the answer.

The frog croaked.

I screamed and slammed the door shut.

"Wait, Marin! Do not leave me!" the frog cried outside the door. "I know you hate frogs, but please? Beshrews, I might hate frogs too after this. This body is exhausting. I jump so high, and only go so far. Marin, are you still there?"

I stood on the other side of the door, recognizing the voice of my husband. On one thing, we agreed. "This is a nightmare," I whispered. The man I loved had been turned into the thing I hated.

My tongue absently went to the hole in my mouth where I had lost my tooth earlier. Feeling at the gap and tender gums, I nudged another tooth. It wiggled loosely.

Fear spiked through my heart as I realized the truth.

It was a nightmare set on the most beautiful seaside.

I was dreaming.

Even after pinching myself, I remained in the dream where my husband was a frog. I slapped my cheeks, yet the nearby seashore continued to wave in and out.

Ignoring Ranae's froggy voice outside, I made my way to the bedchamber. "I will lie down and go to sleep. Then, when I wake up, this will all be over."

"It will not work, Marin," Ranae called from outside. "We are in a deeper sleep. This is no normal dream."

As if the incredible details of this dream were not enough to prove that. No matter. I had no other ideas, so I had to try.

"Good night, Ranae," I murmured, laying down on the softest bed I had ever known. "When I wake, I will find your arms around me. I will tell you of my dreams and we will begin the day with a laugh."

Chapter 4

MARIN

Ranae's froggy voice continued to call to me in the bedroom. I shut him out, forcing away the images of amphibians and loose teeth. It was a dream. Only a dream. I would fall asleep and wake with my manly husband and no holes in my smile.

I succeeded in falling asleep, though failed on every other account. When I awoke, another tooth was loose in my mouth. I sat up to spit it out as something plopped onto my lap. A frog.

Screaming, I tossed my blanket to throw the little monster across the room.

The voice of my husband yelled back as he smacked against the wall.

"Get out of here!" I screamed at the creature.

"Marin, please—"

"Why is this happening?" I cried. "Why are you a frog? Why are my teeth falling out? Why am I here?"

"Beshrews if I know," he shouted back with his admiral tone while his froggy mouth simply croaked. "By the goddesses, just listen to me for one beshrewing second, then we can make these beshrewing beshrews stop!"

I blinked at the frog. Ranae never talked to me that way before. I knew sailors could swear up a storm, though Ranae had always held his tongue around me.

Go figure, as a frog, his tongue was looser.

Ranae let out a little croak, almost like a shy clearing of his throat. "That might have been uncalled for."

"To put it lightly," I said, still in shock. That was probably the closest the admiral would say to "sorry."

"I hate this body as much as you do," he said. "Jumping around, my eyes pointed in different directions, an annoying desire to eat bugs—"

"Please, stop." Each of his descriptions tested my gag reflexes.

"Worst of all," he said, "is your hate for me."

I wanted to argue his words, yet managed to only work my jaw wordlessly. I did not hate him. I simply detested the sight of him.

"Marin, please," he croaked. "Look at me."

I clenched my teeth, feeling another loose one, then swallowed back the bile. Squeezing my eyes shut, I took a deep breath. Opening my eyes again, I steeled my nerves as I turned towards the muddy brown, bumpy, webbed, bug-eyed, wide-mouthed thing.

Something wet slid down the side of his neck. Was it a tear? As much as the thought of mucus disgusted me, I hated the thought of him crying even more.

"Please, do not push me away again," he said. "I need you."

"Ranae, I—" As much as I wanted to argue his words, to keep him near me and say that I never wanted him to leave, I could not bear the sight of him. The protruding eyes, blubbery body, disproportional legs… One of my own tears escaped my eyes.

"I love you, Marin. I always will. The last six months of being married to you have been my happiest—no contest—despite the guilt that ate at me, saying that I brought you down and you deserved better."

"No. Stop lying to yourself," I said. Those words I would argue. I would not allow him to taint the beautiful time we had spent together. I cherished our marriage and never thought of him as inferior. "If you love me and think I deserve to be happy, then we will work together to break this curse."

His eyes twitched back and forth, as if he was undecided whether to focus on me with his left or right eye. Ugh, he made me want to puke.

44

"Good," he said, "because I may know how, but I need help."

"How?" I asked, almost desperate enough to step closer with eagerness. Almost.

"We need to sail to the Well of the World's End, then take a drink from it using a sieve."

I blinked at him and sorted through his words. I rarely questioned authority and orders, except this was absurd. "We need to drink from the Well of the World's End…using a sieve?" Sieves were used for sifting flour and pebbles. They had holes. How were we supposed to drink from one? Not wanting to sound argumentative, I simply asked, "How?"

"First, we need a ship," he said.

"Yes, that much is obvious. How are we supposed to drink from a sieve?"

The frog held up one of his webbed front feet. "I can coat it with my mucus to keep the water from dripping through."

Mucus…Frog mucus…Drinking from a sieve… Coated. With. Frog. Mucus.

Outside was too far away. I threw up on the smooth wooden floor of the bedchamber. A tooth came free and added blood to my vomit.

"Ew," Ranae said. "And you call me the disgusting one?"

I wiped my mouth and cried, "You are what made me vomit!"

He may have winced. I was too busy not looking at him to notice.

My instincts wanted to ask a maid to clean my floor mess. As if this nightmare would allow such a luxury. Biting back my complaints, I found a towel from the next room to clean up the mess. Ranae simply watched.

"We should focus on step one of getting a ship first," I said, focusing on cleaning. "How do you know about the well?"

"That, I do not know."

I disliked that answer, though what could I do about it? "Whoever designed this nightmare, I give full marks for detail. However, it detrimentally lacks in pleasantness."

"Agreed," Ranae echoed. I was in no mood to take the towel all the way to the shore for cleaning, so I left it outside.

"Hold on," I said, remembering something. "I might know where we can find a ship."

Returning to the kitchen, I did my best to ignore his hopping after me. I sifted through the counter pile of papers, briefly amused by the name Maureen Irving. With my higher status, Ranae had taken my surname instead. At least in this dream, I could take his name to demonstrate my love and respect for him.

I searched the envelopes for the word that caught my interest before. There was also the picture of me with the boat. Did I own that boat? Where was it docked?

An envelope gave me a clue: Maryport Marina. Where was that?

"Marin, there are maps down here."

I started to bend down to look under the counter, until I realized that action brought my face closer to the frog. I paused.

"What?"

"Could you...back away?"

He tilted his flat face at me. "Are you scared I might jump at your face?"

"Yes."

"I will not."

I clenched my teeth, very aware of the three missing. "Please."

With a croaking sigh, the frog jumped back. Satisfied, I leaned down to pull out a box of maps from behind the recycle bin. They were all rolled, colorful, and made of some glossy material or crisp paper. I unrolled them and used random devices from the counters to weigh down the edges. The more I saw, the more I realized, "I have no idea where we are."

"Let me see," Ranae said. It was my only warning before a frog jumped onto the kitchen counter.

I screamed and shoved myself away.

"What?" he asked.

With my back against the doors of the cold box and my hand to my chest, I struggled to calm my heart. "I will never get used to you being a frog, and frogs do not belong on cooking surfaces!"

He grunted. "Unless we are the meal."

"Ew-ew-ew!"

"Are you going to puke again?"

"Do not push me," I said, resting my other hand to my head, willing it to cool. Cleaning up my own vomit was an experience I wished not to repeat.

Steeling my stomach, I examined the maps again. One labeled the Maryport Marina next to the Lake District Coast Aquarium. Another map detailed a large island, called Isle of Man. Yet another showed a great city port named Belfast, Ireland.

I never heard of any of those names before. "Is the Well of the World on any of these?"

His beady eyes twitched over the maps. "Warning, I need a higher vantage point." He jumped to look at the maps from above, like a normal human. The jump only gave him a second in the air, leaving him to jump, over and over to gain the scope he wanted.

I had to close my eyes and turn away during his jumping.

"Are you done yet?" I asked.

"I could always sit on top of your head."

I grimaced and shuddered.

He jumped one more time, then made a soft rumbling sound. "These maps might be outdated. Why else would they be off the ship and shoved in a dark corner?"

"Outdated or not," I said, "I doubt that we are dealing with familiar waters."

The frog nodded. "I say we eat lunch, then head outside. Someone might direct us to the marina, where they are sure to have accurate maps."

That much, I could agree. After throwing up with an empty stomach, I was starved. I opened the doors to the cold food storage and pulled out a few plant-looking things. The leafy greens were bland, yet crunchy. Not much different from Somnus's leafy greens.

I recognized one piece of fruit though. An apple. I took a bite and paused. It was so juicy and sweet!

I took another bite and heard a crack. The sound came with a sick feeling within my jaw and echoed through my skull.

"Agh!" I cupped a napkin under my mouth and faced downward, spitting out my food. In the middle of the slightly mushed apple chunk was a piece of white bone.

I rolled my tongue through my mouth. Sure enough, one of my molars had chipped.

I stared at the white bit in my napkin for a gross amount of time. I felt the gap in my teeth just as I felt the napkin in my hand. Had I chipped these teeth in real life, or were these just part of the dream?

"Are you all right?"

"I broke another tooth," I said.

"Another one?"

"It is my fourth one already. Goddesses, I hate this dream." Breaking my teeth on forgotten bones and the filthiness of butchery were two of the many reasons I removed meat from my diet. Almost every meal included a small piece that had escaped the deboning process. It was like biting on a rock when I expected something squishy. Then there was the disgusting task of spitting it out, terrified that I might accidentally swallow it and choke to death on my own food.

"At least you have teeth," Ranae croaked.

I took another bite of the apple, chewing more carefully this time. "After lunch, I propose that we venture forth to find the location of the marina. If I receive mail from there, I hope that means I have connections to a boat."

Chapter 5

EMER

"I want to explore the docks before crossing it off the list of possibilities."

Caden and the others shared worried glances to Emer's request.

"What if," Emer suggested, "I go in with a compass. Maybe I can hold onto a rope secured to something outside the mist."

Mica shrugged. "I'm in favor of the rope idea."

Emer smirked, thinking of a moment in England when Mica had saved her by packing a coil of rope.

Leo folded his arms. "I think this whole thing is foolish. If you want to wander through the mist, go ahead, but I'm keeping the horses and carriage outside the thick of it."

Caden shrugged. "That's not a bad idea. We'll need someone in the clear. In fact, I suggest we split into three groups. Leo, Thachuma, and Jesse can stay with the carriage where the visibility is enough to see to the next block. Shinópu and Mica can stand farther in—just at the edge of Leo's sight. They will hold one end of a rope while Emer and I hold the other, exploring the docks. As much as I don't want to risk Emer in the mist, she's the most likely to recognize any clues left by her sisters. I will accompany her in case anything happens."

Leo nodded despite his frown.

Mica said, "Sounds like a plan."

"Be careful," Jesse added.

Emer gave Caden a determined smile, and they headed south, towards the lake.

They didn't need to go far before the mist thickened and their visibility clouded. Leo pulled his horse to a stop.

"This is as far as I go. Only take what you need. I don't want to be left without supplies when you loons get lost and die in there."

Caden grunted with annoyance, but pulled his horse to a stop and dismounted. "Heaven forbid we take a detour to shorten the rest of our travels. How about this, Leo? You can set up camp, rest the horses, and enjoy a lunch break until we return. If we don't return by night fall, I give you permission to take the carriage and storm back to Uldra."

Leo grumbled. "As if I would be welcomed when I returned to your homeland without you?"

Mica chuckled. "It's good to hear how much you need us. You make a man wonder sometimes."

Caden reached up to help Emer dismount. She smiled, appreciating the courtesy and remembering times when he had helped her up from the low seats of England's vehicles.

Jesse wished her good luck again as Mica removed a coil of rope from his saddle.

"Thachuma," Mica called to the dwarf cook. "Shinópu and I will only go to the edge of your sight at that shop corner, but keep an ear open for us. We all know how Leo's hearing is."

Leo leaned back with casual interest. "Did you say something?"

"Exactly." Mica grinned and winked at Thachuma.

The fairies in Emer's stomach relaxed slightly at Mica's humor. The last time she had approached the docks, the mist had swallowed everything in sight. Similar to last time, the trees stilled as they walked farther into the white. No breeze stirred the debris. No critters scattered from their approach. Buildings became forms of shadows in the distance.

"Good thing," Mica said, his cheery voice loud in the eerie silence, "we came during the day."

"Good thing," Caden muttered to agree.

The silent dwarf prince only became more silent, walking with barely a whisper. His stealthy hardness reminded Emer of the stories told by the Huiess princesses about their king's assassins, silent as shadows and deadly as monsters. It helped little to ask her father about them as he confirmed the stories with facts.

"Be careful," he had warned, "of a knight that is too still." Or had he meant "night?"

Emer shivered even in the daytime as the mist grew thicker. They reached the edge of Leo's sight, looking back to see his form—a mere shadow—discernible only by his restless pacing. Ahead, Emer knew the loading bay separated them from the piers, but the great ships were lost in the mist.

"Alright," Mica said, dropping the coil of rope. Picking out the ends, he handed one to Caden and kept the other. "Don't get lost in there. I know you have the directional senses of a rock, but as long as you hold onto the rope, you should be able to find your way back."

Caden smirked in reply. He held the rope to Emer, gesturing for her to take hold of it. She grabbed the rope behind Caden's hand, standing beside him with the rope between them as they stepped farther into the mist.

Turning back to Shinópu, Caden said, "If any trouble rises, this guy—" he gestured at Mica "—becomes a hopeless mess. We're counting on you to keep him safe to lead us back."

Mica stuck out his tongue at his friend, barely visible as the mist clouded the space between them. "If Emer wasn't going with you, I'd be tempted to tie my end to a cart of manure. Hey, Shinópu, want to help me find a cart of manure?"

"Nah-ah," Caden laughed. "You can't see it, but I'm wagging my finger at you. Don't forget, we're in the presence of a princess. Best behavior now."

"Same to you," Mica called. "I know what happens when you two go off on your own."

By most accounts, Caden had ignored the last jab. Emer knew otherwise as she stepped beside him and saw his neck burn red. They had only gone a few steps, but Mica and Shinópu were already barely visible. They reached the docks and the mist became thick enough to whiten Caden beside Emer. Afraid of losing sight of him, she slipped her hand up the rope to hold Caden's hand instead. She couldn't quite catch the meaning of his quick smile and glance.

Emer's body began to weigh heavier. Walking upright became a chore. She had enough energy to set a sail, but the process would be sluggish. It became hard to focus when her desire for rest slipped between every thought for her sisters.

"Leo said," she recounted to Caden, "your original plan was to sail to Noz Isle…to ask Tanzi for help against the ogres. How did you plan to sail with these lethargic feelings?"

"We, er," he slurred with drowsiness, "didn't know about the curse on the lake…until our last trip from Uldra. We ran into some…local tradesmen. They told us about the curse."

One more dock over would be the berth of Ranae's old ship, *Liverthas*. It was Somnus's largest ship, fit for war, and suitable for quick speeds.

They reached the edge of the dock when the rope tightened.

"End of the line," Caden said.

The mist hid any ships secured to the dock.

Emer bit her lip in frustration. "We came this far to stop here? Hold onto the rope with one hand and stretch me outward."

"I don't think a meter or two will make much of a difference."

Emer grumbled. He was probably right. She bent to examine the wooden planks below her. "We are on the dock. There is only one way on and off. I should not become lost if I wander from here."

56

"I don't think that's a good idea," Caden said. "Is the mist making you tired? You might not be thinking straight."

"Do you have any other ideas? It is a straight dock. How lost could I become?"

"You could fall off," he said. "You'll be going farther into the lake, where you'll likely become drowsier. If you fall asleep, you could slip into the water and drown."

She was too tired to argue. He had valid points, but it infuriated her to come this close without answers.

"I will be right back," she said, dropping his hand and stepping into the white.

"Emer!"

She moved quickly out of reach and sight until a plank creaked with age. From there, she stepped carefully, feeling her way forward with her feet before settling her weight. "Keep talking," she said. "As long as we can hear each other, we may know that we are both awake and safe."

"Theoretically," Caden grumbled. "You should be the one to keep talking. We both know I'm safer with the rope than you are."

"Yes, I suppose. Though you sound a little more alert now that you have something to worry about."

He mumbled something inaudible, then asked, "Do you see anything? An anchor or tying post?"

"Nothing yet," Emer said, feeling her way to the edge of the dock. She remembered the lake in constant motion before. Even on the calmest days, people called to one another on the docks, music played from the nearby beach, and little waves splashed against the dock posts and boats.

Only silence accompanied her as she tested each plank with her foot before shifting her weight onto it. No harsh weather pushed the waves, and no boats stirred the waters. If life rippled underneath, the silence said it was either hiding from her…or hunting her. She crept further down the dock, searching the tying posts for a rope that anchored a ship to the dock.

She found it, but the rope didn't reach upward to the high top of the ship's railing. It went down. Emer felt at the rope, testing its tightness. Yes, it was still tied to something, but what? Emer leaned over the dock, supporting herself on the tying post and the rope. She still wasn't close enough to see the other end of the rope.

"I…I need to go in the water."

"What?" Caden shouted back.

"I need to—" she paused for a yawn "—go in the water."

"I heard you," Caden said, "I just think it's a terrible idea!"

"The rope is anchored," she called back, "but I cannot see the ship."

"Just come back! If you see the rope's tied, we can safely assume their ship is still here and they didn't escape via the water. We can return to Mica and Leo and search the city."

It was an assumption that left them with no more clues. They couldn't find her sisters simply by the rule of elimination. They needed clues where to go next. More to herself than to Caden, she said, "I need to know what happened."

Slowly, she removed her boots and stockings. Holding onto the rope anchor, she slipped off the dock and into the water.

"Emer!" Caden shouted.

From the dock, she thought the water looked white. Up close, it was black. No light reflected into or from its depths. She remembered the lake being warm during the summers, but now it chilled her bones. At least the cold helped shock away her sleepiness.

"Brrr," she chattered, partially to vocalize her chills and partly to let Caden know she was still alive. For now.

She pulled herself along the rope, which stretched above her head. Soon, the dock was swallowed by the mist. It was just Emer and the water. She squeezed the rope, climbing forward hand over hand, terrified of slipping and becoming lost.

A large shadow grew in the mist as she dragged herself through the water. Wood. Dark, decayed, and rotten, but it was definitely the remains of a ship. Creeping closer, she spotted tints of green. Moss?

Emer reached the edge of the ship. It had sunk, leaving its decayed main deck less than a meter above water level. The top of the ship railings had broken off, leaving a row of posts jutting into the air like crooked teeth to frame the sunken ship. Emer released the anchor rope to grab the posts, pulling herself onto the ship then along the side, farther into the lake.

"The sh-ship's name should be eng-g-graved on the wheel," she said, hoping Caden still heard her despite her shivering.

Hand over hand, post to post, she made it to the quarterdeck stairs. The unsubmerged deck of the ship was overrun with moss and roots that curled around the decayed wood frame. Emer followed the soaked roots with her eyes and hands as their branches disappeared in the mist. Beautiful trees had made a home from the wasteland of her civilization.

"W–w–wonderful trees," she chattered, "c–c–could you help me f–find the w–w–wheel?"

Wood creaked somewhere above her in the mist until a leafy branch lowered into her view. She left the post to grab hold of the branch, letting it drag her through the water to the middle of the ship's deck.

The curve of the broken wheel poked just above the surface of the water. She bent close and felt at the grooves in the wood where pockets of moss grew.

Liverthas.

Confirmation. Her sisters wouldn't leave by water without taking Ranae's favorite ship. Even if it answered that question, it left open a hundred others. Where else had they gone? Why hadn't they taken Ranae's ship? Had it already sunk before they could flee? If they fled by land, how far inland were they?

Too many questions. Too many unknowns. Too many options. They all made Emer too…tired.

Her eyelids drooped. As if she was studying economics with her tutor, her head slowly sank and concentrating became difficult. If she could only rest her eyes for a little bit, maybe she could dream of England or the Somnus she used to know. She just wanted to *return.*

She closed her eyes, finally giving in to the lethargy. She was so tired. Tired of not knowing what happened, tired of feeling lost, and tired of feeling like it was all up to her to fix everything.

Her shoulder bumped into soggy wood.

Emer blinked her eyes open, finding herself at one of the ship's railing posts. The tree had pulled her back to the edge. She must have spoken her desire to "return" aloud for the tree to obey.

"Thank you," she said, grabbing the post and rubbing her eyes awake. She needed to get back. Return to land. Return to wakefulness.

An odd sense of déjà vu played in her mind as she remembered the need to wake up and return home.

She pulled herself along the posts again when a light caught her eye from under the water. It was just below her feet, but she would have missed it without the perfect shimmer of light. With her hand on the post, she lowered herself in the water, reaching with her feet for the object. Most of the wood was overgrown with moss, molding the object to the ship.

"Moss beneath my feet," Emer said, "I thank you for holding onto the shiny object. Will you release it now?"

The moss pulled away, allowing Emer to wedge her toes underneath the object and catch it between her feet. Bracing her weight on the post, she raised her feet above the water.

A silver comb. Five cats decorated its ornate head with disproportionate bodies and faces. Emer recognized it and grinned with hope.

"Emer!" Caden shouted from the dock. "Please, answer me! Where did you go?"

"I am here," she called back, pocketing the comb between the folds of her dress. "I found something and am on my way back."

"Good," he said. "How can I help?"

"Keep talking," she said. His voice was comforting and helped her know which direction to go.

"Alright," he said. "I'd feel better if you were the one talking so I'd know you're safe and not drowning, but…what do you want me to talk about?"

"Anything," she said, following her path back to the anchor rope. Post over post, hand over hand until she reached the rope tied to the dock.

"Er, alright. Would you like to hear more about the last hundred years of Somnus?"

"Sure," she said, caring little as long as she heard his voice.

"Really?" he asked, surprised. "Alright, but remember, you asked for it."

Caden began to explain the following wars and rebellions with the excitement of a history professor. If Emer actually had heard all that he said between her focus on not falling asleep, her heart would have ached. Instead, she focused all her energy to climb up the dock post and heave herself from the water. She cursed and chattered her teeth, colder than before. She hugged herself and shivered as she felt her way back up the dock. As soon as she found Caden's form in the mist, she ran. She slammed herself into him, bunching her arms between his chest and her own.

"Emer!"

She sensed his surprise, confusion, and relief as he froze, then wrapped his arms around her.

"You're soaked," he said. "Come on. Let's return to the others and find you something warm."

Chapter 6

EMER

Emer and Caden returned to Mica and Shinópu from the mist, finding Mica relieved and Shinópu sitting on his ankles. The position looked terribly uncomfortable, but the dwarf prince seemed at peace.

Mica stepped forward to greet them. "Thank you for not losing yourselves in there. It didn't dawn on me until after you left that if we lost you both, we'd be stuck with no other option but to return to Uldra without its prince and without Charlotte, leaving us with no alliance and no treaty. So, er, neither of you are allowed to die, understood?"

Emer smiled and Caden gave his friend a light punch on the shoulder. "Tell that to Emer. She was the one who let go of the rope."

"You let go of the rope?" Mica gaped.

"Yes, and it made all the difference. I found a clue. We should rejoin the others, then I only need to tell you once."

Back into the clearer areas, Leo practiced his punches against a tree trunk.

"Now," Emer pouted, "what did that tree ever do to him?" She was half tempted to tell the tree to grow tougher or to splinter.

Thachuma added a log to a developing firepit, and Jesse stitched a new seam in one of Charlotte's gowns.

"Leo," Caden shouted to compensate for Leo's hearing loss. The angry former Prince of Braeder stopped, halting Emer's plans of vengeance.

Leo scowled. "Took you long enough."

"It wasn't a waste of time," Caden said. "Emer found something."

"Yes," Mica said eagerly, "tell us. The suspense is dreadful."

Emer waited until Thachuma and Jesse gathered before she pulled out the comb.

"What is it?" Thachuma asked.

"A comb?" Leo scoffed. "That's it?"

Emer gave him a pointed look. "This is no ordinary comb. This comb was owned and worn by Garnet."

"Garnet?" Caden asked for confirmation. "Then Garnet was on the *Liverthas*. Does that mean we need to search the lake? Devils, I hope not."

"No," Emer said. "The *Liverthas* was still docked when it sank."

Leo scoffed. "How is this a clue to her whereabouts? All it proves is that your sister misplaced her comb."

"It proves," Emer said, "that Garnet was headed to Lithus. Bear with me as I explain. This comb was given to Garnet by one of the lords of Lithus. She hated this comb, with its disproportionate animals with human faces, but she always wore it when going to see the lord."

Understanding lit Caden's eyes. "Garnet's comb means they were headed to Lithus before the ship was grounded. The question is, did they continue to travel west by land, and did they reach Lithus?"

Emer sighed. "I cannot say. But now we know their destination. It makes sense for them to go to Lithus, since that is Ranae's hometown. You said Marin sleeps somewhere along the Somnus coast. If we continue to travel westward to Lithus, keeping an eye open for odd phenomena similar to the thorns that surrounded the castle, then we may find Marin."

"Then let's go," Leo said. "The three of us already had our lunches. The rest of you can eat on the road."

Mica whined, but Caden gave him a nudge. "He's not wrong. We took this detour to save us time in the future. The sooner we find and wake the princesses, the sooner we can return to our people. They need us." As a somber afterthought, he added, "No more distractions."

"Right," Mica muttered. "Responsibilities. Shrooms."

Emer smirked at his replacement word for "Beshrews." It was the kind of thing Pearl would say if a harsh word ever slipped from her lips. Emer gave him a sympathetic smile and pulled herself onto Caden's horse as before.

They rode westward, less concerned about catching the smallest of clues to finding the other princesses.

"Emer," Mica asked, shuffling like a sheep on his horse. "Did Pearl have many suitors?"

Emer stopped herself from speaking the first answer that came to her mind. She studied Mica's shyness and kept her eyes from rolling. Of course he was infatuated with her little sister. *Everyone* was infatuated with her little sister.

She shifted to peek at Caden, suddenly worried about his interest in the subject as he retrieved his parchment and charcoal for notes.

"Pearl," she said, "had only finished her first season of courting when I was poisoned. I cannot say if anyone worthy of her affections expressed their interest in the time between my poisoning and hers."

"Anyone worthy?" Caden repeated. He let his horse follow its own instincts to stay on the path while he set up a board to hold his parchment for writing. He paused as if struck by a memory. "Taking notes while traveling was a lot easier in the backseat of a vehicle in England. Not only were the roads less bumpy, but you were less distracting when you sat farther away." He spared Emer a glance as his neck burned red. "So, did you have trials for your sister's potential suitors to pass?"

"No," she said, "but it was my natural duty as her older sister to look out for her."

"What about Princesses Garnet and Aquamarine?" Caden asked. "Or your parents? Wasn't it their job to filter out wrongful suitors?"

"Pearl was particularly close to our mother," Emer said, "but Mother had a hard time accepting Pearl as a growing woman. Also, most of Pearl's experiences with courting were at the midnight masquerades on Noz Isle, which our parents never attended—or even knew about. Then Garnet was preoccupied with learning how to rule the kingdom, and Marin was usually away at the docks. That left the job to me."

"Alright," Mica said. "Then what kind of man would you approve for Princess Pearl's attentions?"

Emer smirked back. She didn't have a specific list, more of an idea, but she wanted to contribute to

Caden's notes and analyze Mica's shy interest in her sister. "First of all," she said, "he needs to see her for more than her beauty. Everyone thinks she is beautiful, but not everyone knows why. It is because of her sincerity."

"What do you mean?" Mica asked.

Emer explained, "She genuinely cared about the people. She never said a mean word about anyone, no matter their station or situation. A man worthy of Pearl would need to appreciate her for her kindness, but also have the thoughtfulness to know when to restrain her."

"Restrain?" Caden asked, making a note.

"Pearl would give away the very clothes off her back if she thought someone else could use it. She needs someone to remind her that she also needs clothing and food."

Mica puckered his lips thoughtfully. "I see."

Caden continued to write snippets of Emer's words. Clearing her throat, she leaned closer to whisper, "Are you sure you need to write this down? I think Mica will remember it all well enough for you."

Caden chuckled back, but kept his attention on his parchment. He shifted in his seat and occasionally glanced back at Emer when he paused between notes.

Why is he acting uncomfortable? Is it because of our conversation about Pearl?

Emer took a deep breath to steady her nerves and shift her mindset. "Is there anything you would like to know about Marin?" she asked.

"Oh, yeah." Caden shuffled for a separate parchment roll. "She was married to the navy admiral, right? Is there anything we should know that might help us look for her?"

"Marin was akin to a second mother at times," Emer said. "No matter the situation, she always followed the rules. Her one exception was the midnight masquerades, because it was an excuse to sail with Ranae to and from the island before they officially courted. Garnet and I worked on her for weeks before convincing her to sneak out of the castle. She could also be as stubborn as a mule when it came to butchering practices and protecting the lake."

Caden continued to write bits of her words. Emer waited for him to finish recording his thoughts before asking, "What are you thinking?"

He frowned as he studied his notes. "While this is all interesting, I don't see how it helps us find either of them."

"Maybe we should spread out a little," Emer said. "We will cover more ground and be more likely to spot odd phenomena if we travel apart."

Caden nodded. "As much as I want to stick together, it's not a bad idea. We can split into three groups. Emer with Thachuma and Jesse. Mica with me, and Leo with Shinópu."

Emer frowned. "Why can we not stay in the pairings we already have?"

"As Mica mentioned, it's not a good idea for you and me to be paired when we separate into groups. If something happens to both of us, our kingdoms have little hope against the ogres."

"Oh," Emer said, trying not to connect his willingness to part with her to his interest in her. "I had hoped to discuss our shared dreams of England."

Caden twisted in his seat, seeming to study Emer. She squirmed under his probing gaze.

"In that case," he said, "Shinópu stays with Thachuma and Jesse on the carriage, and Mica goes with Leo."

"Lucky me," Leo grumbled.

"Ah, come on." Mica grinned at the hunter. "With your eye for hunting and my eye for detail, we should be the most effective pair."

"Exactly," Caden affirmed.

They agreed to reunite before sunset as they separated their groups and began to widen their distance. Mica and Leo took the mistier left while Shinópu joined the carriage to explore the right.

72

They traveled only a block or two away from one another, catching glimpses of each other between buildings or road intersections. It was during the long stretches of buildings that Emer felt nervous.

What if they drifted too far apart? What if they lost each other? What if one of the groups fell behind? What could she discuss with Caden while they were basically alone?

"I wish we had a way to communicate with them. Do you remember the phones in England?"

Caden nodded thoughtfully. "They were truly a marvel."

"Yes," Emer said. "Caden, if you have the memories of Honorable Caden who grew up in England, do you know how phones worked? Is there any way we could create them here?"

He rubbed the back of his head. "I don't know. I mean, I have a vague understanding of phones as communication devices and some historical concept about phones having cords attached to them. I have a memory of tying a string to the bottom of a metal...cup? While Mica had the other end, connected to another cup, we talked to each other through them. Does that sound crazy?"

"A little," Emer giggled. "Then again, everything about their technology seemed a little crazy and magical."

He joined her light laughter. "I can't say which is more incredible: their phone technology or your plant magic."

She smiled, glancing at the nearest vine dangling from a tree branch. One of its leaves curled into a funnel, almost like a speaker. "What about a combination of the two?" she pondered aloud.

"Huh?" Caden asked.

Emer asked him to stop his horse rather than attempt to explain. How could she explain when she hardly knew what she was doing? All she had was a vague idea in her mind that begged to be experimented.

She hopped off the horse and walked over to the dangling vine.

"Dear vine," she said, "where are you rooted?"

She closed her eyes and allowed the plant to speak back to her with an image of where it fed from the ground. Opening her eyes again, she followed its trail to the spot it showed her.

"Perfect," she said. "Can you split off a second branch to create a second end?"

As soon as she asked, the vine began to grow a second stem from its base. Caden dismounted and tied his horse reins to a nearby branch. Retrieving his charcoal and parchment, he came to stand beside her, watching and recording the process.

74

"Are you creating a phone line…from a plant?"

"Hush," Emer said. "Dear vine, you are alive with beautiful feelings and desires to help. If you create a funnel with your leaves at the ends of your two branches, could you carry sound?"

The vine quivered. Unsure of its capabilities, Emer asked Caden to remain at the base while she went back to the hanging part. The end had grown thick leaves and curled them in a way to create a blooming funnel.

She caressed the shape, amazed by its sturdiness. "Perfect."

"Beshrews, it worked!" Caden's voice echoed back to her from behind the tree *and* through the vine. "But we can't come back to this spot every time we want to talk through a phone. It kind of defeats the purpose when you're close enough to hear even without the vine."

"Yes," Emer said, "but I can form this type of vine again and encourage it to grow longer."

Caden grunted. "It's a far cry from the portable devices used in England."

"One step at a time." Emer laughed lightly as her mind considered how to improve the system. The phones of England had been more than com-munication devices. They held maps, detailed image creators, and libraries worth of information. And almost everyone carried this access wherever they went.

How can I make this vine phone portable? Cutting the vine would kill it, and Emer couldn't influence dead plants.

"Marvelous vine," she said, "we would like to carry you with us. May I have your permission to plant you in a pot?"

Caden's voice echoed back to her. "You're asking a plant for permission to replant it?"

The vine answered with a sense of sadness to leave its home, but also a happy thought to be useful in a way no other vine had. Emer stroked its stem fondly.

"Thank you."

Caden yelped as the vine drew back, pulling away through the tree limbs. Emer followed it to its base where it had coiled itself like a long rope.

Emer smiled at it. "Feel free to grow as long as you want as I prepare a pot for you." Then she went to a fern with long leaves. "May you form a bowl with your leaves? I could use Caden's sweaty helmet with its holes—" Caden guffawed in the background "—but your leaves would be much healthier and far more beautiful as a pot for the vine."

The fern agreed as it wove its leaves together to create a thick basket. Emer thanked the fern and asked for permission to pluck its leaves to free the basket.

76

With her basket prepared, she dug around the base of the vine until she had a sturdy grip. She wiggled the base, feeling its looseness in the soil, then uprooted it. After replanting the communicating vine, she and Caden situated its coils on his horse. The vine had taken full advantage to grow while Emer created the basket. Caden estimated the length of the vine to stretch at least a hundred meters.

"We should hurry to catch up with the others," Caden said. "We lost travel time, but again, I think this may save us time in the future."

Chapter 7

MARIN

Leaving the house on the shore was tricker than I expected. I rummaged through the house wardrobes until I found a long dress that best resembled a chemise despite its striped pattern and croppings above my elbows and ankles. The closest option to a kirtle I found was a long black knitted top that opened in the front with buttons. At least the sleeves covered my elbows. Thankfully, the house was equipped with a set of boots that covered my calves. The boots were made of some material other than leather and had several buckles with no purpose. What a waste.

I geared myself with a bag that had a large outside pocket for Ranae. I filled the inside with a few maps and some provisions, including food for two days and colorful papers that looked like currency from the bedchamber.

Finally ready, I left the house to walk up the road where those strange vehicles roared by. Looking carefully, I spotted people sitting inside the vehicles. With that knowledge, I began to wave at them as they passed by. A few smiled and waved back. Some ignored me. A couple even stared at me, confused. No one stopped.

Where were they all going, and why did they need to be there so quickly?

I stayed on the road and kept to the seaside whenever it branched. This led me down some nicely paved walking trails. After wandering down the paths for several minutes, I crossed ways with a young couple on a stroll.

Their clothing was scandalously limited and revealing, yet they were kind and pointed out my location on one of the maps. I had been correct to assume I was in Maryport. With that, I asked about the location of the Maryport Marina. The kind, though slightly confused, people directed me farther up the road. Thankfully, they said, "It's not far."

I found the marina, with dozens of boats similar to the one in the picture on the kitchen counter. These seemed to be boats for personal use without a single warship near the docks. In a second docking bay berthed larger boats with more unfamiliar parts. They seemed better for fishing than warfare. Was this dream place in a time of peace? What a nice thought.

However, could any of these vessels weather the deep seas to take me to the Well of the World's End?

Only one way to find out. At least, only one smart way.

A building between the docking bays looked important enough to hold some information. I went inside, and a little bell announced my entrance. Cute.

"'Ello," a man said from behind a counter. The attendant wore a checkered shirt with an odd blue kirtle with straps more than sleeves and a large pocket in front. His scalp was bald, though he more than made up for his lack of top hair with his scraggly peppered beard. He set down a thin book and straightened his spine with a crack.

"Hello," I said, approaching the man. "I need a boat that is strong enough to sail into the deeper waters, yet simple enough to be manned by one person."

"Ya lookin' for a bluewater cruiser?"

I narrowed my eyes, unfamiliar with the term. "Is a cruiser strong enough to sail into deeper waters, yet simple enough to be manned by one person?"

He chuckled, a little nervous. "Woman, if ya don' know what a cruiser is, ya shouldn' be goin' out to deeper waters by yerself."

"I have some sailing experience," I said. "Simply not with your style of boats."

"Oh, really?" He leaned on his forearm and hunched over to give me a skeptical eye. His nearness emphasized his scent of cinnamon and soap. Even the dock workers were clean in this place? He asked, "What kinda boats are ya used to?"

"E-eh," I stammered. "I am unsure what they may be called in this area."

"Uh-huh." His skepticism deepened.

I huffed. "The ship I am most familiar with is the *Liverthas*, a flat-bottom ship of one hundred fifty meters long and sixty meters wide. It has thirty battened sails mounted on nine masts. With its six decks, it houses a thousand naval soldiers, plus a hundred crew members with their families. It also carries thirty full-sized cannons to be the king of the Imazhin Lake. Now, I understand that such a ship would be impossible to man by myself, so I would be happy to take a 'cruiser' of about ten meters with full keel, a strong rudder, and one or two masts."

My bag croaked with approval.

"Wha' was tha?"

Rather than acknowledge the frog in the room, I pretended the man was hard of hearing. "I said that I would be happy to take a cruiser of about ten—"

"I heard ya. Le' me pull up wha' I got in blue-water sailboats."

He clicked away at a clackety board before turning an odd box towards me. The box displayed images of a variety of the most sleek and beautiful ships I had ever seen.

"These are lovely," I said. "While larger ships are more work, I understand they are also faster by nature."

"If yer goin' to deep seas, ya wan' somethin' based on a design of thirty to fifty years old. They don' make boats the way they used to, ya know? Cheap and flimsy materials aren' meant to last. These older boats were designed back when weather predictions were less accurate—not like they're always accurate these days anyways. Anyhow, this is wha' I got in pocket cruisers. They're cheaper and small enough to man by yerself. They're not as fast or spacious, but if yer by yer lonesome, they ain' half bad."

"This Albin Vega looks sturdy. How much for it?"

"I have one on sale at ten large."

"Ten what?" I asked.

"Ten thousand quid."

I flipped through the paper money. The largest bill said a hundred. I held it up. "If I have five of these, how much more do I need?"

He raised an amused eyebrow. "Nine-thousand-five-hundred. Tha's basic math, woman."

Goddesses of plenty, I was poor! Not that I expected a boat to be cheap, though I hoped to afford at least a personal rig.

"We can set ya up for monthly payments, if tha's more manageable."

"How much would that be?"

"We start as low as three hundred per month."

I filtered through my money. I hoped to be back in Somnus before a month. "Deal," I said.

"Brill. We can start yer forms righ' away then. Wha's yer name?"

"My full legal name?" Using the name on the envelopes of my current living quarters, I said, "Maureen Irving."

The man slowly sounded out my name as his fingers clicked away on some board of letters. "Oh hey," he said. "Looks like yer already in the system. Did ya know yer Centaur's fit for deep waters?"

"My what?" Since when did I have a centaur? And since when did they swim deep waters?

"Yer Centaur twenty-six Westerly, out on dock twelve."

I really hoped it was not a centaur named Westerly, aged twenty-six, hitched to dock twelve.

If it was a boat I already owned, that could be equally embarrassing. How could I excuse the last ten minutes of conversation?

"Oh, yes," I said with a little smile and shrug. "I was just curious if you had any other suggestions for me. I think I will go look at my centaur before I make any decisions. Thank you."

I made a quick exit and hoped the man left me alone as I walked down the pier. It branched off multiple times to smaller docks, housing dozens of little white boats. I had never seen any boats like them before, yet each one was unique in size, style, and craftsmanship. The only similarities were that most of them were white and framed with metal poles. They were the right sizes for fishing boats, leading me to wonder what their larger boats looked like.

Goddesses, how would their navy compare to ours?

Dock twelve anchored the white boat from the kitchen picture. *Liberation.* I set my bag on the dock and opened it.

"Please," I said, "wait until I step back for you to jump out." A frog jumping out of my bag with my face overhead would give me nightmares for weeks. That terrifying thought haunted me a little more, as I apparently lived within a dream for two days already.

I stepped back as webbed feet grabbed onto the bag's lip. Poking his little brown head into the air, Ranae jumped away from me, onto the dock.

"What do you think?" I asked, waving towards the boat.

"Hmm." The frog nodded in approval. "Hard to know its speed without seeing the sails, but based on its size, I guess it might take us a few days to reach the well."

"It seems," I said, "that we have our very own boat to explore. Shall we take a look?"

If the kitchen picture was not evidence enough, each step closer proved that the centaur was a boat unlike any I knew from Somnus. Only about eight meters long, it had an open stern with seating and a long stick for steering the rudder. The front two-thirds of the boat was enclosed with a cabin. It was built not from wood, though of some metal. The white coloring was quite fetching.

"It is a far cry from the *Liverthas*," Ranae said, "but I am more than curious about this style of boat."

I opened my bag to let him hop back in. Instead, he took a great leap from the dock straight onto the boat.

I shuddered at the sight. Disgusting creature. Poor Ranae.

Following him onto the bow, I was surprised at the boat's sturdiness. None of Somnus's fishing boats of this size were this stable in the water. The deck was rimmed with bench seating of grey wooden slats.

"Do you see the way into the cabin?" I asked.

The frog stopped hopping halfway down the stern to look into one of the windows. "It looks like the door is over by you."

I turned about, searching for a latch. Yes, there was a wooden door. Except there was no knob, and the only way I would fit through it was on my hands and knees.

The frog jumped to the top of the cabin to check out the bow. "Oh," he said. "I think this is a sliding hatch. Goddesses, it is like a puzzle box. I suppose that keeps it sealed from water. Intriguing."

I grinned at my admiral. "I would tell you not to get any ideas to apply to our own ships, except that would be impossible and hypocritical of me. Can you imagine ships like this on the Imazhin Lake?"

Ranae muttered half to himself, "I really want to see the interior of this thing."

"Me too." Sliding the lid back, I then had a handle to push the wooden section down, revealing the cabin inside. I stepped down the odd half-step to the full step, then down to the cabin floor. The space was tight, though well used. Both sides were lined with benches covered with cushions. The bottom cushions looked loose, and—yes, they were detachable to reveal an assortment of amenities underneath. The back cushions even rotated downward to create shelves and opened to the boat's inner mechanics.

"Ranae!" I called back to my husband. "I think you want to see this!"

The little frog hopped inside. Such creatures did not belong in the living space. I forced myself to turn away and find a distraction. Thankfully, this strange boat provided a lot to occupy my attention.

Returning to my explorations, narrow cubbies above the seats slid open for storage space. A wooden table blocked half of the walkway, yet its single metal leg allowed it to change angles. On the starboard side, the seating ended early to make space for an in-built bucket with two faucets. I turned a knob, surprised by the running water. Who needed running water on a boat? Unless it was fresh? How did that work?

I turned around, wanting to ask Ranae to have a good look at the piping, then nearly screamed when I saw a frog's beady eyes in the dark cavity of the boat.

"What?" he asked. "What is it?"

"Sorry," I said with my hand to my heart. "I cannot accept that you are a frog. I hope you change back before I grow accustomed to it."

He ribbitted with a chuckle. "Me too, darling. Have you seen this piping? This system is ingenious. Do you think there are architectural drawings? That would be useful."

"If I find any, I shall let you know." I continued my explorations of the boat I apparently owned, opening drawers and cupboards, reaching a closet and what appeared to be a v-berth triangular bed taking all the space at the bow. Again, no space was wasted, as a few books lined the lip beside the bed and more supplies stored underneath the mattress.

While I knew of naval families who spent days on the *Liverthas*, I had never seen a small boat with such efficient space. Yes, even if it took us several days to reach the well, I imagined the time would be…cozy.

In one of the cubbies, I found a booklet titled "The Westerly Manual" which I found incredibly convenient. I flipped through the pages, grateful for the diagrams as I recognized only half of the words.

"How thoughtful of them to write out instructions, as if they expected foreigners to try manning this craft."

I made myself comfortable and read through the manual while Ranae hopped inside, outside, and all around the boat. I kept my pages high to keep the creature from invading my visual space.

I was halfway through the booklet when Ranae's voice interrupted my reading. "I think I have her figured out. Sailing with just the two of us will be tricky, but manageable."

"A'righ', A'miral," I said, mimicking the accent of a dock worker. "Wha' say ye of our ship?"

A croaking version of my husband's voice echoed from the boat's innards. "Whoever built her put a lot of thought into her. A few of her mechanics confuse me. Something tells me that they help the ship run without wind. I have no idea how I know that. She seems sturdy, though the best way to know is to test her. Want to try a test run before we venture out?"

As much as I wanted to find our way home as fast as possible, setting sail through unknown waters on an unfamiliar ship was unwise. A test in shallow waters would be best.

"Aye, aye."

We went back to the dock to untie the anchor ropes, using the rudder and poles to slowly push ourselves out of the marina. As soon as we were free from the dock, we drifted in the calm bay.

"You said this boat has something to help us sail without wind?"

"Yes," my husband said.

"Please, do not say oars, because I am the only one strong enough—"

"No, no," he said. "There is something about this boat—about the boats of this world…"

I tilted my head, waiting. "Is this information akin to your unexplainable knowledge of the well?"

"Yes," he said. "This boat has a…an underwater windmill? You put a key into a hole on deck, then turn it to make the windmill thing spin in circles, moving us forward."

I raised my eyebrows and rummaged through my large bag to retrieve the ring of several keys. "I bet one of these will work. If all it requires is turning a key, I believe you may have the strength for that."

"Yes, I may."

I huffed. "You would think that this world, with all its fanciness, would find a way to make the water itself move their boats."

Ranae chuckled. "No, actually, it makes sense. As long as men have been on the sea, they have sought to tame it, but she is a wild mistress who cannot be tamed."

I shook my head at him. "You and your mistress of the sea. I hope you understand how fortunate you are to have me as your wife. Not every woman is willing to share her husband with a mistress."

"The sea is a demanding mistress, true. Almost like a force of nature."

I gave him the stink eye, then quickly looked away. It was much easier to talk to him without seeing him as the frog that he was.

He hopped to the deck floor with the key ring and grunted to himself as he tried one key after another into the slot. Eventually, one slid perfectly into the hole and Ranae croaked with pleasure. His front legs were too weak, leaving him to use his hind legs to turn it sideways. A low rumble erupted below our feet and the boat lurched forward. We sped through the waves with the strength of a full rowing team. How?

"By the goddesses," Ranae cursed, then hopped into the cabin.

"What is it?"

"Can you remove the board with the stairs?"

I jumped into the cabin and found that the steps could be completely removed, revealing the strangest piece of machinery I had ever seen. The deformed metal box rumbled like a broken cart over a dock, part of it spinning faster than sight.

"What is it?" I asked again.

"An engine," Ranae said.

I raised an eyebrow at my froggy husband. "How do you know all this?"

His stomach bulged with a deep breath. "That, I do not know."

I pouted my lips, dissatisfied, though recognized that the admiral rarely liked to admit ignorance about anything. He was the admiral. He needed to know all the answers. He needed to give commands with assurance, no matter how much he doubted himself. If he doubted his commands, then his crew would doubt him, and then he was one step away from mutiny.

The frog jumped back to the deck, then hopped to the boat's rim.

"I want to see it."

"What? Are you jumping in?"

"At least I have no coat and boots to worry about keeping dry." With that, the little frog jumped overboard.

"Ranae!"

The boat moved too quickly. Would the frog be able to keep up with our pace? How would I turn off the machine if he could not? I could try turning the key again. What if that only made the boat go faster?

I lowered the ladder into the water for my husband to join me if he could. Seconds passed and no little detestable brown head popped into view. The seconds ticked into minutes.

"Come now," I whispered. "Swim faster, find a current, anything to come back. I cannot do this alone."

More seconds turned into minutes. No frog in sight. How long could frogs stay underwater? Or had the boat gone so quickly that he was too far behind?

Another painful twenty seconds passed as I searched the sea behind me for any sign of the animal I hated most.

A little brown head bobbed above the water.

"Ranae!" At least, I hoped it was Ranae. I assumed frogs preferred shallow waters, though who knew if the frogs in this world had different habitats?

"Marin! Thank the goddesses! Pull out the key! Stop the boat!"

"Aye, Admiral!" I scampered around the deck to grab the key and yank it out. The gurgling sound sputtered and stopped. Calling back to Ranae, I said, "I stopped it! You can come back to the boat now."

"Hold on," he said, "I want to see it now that it stopped. I order you not to touch that button again."

Order? Yes, I had addressed him with his rank earlier, though I was a princess. The only people who could give me orders were my parents and Garnet when acting as future queen.

I stewed on that thought until the frog hopped onto the ladder.

"Ranae! Are you alright?" As much as I wanted to go comfort my husband, his wet and webbed figure kept me back.

"Goddess of Water," he swore, "that was a collection of bizarre experiences."

"What happened?"

"As soon as I jumped into the water, I…goddesses, this body was *made* to *swim*! The power of each stroke, the capacity to hold my breath, even the shape of it. I was probably the same speed as my human form, but I moved through the water like never before. It was incredible."

"Please," I said, "you cannot tell me that you want to remain a frog because of its swimming capabilities."

He chuckled. "No. Even if swimming as a human from this day forward will feel sluggish and awkward, I want you to look at me without cringing."

I cleared my throat, suddenly conscious that my eyes were currently averted from him. I tried to prove him wrong by glancing at him. Nope. Instinctual wince, then averted eyes again.

He let out a low croak. "Anyway, there were too many bubbles for me to see the machine clearly. Then, my frog swimming was too slow to keep up with the boat. I fell behind and swam as hard as I could. Marin, I was terrified to lose you."

"That thought occurred to me also," I said. "I was unsure how to stop the boat."

"Good to know you still care at least a little. I must have hit a current as I started to catch up. I got a look at the machine while it was stopped. It is like a windmill under the water, its blades rotating to push the water away. I managed to slip through for a closer look, but cannot say exactly what makes the blades turn. I wish you could have seen it. The machine is incredible. And to think, it made you travel faster than I did with these powerful legs."

"Yes, very exciting," I said. I was simply glad to have him on board again.

Odd that I could ever have such a thought about a frog.

Chapter 8

MARIN

Ranae and I considered sleeping on the boat, though after docking the Westerly, there was still enough daylight to return to the house where we first began this bizarre dream. I took the manual with me to read before bed. With Ranae as a frog, I refused to let him sleep in the bed with me. He was lucky to have the whole sofa to himself, considering his mucus residue and plopping jumps and croaking breaths.

He woke me in the middle of the night with his croaks. Goddesses above, I never thought I would prefer the sound of Ranae's snoring.

I eventually drifted back to sleep, then dreamed of our wedding day.

Everything had been better than ideal. Ranae had wanted a ceremony on the *Liverthas*, though royal tradition placed our wedding in the chapel right outside of the Somnus castle. It was where I had grown up learning about the goddesses who created our world, giving me many fond and peaceful memories of the place. Not that I had the audacity to argue with my father either way.

Ranae wore his admiral ceremonial uniform and Elisa had sewn a beautiful gown of sea-foam green, embroidered with gold and lined with white lace. It made me feel like the queen of all Rezhina.

We exchanged candlelight, vows, and rings in front of the chapel for all the courtiers to witness. The sun shone brightly all day, with only a mild breeze to stir the air of the late harvest season. The festivities of dancing and entertainment continued through nightfall. It was almost as festive as the midnight masquerades on Noz Isle, except here I could talk about politics and environmental policies. Plus, since it was my wedding day, no one verbally disagreed with me.

Yes, the entire day had been ideal...to my recollection.

In my dream of that special day, I remembered a part I had hidden away, a small piece of conversation that I had forced myself to forget.

Lord and Lady Lance had come to congratulate us during one of our breaks during the feast. Lady Lance's stomach bulged with their ninth child.

"Lady Lance," I greeted her, "how are you still standing?"

"With effort," she said, allowing a hint of her pain to slip behind her grin. "My day of celebration will come soon enough. Today is all about you, and we are happy for you. Both of you."

"Thank you," I said. "Help yourself to the salad bar and desserts. You eat for two now."

"Maybe three."

"Twins?" I asked. That would explain the size of her stomach.

"Nothing has been confirmed yet, but after eight pregnancies...a mother knows."

After a couple more pleasantries, they bid us one last congratulation, then walked off towards the banquet tables.

"Ten children." I shook my head in awe. "Do you think ten is too many for us?"

Ranae choked on his own breath. He turned his head away to clear his throat properly before returning to conspire with me. "Ten? Goddesses, yes. Can you imagine the work? Any more than two and they outnumber you."

I frowned. "Two is too few. With two, they often compete against each other, hating one another. Then with three, you have a single middle child who typically feels left out, such as the Zhenero princess. Poor Sapphire is neither the heir nor a baby to be spoiled, and no one denies her being a bit...odd."

"Two is plenty. Whoever said a little competition was a bad thing? As long as you have an odd number, you always have a middle child."

"The middle-child effect is less severe with more. Emer is fine between the five of us." I actually considered five children to be ideal, especially being as close in age as my sisters and I were. Yes, we fought as all sisters did. I also counted them among my dearest of friends. "Ranae, as an only child, did you not wish for more siblings to play and grow with you?"

"No." He scoffed. "I had schoolmates for that. With no other children to dote on, my parents could afford to send me to the best schools and teachers. I highly doubt that I would be the man I am today if my parents had more."

I could hardly argue that I wanted him to be anything less than the man he was—the man I loved. "Except," I said, "as children of the royal family, our children will have access to the greatest teachers and opportunities, no matter how many we have."

"Can we discuss this another time?" he asked, cringing. *Cringing?* "Today is meant to celebrate the two of us."

His attitude towards the subject kept me from bringing it up again until we entered our new bed-chamber together. Our first night of marriage was spent in a heated argument as Ranae confessed to taking herbs to ward against pregnancy.

"You do not want children?" I shouted despite my earlier attempts to keep our argument secretive. "Fine! Then you can sleep on the *Liverthas* until you want me as your wife!"

* * * * *

I jolted awake, sweating and shivering at the same time. Going to the water closet, I washed my face, surprised to find moisture and redness in my eyes. The memory surged back through me and a sob broke free.

Our fight that night had been so awful that I went to Garnet afterwards. I asked her—begged her—for a tonic to help me sleep. I wanted to dream away the nightmare of my broken heart. It helped…until I woke up. The day was worse than the night as I hid away in my room. I wanted to see no one, ashamed of our fight, embarrassed and feeling hideous that my husband would not love me.

Ranae visited, of course. As if to win my love all over again, he brought me flowers and sang songs from outside my window.

This lasted a whole fortnight, until Tanzi referred me to the apothecary beyond our castle walls. I

100

understood little about my youngest sister's enthusiasm for his experimental potions and remedies; however, I was desperate. He first gave me a potion to help me forget the pain. The memories remained, yet they hurt less, enough for me to brush them aside and ignore them. Next, he gave me a love potion. It came with a dozen disclaimers, except I was using it for someone I already loved. All it did was make me love Ranae even more than the hurt he caused me, to love him and yearn for him more than my desire to nurture a small one with his eyes and my smile.

Still, I went back to Ranae only with a deal.

"I will accept the preventative herbs, if—" I paused for emphasis "—and only if you promise me that someday you will bless me with children."

He clenched his jaw before agreeing. "Someday."

The potion of forgetfulness worked. I had not thought of that argument in months, yet it returned to me clear as day with the single dream.

Wiping my face clear, I stepped from the bedchamber. No meal waited for me at the kitchen table. I sighed and rummaged through the cold storage for something to eat. Thankfully, my back was turned, washing carrots, as Ranae's croaking voice neared.

"How did you sleep, Darling?"

"I managed to fall asleep again after your croaking woke me. Then I dreamed of our wedding day."

"Did you?" he asked. "I did also. It was just as I remembered it."

I smiled. "Yes, it was lovely, for the most part. I suppose it should come as no surprise that we share dreams while we share this dream in Maryport."

"So it seems."

I scrubbed the carrots with extra vigor as I debated with myself. Should I bring up the rest of the dream? No, it would only start a fight. I never wanted to fight with Ranae again. Except the issue was fresh in my mind. If I let it fester, it would grow like mold.

I spun on my heel to face the…frog. Nope. Back to the carrots. I grabbed a knife and began to chop them. I wanted to cut something, hoping it would sever my frustration.

"Do you remember," I asked, "the promise you made?"

Silence.

I angled my face towards him, keeping my eyes on the carrots. "Ranae?"

A small croak. "I remember."

He might have forgotten until the dream had reminded us both.

If he hoped I would let the topic drop with that, he was wrong. "You realize the longer we wait, the

102

harder it will be. When did you plan to fulfill your promise?"

"Soon."

"How soon?"

"Not now, obviously," he croaked.

"Obviously," I grimaced. "Ew." My carrots were cut to thin slices, and I popped one into my mouth. I ground my teeth and one popped out. "Ugh! Again?" I complained, spitting out the loose bone. Another molar. My tongue automatically felt at the fifth hole in my mouth. At this rate, I would lose all my teeth within a week.

Ranae grunted. "Which curse would you prefer? Losing your teeth or your ability to walk on two feet?"

I groaned. "How can such a beautiful place be such a nightmare? How soon can we set sail?"

"I have nothing to pack," my husband said.

"Right," I said, mincing the rest of the carrot slices before popping them into my mouth and sucking on them.

I readied myself with another long chemise-like dress—a light blue one that paled my skin—and covered its lack of sleeves with the same black knitted top as the day before. I packed my largest handbag with the remaining food from the storage and anything else I thought we could use. Ranae hopped into my bag, and we walked back to the marina.

Liberation waited for us like a white chariot. I reviewed some of the manual instructions, comparing the diagrams with the objects indicated on the boat.

"According to these maps," Ranae said, "we want to go two-forty degrees west before cutting north-west to sail around Ireland."

"Aye, aye," I said. Reading from the manual had made the whole boat seem more complex, yet applying the instructions was simple enough. We drifted out of the marina and into the open waters. I set our sails and pointed westward. Clouds billowed on the edges of the horizon, though straight ahead the way was clear. Almost like they had parted the way to let us through.

"Look," I said. "The clouds are making way, welcoming us home."

"Excellent," he said, "except we need to adjust our heading southward along the shoreline until we can find a good current."

"Why?" I asked. "I thought you said that the Well of the World's End is northwest."

"Yes," he said, "but sailing directly northwest will run us into land. We need to go around it. Hence, set the sails southward."

"According to the maps, we can sail west with only minor adjustments around the land. If we go south, we will lengthen our time to find the well. Do you enjoy being a frog that much?"

The frog stared at me with his dead-pan eyes and slowly inflated for a croak.

"Did you just…sigh at me?"

"Maybe. My expressions are frustratingly limited in this form."

"Then let me sigh back," I said, failing to not feel offended. "Why ever should we travel south when we need to go northwest?"

"Because," he said, "we should stay in shallower waters while accustoming ourselves with this craft. Also, the waves are square going west."

"The waves are square?"

"Yes. Square waves are a sign of crossing currents. It is better to ride with the currents and no sails than to battle the currents with full sails."

I folded my arms. "We would waste time to sail south then turn directly west, doubling back to go northward."

The frog croaked. "Will you force me to pull rank as Admiral of the Somnus Navy?"

"Pull rank all you want. I am a princess of that navy and you are a frog. I say we sail directly for the well."

"That is a mistake."

"Too bad," I said, walking up the stairs to the steering, "because I can move faster, have greater strength, and I have thumbs."

My husband muttered something angry.

I leaned back to give him an exaggerated smile. "What was that, my sweet?"

"Just a curse on this frog curse."

"Truly," I mumbled in return. With Ranae as a human, I would be more than content to let him do the hard work while I snuggled with a book in the cabin. Also, I missed his handsome face. It was a true travesty to have his fine physique replaced with a detestable amphibian.

I worked the sails until I was pleased with their angles in the wind, then set the rudder before checking on Ranae in the cabin again.

Ranae flipped a switch and sound erupted from a black device on the port side of the boat. It was music, though unlike any music I had ever heard. A woman sang with a nasally voice and deep drums keeping rhythm. Unknown twangy instruments accompanied her song of, "Bad girls wear high heels to warn you that they're comin'! Click-clop and you know who makes the town go runnin'!"

I stared at the black device with its knobs and arrow buttons. What would happen if I pushed one? I tried an up arrow. The music immediately changed to a sound like foaming water. It was consistent, and I could pick out hints of the twangy music continuing in the background. I pushed the button again. I had expected the foaming water to overtake the music entirely. Instead, a new sound came through. People talking. They spoke quickly and with exaggerated voices, talking about…furniture? They kept repeating the word, "sail." I pushed the button over and over, hearing snippets of music between numbers of foaming water. It was like taking a book off a shelf, reading one sentence, then grabbing an entirely different book for another sentence.

"Intriguing," I said. "Is it a storage of words and music?" I pressed another button on the bottom row with the number one. The music instantly changed to words.

"Clear skies, a northwest wind of ten to fifteen kilometers per hour. It's a beautiful day for sailing, isn't that right, Johnny?"

"That's right. This is one of those days I'd take my mates with me for some easy fishing. Enjoy it today, because this weekend's supposed to get hairy."

"Not storage," Ranae said. "These men are speaking right now. Instead of sending flag signals from ship to ship to communicate, this world has found a way to send entire voices."

"Intriguing," I said, looking over the box to see how it worked. Despite my analysis, I still had no idea.

I preferred to stand on deck, where I understood at least the wind and sails. Our progress was almost as slow as rowing. Studying the waves, I had to agree with Ranae. We were stuck between crossing waves. Obeying rules was usually easy for me. Taking orders from a frog, however, tested my tendency to follow without rebellion. I changed our course southward and immediately we gained speed.

Chapter 9

MARIN

The waters were fairly calm, as the speakers from the black box had claimed. I relaxed on deck, enjoying the spray of the water, the smell of salt, and the wind against my face.

A frog climbing from the cabin startled me. Ranae. At least I held back my scream that time.

He looked over the sails and rudder position with an approving nod. We sat in silence, feeling the waves gently push us up and down. A few more white sails dotted the shoreline as others joined the waters.

Ranae's froggy stomach expanded slowly until he let out a small chirping noise.

"Enjoying yourself?" I asked.

"Very much," he said, closing his eyes. "The sea is peaceful and quiet in ways no other place is. Away from the shores, you leave even the birds and bugs behind. Only you, the sea, and the sky remain."

"And the fish below."

"Eh." He verbally shrugged. "They only matter if you fish. If all you care about is transportation or a moment to relax, I can think of no better way to connect with the goddesses without distractions."

I smiled, listening to his voice and watching the waves rise and fall. It truly was peaceful.

A young voice interrupted the foaming water sounds coming from the black box. "Pan-pan, pan-pan, pan-pan."

Ranae turned to the box. "A distress call?"

"It sounds like a child," I said, stepping closer to hear.

The box continued, "This is *Geopende, Geopende*—"

"It's Dutch," a woman's voice interrupted. "It's pronounced heh-O-pen-de."

The younger voice tried the new pronunciation, then spelled the boat's name to clear any confusion. "We're at 54.5157 and -3.69235. We ran out of gas, and we're stuck out here. Can someone come tow us back to land? It's a little far to swim—"

"We need to return the boat. It's a rental," the woman interjected.

"There are two of us on board—"

"A woman and child! Repeat, we have a woman and child on board!"

110

"Mum! I'm not a child, I'm a man! And you're messing up the pan-pan call. Where was I? Er…"

Ranae croaked a sort of chuckle. "First timers?"

"They mentioned their boat was a rental," I said, unrolling our map. "What were their coordinates again?"

"54.5 and -3.6 about."

The man-child started over his pan-pan call, repeating the numbers as I found our own location on the map. "I believe the port town we passed was Workington. That puts us about 54.6 and -3.5."

"Any developed society with distress calls will have rescue boats," Ranae said. "Pan-pans are not maydays and not life threatening. There is no need for us to go out of our way and tow them wherever they need to be."

"They obviously need help, and we are close by. In fact—" I paused to leave the cabin and search southward. A small white boat without sails loitered within sight. "They are probably right there."

Ranae mumbled something about not having the time, though I decided it was a good time to pull rank again. "It is the *human* thing to do."

Turning on the engine, I directed our boat towards the distress call. The white boat I had spotted earlier was indeed the two people in need. As we neared, the woman on board waved her arms and jumped up and down for our attention. I cut the engine to slow our approach and lessen the noise for communication.

Their boat was about two meters shorter than ours with no inside cabin. Instead, it had a simple platform for shade over the steering functions and two chair-like seats. The woman fiddled with something out of sight. The engine box, attached to the back of the boat, sputtered and died.

"Ahoy!" I shouted. "You made the pan-pan call?"

"Yeah!" the boy shouted. He seemed quite pleased with himself. He was maybe twelve years old, wore no shirt and mere trousers that cut at his knees. His mother wore trousers, a colorful shirt, and a yellow hat with the widest brim I had ever seen.

"We're the Pooles," the woman said. "This is my son, Scott. Can you help us? It seems we've thrown a spanner in the works."

"We can help," I said, unsure about her explanation while angling our boat to drift beside theirs. "We have strong sails and an engine to tow you back to shore. I believe Whitehaven Port is only five kilometers north."

"Thank you," Mrs. Poole said. "We sailed out from Workington, but Whitehaven should be fine. I had no idea sailing could be so much work."

"We weren't sailing, Mum," young Scott said. "We don't have sails. *She's* a sailor."

He looked at me with open admiration while Ranae scoffed. "Takes little to impress a twelve-year-old."

"Is that a frog?" Scott asked.

I blinked. "You heard Ranae?"

"It's your pet? Wow!" The boy's admiration turned into awe. "How did you train it to stay with you?"

"Pet?" Ranae barked. "I was not trained! I am the Admiral of Som—"

"Wow, he's a loud one," Scott mused. "What kind of frog is he?"

Ranae snapped his wide mouth shut. Apparently, only I understood his croaks for words.

Unsure of Ranae's "breed," I said, "Who knows? Shall we hitch you to our boat for a tow?"

"Sure," Mrs. Poole said. "Whatever you need to do. Just get us back to port." She opened compartments, then closed them, obviously trying to help without knowing how.

"Here," I said, retrieving our rope and tossing the end to them. "Do you know how to tie a bowline knot?"

"I do!" Scott said, jumping forward.

"Good. Tie it to your front hitch." Meanwhile, I secured the line to our stern to drag them behind us.

Mrs. Poole hugged herself and watched us work. "Thank you," she said with a small voice.

"Of course," I said. "If I may ask, what were you doing out here by yourselves?"

Mrs. Poole landed loving eyes on her son as he expertly tied a bowline. "He loves boats. I saved up all season to rent this rig for his birthday and thought we could handle it. I can drive, but I don't know the first thing about boating. If his dad was still around—" She finished with a huff, and my heart went out to her. "I guess this is what I get for trying to be fun."

"Are you kidding?" Scott laughed. "This is the best! I got to use the radio and make a pan-pan call! And I got to meet an awesome sailor with a real sailboat and a pet frog!"

I joined his laughter, and Ranae ribbitted.

"Oh, yeah." Scott put his hand under his chin in a thoughtful pose. "I should probably make a radio update that our call was answered."

His grin broadened as he picked up a corded device near their steering and spoke to it.

Meanwhile, I adjusted the sails and rudder to turn northward. That quickly caught Scott's attention again, and he asked to come aboard. "What are you doing? Can I see?"

114

With a confirmation nod from his mother, he hopped over. The boy asked many questions, many of which I had to relay from Ranae's answers. With our engine roaring, Mrs. Poole remained behind the wheel of her own boat to keep it on course with the tow. The work became simple at that point, and Scott became distracted by Ranae. He was rather distracting, after all.

"What kind of frog is this?"

I turned, ready to tell Scott again that Ranae's breed was unknown, when I realized that Scott spoke to something else. The boy held a flat rectangular stone between his face and Ranae.

"Huh," Scott mused, his eyes reading from the stone. "He's a karpathos frog, native to the Greek island Karpathos. They're the most endangered frog species in Europe! Wow! Did you rescue him?" he asked me. "Are you someone who saves animals and fights against poachers?"

I blinked with too many questions in my mind. First of all, what was that rectangular stone? Second, how did it know Ranae's species, and third, were there more people like me?

To answer his question, however, I simply said, "Yes, I fight for the animals."

"That's so awesome! I want to be a marine biologist someday. Well, I'd be a sailor if I could, but there aren't any real jobs for sailing ships anymore unless you're a pirate. So, marine biologist it is! I want to see the world and help the sealife. Mum and I go to the aquarium a lot, and I can name every type of fish!"

"Incredible," I said. I could pick apart "marine biologist" to understand it as someone who studied sealife, though what was an "aquarium"? Carefully wording my questions to not sound completely ignorant, I asked Scott about his favorite parts of the aquarium, what he liked to do there, and the history of the aquatic facility.

Incredible, indeed. Could we create a place in Somnus to study and nurture sealife? Thinking of Ranae as an "endangered" species, could we expand it to land animals too? Unlike Ormio's menagerie, its purpose would be to preserve and shelter the animals, not merely for human entertainment.

I was left with much to ponder by the time we dropped off the Pooles. They both thanked us many times over as I waved goodbye and set back out to sea.

We turned southwestward again to reclaim speed, then after about fifteen kilometers of sailing per-pendicular to the shoreline, we turned due west. Beyond the range of the square waves, we left the land behind again. According to the maps, we were leaving the Solway Firth to the middle of the Irish Sea, just above the Isle of Man. When we reached the deepest

116

section of a hundred and twenty meters, we turned northwest, following the North Channel between Scotland and Ireland.

We reached the northernmost point of Ireland and anchored ourselves for the night around Malin Head. I spent most of the evening browsing through the selection of books stowed by the bedding. An aquarium and marine biologists might help the preservation and sealife of Imazhin Lake, though there was also the issue of the waste dumped into it.

One book addressed past environmental issues about a great city called London. Like the Westerly manual, I only understood the basics, though the basics were enough to teach me that the city's filth had invited rats that carried a plague. I read in terror about the deadly circumstances that followed. In this dreamland, even their history seemed fictional. Either way, I gained a new fear for the future of Somnus if we continued unchecked.

At least the book had a happy ending. With the help of piping out the waste, well-paid cleaning forces and management, the city of London became clean despite its ever-growing population. The flowing River Thames did its job too, by moving and cleaning "biodegradable" waste to larger bodies of moving water. Could the kingdoms of Rezhina extend the

Imazhin Lake to give it a proper flowing outlet? Maybe if everyone worked together…

It was hard enough to convince my own kingdom to work with me. I groaned and set the book aside.

Wanting to stretch my legs and distract my worried mind, I went out to the deck. I stared westward at the line of blue that was so flat that it curved. Such a sight was impossible in all of Rezhina Valley. We truly were sailing towards the end of the world. The sun dipped into the never-ending expanse of the ocean, casting a marvelous red glow across the sky.

"Ranae! Come look at this beautiful sunset!"

Tiny plats of webbed feet on metal announced his approach. I kept my eyes on the horizon, amazed by the colors.

Ranae released a long and slow croak. It almost sounded like a broken rocking chair. I laughed and broke my staring contest with the sun to smile at my husband. Maybe I was a bit blinded from the sun as it almost looked like the frog smiled. He settled back on his haunches.

"Sailor's delight," he said. "We should have calm seas tonight."

Chapter 10

MARIN

Sleeping on *Liberation* was like being a baby in a cradle. The waves rocked us back and forth through the night, filling my dreams with memories of days spent with Ranae on *Liverthas* or the smaller boats we borrowed to sail to and from Noz Isle. Since the masquerades went all night, the best time to catch sleep was during the boat rides before and after the dancing.

I woke up, half expecting to find myself in Somnus, whispering with my sisters before we snuck back into the castle.

I stretched and walked up the steps to check the rigging of *Liberation*. The same sky that helped relax me to sleep greeted me. Only a few clusters of clouds spotted the open red sunrise.

"Ranae!" I called back into the cabin. "We have a beautiful sunrise!"

He jumped up the stairs and stuck to one of the railings.

"Beshrews," he cursed.

"What is it? You said we would have calm seas last night because of the red skies."

"That was sunset," he said, his voice extra gravely. "Red sunrises are another story. Secure the lines. We have a bumpy trip ahead."

Confused as I was, I trusted Ranae's sailing experience. I obeyed without a second thought, going about the usual morning check-ups with extra care.

We set our sails and pulled up our anchor lines. The strong winds blew the wrong way. We started the underwater mill, then worked on deck together. Ranae hopped to the bow, grumbling about not having the strength to pull the sails or direct the rudder. Instead, he commanded me about like a true navy man. Loosen the sail. Shift the rudder to the starboard. Tighten the sail. Not that tight! Shift harder to the starboard.

The work was exhausting, and my arms were sore by the time thick clouds covered the high sun.

My stomach hurt from skipping breakfast and dinner the night before. I started on a soft peach until another tooth came free. Ugh. Maybe I could save my teeth by eating only liquids. In Somnus, I knew an elderly gentleman without teeth. He said it was surprisingly easy to gum his food. The thought of pulling my remaining teeth made me more squeamish than Ranae's froggy curse. I prayed to find the well before the hunger clawed at my stomach, though it seemed the emptiness already cried for sustenance.

The winds and choppy waves continued to batter against us as the rain began. The winds picked up, and I struggled to roll the mainsail into the boom. Such a job normally required at least two expert sailors. I was no novice, though never before had I sailed in such weather. The waves continuously rose above the deck, splashing around my ankles. Ranae's croaking commands to move faster only raised my stress and irritation.

"If we were a bigger boat with more sails," he said, "or with a more powerful underwater mill, we might have been fast enough to escape this storm."

"If we were a bigger boat," I argued back, "we would need more people. This Centaur is already more than I can handle by myself." I hoped Ranae would catch my heavy hint to find some way to help. Unfortunately, there was only so much he could do with his little froggy legs. Frustrating frog curse.

The waves grew taller than the mast, tipping the boat sideways as the current carried us into its belly. I gripped the slippery railing with my soaked hands.

"Ranae?" I shouted, hoping for instructions. What could we possibly do against such giant foes?

"The engine is off! Into the cabin!"

Ranae jumped for my arms as the water smashed across the deck.

"Ranae!" I screamed, almost letting go of the railing to reach for him.

The water cleared, streaming off the sides.

Ranae was nowhere to be seen.

"Ranae!" I screamed. I called for him over and over until another wave crashed over the boat.

I sputtered, tightened my grip on the railing, and wiped my eyes free of the salt.

"Beshrew you, you beshrewed storm!" I yelled, feeling like a true sailor, swearing up a storm within a storm and helpless in the face of the overpowering ocean. "You cannot take him from me! You hear me! I am Princess Aquamarine Reo Irving of Somnus, and I demand you give him back to me!"

In response, the waves grew taller, almost to spite me. I gripped the railing as if my life depended on it—it probably did.

The wave hit and threatened to pull me away. If any part of me remained dry, it was now drenched with the rest of me as the boat rose through the wave. For one terrifying second, the whole boat was under water. In that brief moment, my feet floated. The sensation was both freeing and terrifying as I floated in the wave that swallowed the entire boat.

The boat rose, breaking free to the surface and slamming me down to the deck.

"Ow," a frog croaked.

"Ranae!" I cried. There may have been tears on my face. I was too wet to know the difference.

"Is the mast secured?" he asked.

"Yes!"

"Good! Now, get in the cabin!" he commanded.

"Aye, Admiral!"

No time to bicker over rank. I opened the hatch and slipped through with Ranae in my hands. Closing the hatch behind me, I stumbled to one of the side benches. I lay there as the boat rocked violently through the waves. We were at the mercy of the storm. At least we were together.

"I thought I had lost you," I cried.

He croaked with a heavy swallow. "I thought I was lost. Then, like a miracle, a wave picked me up and carried me straight to you."

"Miracle," I scoffed. "This storm wants to kill us, and you still bless it?"

"It brought me back to you."

"It did." I sniffled. The fears of losing him and of the dangerous storm made me want to hold my husband. I wanted to be held by him. I missed his large arms that made me feel protected and loved.

"Ranae," I whispered, barely above the roar of the waves. "Can I hold you?"

He croaked, and I winced. "While I am a frog?"

"I know! Just come here! I fear for my life right now, and I need the comfort of a living *something* amidst this hateful ocean!"

Ranae probably meant to jump onto the seat beside me. However, a lurch from the waves moved his landing position. He landed in my lap.

I screeched. Instincts died hard.

"Sorry—"

He made to jump off. I grabbed him first. I ignored the bumps, the warts, the mucus, and simply held him to my chest. We sat there for a while as if to wait out the storm. As if. The waves became stronger and tipped us sideways, back and forth, back and forth, back and forth.

"Marin, you are trembling."

"As I said, I fear for my life," I cried.

"Sometimes," he said with a low croak, "these can be the most spiritual moments with the water."

"How?"

"We are at the mercy of the water goddess. We have done all that we can, leaving no question about our fate. Whether we live or die, it will be by the hand of the goddess. Our lives are in her hands."

"I wish her hands were calmer."

My husband chuckled, bouncing his chest against mine. Any other time, such a feeling would have sickened me. Tossed about by the waves as we were, stronger forces threatened my stomach.

"Calm," I said, remembering the mantra I used with Garnet whenever one of her anxiety attacks rose. "Breathe in…breathe out. Be calm. Imagine the little waves of the shore, washing up your feet, then drawing back. Breathe in…breathe out." I imagined the waves rocking me with love instead of anger, like a mother rocking her baby to sleep. My pounding heart became a regular drum.

"Marin?"

"Hmm?" I asked, finally at peace.

"It stopped."

"What?"

The frog wiggled in my hands to jump to the hatch. He wanted to go outside? In this…storm? The boat was still, and the roaring waves were gone.

"Can you open it?" he asked.

I slid open the hatch to peer outside. The rain continued to drizzle, though the waves were as calm as our first morning.

"Mercy from the goddess?" I asked.

Ranae croaked. "No, this is a straight miracle. In all my years of sailing, I have never known such a great storm to dissipate so quickly. It was almost as if it was called away."

"Or demanded to calm down."

The admiral scoffed. "You think you can command the seas?"

"This is a dream, is it not? Perhaps I have more influence here."

"And you made me a frog?"

"And lose my own teeth. Yes, we have already concluded this dream is a juxtaposition between wishes and nightmares. If the water is at my command, then I would tell it to sail us hastily towards the well."

A thud hit our stern as an unseen wave shoved us forward. Unprepared, I fell to the deck, and Ranae croaked with surprise.

Standing again, I stared at the water that bubbled behind us as if the underwater mill was on. Ranae turned to me with his buggy eyes.

"Did the sea just listen to you?"

"It seems so," I said, breathless. Surely, it was a fluke. "Waves of the sea," I called, "stop the boat."

A wave hit our bow, stopping us as if we hit land. I nearly stumbled again, though I caught my balance with the rigging.

126

"Goddesses of stars and spirits," Ranae cursed. I was half tempted to echo his profanities from Ormio and Huiess.

I could command the water. This would have been helpful to know when we first set sail.

"If the waters are with us," I pondered aloud, "we should probably sail directly towards the well again. No worries about upcoming storms or crossing currents."

Ranae croaked, a guttural noise that I came to recognize as a scoff. "Fine."

"No attempt to pull rank as admiral?" I teased.

He scoffed again. "Even if you lost your princess status in this world, you control the very seas. So long as we sail, no one outranks you."

I grinned back.

"Waves," I called, "sail us directly towards the Well of the World's End!"

Chapter 11

EMER

Engulfed in the town of Lithus, Emer walked beside Shinópu. After nine days of traveling, their company reached the outskirts of the town. The city of Somnus had thinned until it blended into the edges of Lithus. They first went to the home of the lord who had given Garnet the comb. Emer reasoned Garnet wouldn't have worn the comb if they hadn't planned to see him, but his house was burnt to the ground. Only two walls remained of the lord's abandoned house, and it still smelled of ash. The rest of the house was overgrown with moss and grasses. They'd camped within the two standing walls for the night, planning to search the town in pairs for signs of Emer's sisters.

With the quiet dwarf as her current companion, Emer's mind had too much time to wander. She wondered why Caden had assigned Shinópu as her partner. In fact, considering the past few days, she had

128

been paired with Shinópu more than anyone else. Despite their time together, Caden hadn't confessed his love for her again since leaving her father's castle. They'd stolen smiles at one another, brushed hands, and shared comfortable conversations, but no more than that.

Did Caden dislike spending time with her? Was it because she kept mentioning the differences between the Somnus she knew and its current state? She thought he'd find such details interesting.

How else could she keep his interest? He liked history. He liked stories. Why did he become flustered as she told him historical stories? It frustrated her.

She preferred to puzzle out how to improve her plant phones. The vines could stretch over two hundred meters, allowing them to search the mists with a tether and communicator. They were also handy while setting camp, as those collecting firewood or food could stay in contact with one end. However, they were impossible to use while traveling through Lithus with its crowded buildings.

Considering obstructions, a massive fallen tree blocked their road forward. It had grown at the edge of a building, then timbered over to crash across the street. There was no way to climb under with its branches hanging down, and climbing over would require both hands and some grunting.

Shinópu climbed up first, testing his weight on the trunk before reaching back for Emer. She took his hand and braced her other against the splintered trunk, prepared for the dwarf's strength to help her upward.

His hand tensed in hers, but he didn't pull her up. Seconds passed and Emer opened her mouth to ask if something was wrong.

He raised his free hand to his pursed lips. Quiet.

Emer listened. It was very quiet. Too quiet? Shinópu tilted his head in slight motions while his eyes scanned the area around them.

"Gaaargh!"

A thick troll jumped from behind a building and landed within reach of Emer. He was well over three meters tall, had small eyes above his long, almost horse-like nose and wide mouth. He wore a leather wrap around his waist that strapped over one shoulder. Most importantly, he carried a giant wooden club.

Emer yelped. Shinópu yanked her to the side, away from the troll, before jumping between them. More voices cried out as five trolls appeared around them. Shinópu moved faster than Emer's eyes could track. He slipped onto the troll's arm to climb up to its shoulder. With a doubled *shing*, he had both of his swords at the troll's neck before the other trolls came close.

"Stop!"

The area became deathly still as his command sank into everyone who heard.

Emer blinked. Shinópu shouted?

"Shinópu!" Caden's voice called around the corner. "Is Emer still with you?"

"She is here," the dwarf said evenly.

One of the other trolls growled, growing anxious as Caden's hurried footsteps neared, the street echoing with more.

A third troll—female, based on its braid and protruding chest—began to raise the log in her hand.

"I wouldn't do that if I were you," Leo said from a nearby rooftop. He had his bow aimed at her head.

Emer found two more trolls ready to pounce on either side of them.

"Beshrews," Caden cursed from around the corner, and she knew he'd come upon the scene. Even with Shinópu and Leo's threats, their teams were matched. Trolls weren't particularly bright, but they were insanely strong. A single hit with one of those clubs could severely injure a man.

Channeling her royal training, Emer took a deep breath. "This is ridiculous. Put your weapons down, all of you."

Every eye turned to her. She fought back the desire to squirm under everyone's attention.

"This good troll was simply coming to greet us." She gestured to the troll who first appeared and gave him a little curtsy. "Good day to you. My name is Emer, and my friend demonstrating a dangerous form of piggy-backing is Shinópu. Please, forgive my friend Leo on the roof. He is hard of hearing and must have confused your welcoming bellows. We know you mean us no harm as we mean no harm to you."

The trolls shared stupefied stares while Shinópu and Leo traded glances.

"Truly," she said, "we can have a civilized conversation without our weapons. Please, tell me, what brings you to this lovely area? I thought trolls preferred the mountains?"

An outlying troll sat down, blocking most of the street, and set his club across his legs. The other trolls relaxed as the female spoke. "We left mountains when humans came."

"All of you?" Emer asked. "Why have we not seen more trolls in the cities then?"

Shinópu's troll watched mutely as the dwarf climbed off his back and sat on his dropped club. Other trolls picked up the narrative.

"We hide in buildings."

"Many refused to leave mountains. Many died."

Emer cupped her fist to show reverence. "How awful. Leo, you said that you caught an extra buck the other day. May we impart it to them?"

Leo guffawed and sputtered, probably wondering how to tell her off, but Caden was first to make intelligent sounds.

"Sure," he said. "I'll have Thachuma bring it right away."

The female troll tilted her head, confused. "You are kind."

"We try." Emer smiled. "The only way we can hope to save the world is one act of kindness at a time."

They chatted lightly until Caden returned with Thachuma and the buck. It was large enough to feed Emer and her friends for more than a week, though she expected it to last only a meal between the group of trolls. Their eyes went wide with hunger and they nearly pounced on Caden and Thachuma as they approached.

"Whoa!" Caden cried out. "Hold on, we're giving it to you. You don't need to take it from us. Just give us some space to set it down first."

They hardly heard him between their hoots and hollers of glee. Emer grinned, warmed by their happiness. The female called out orders to the others to build a fire and soon they all sat around a bonfire. Emer struck up a conversation on matriarchy with the female named Gurtha, Thachuma traded recipes with a troll named Garath, and Mica sat with two trolls watching as he drew sketches of them.

The meal was distributed and the sun set as a new troll entered the camp.

"Kerg," Gurtha called out to him. "You return."

"Sorry," Kerg moaned. He limped badly and cradled his left arm against his chest.

"What happened?" Emer asked, gesturing to Jesse to grab bandages. "You look hurt."

Kerg jumped, noticing Emer for the first time. "Humans?"

"Friends," Gurtha said. "Gave us meat. Tell me, why do you bleed?"

"Ogres," he said.

Every ear close enough to hear perked up.

Gurtha frowned. "Ogres live outside Rezhina. No ogres here."

"Ogres in Rezhina," Kerg said, pointing to his arm as proof. "Hunting. I ran three days away."

Jesse approached with a long strip of fabric. Its vibrant red color looked like one of Charlotte's old dresses. Kerg shied away from her until Gurtha gave him a growl that apparently translated as, "She good. Let her help, you stump."

"I wonder what brought them this far into Rezhina Valley," Emer muttered, eyeing the fabric. Had they

134

heard of Charlotte's death? Kerg said they were hunting. Hunting what? Or whom? Had they come to avenge Charlotte's death? Or were they simply searching to bring Charlotte and Caden back to Uldra?

Either way, Emer made a mental note to avoid them at all costs.

Jesse finished wrapping Kerg's arm and Gurtha gestured at the fire. "Glad you return. Grab meat before Garath eats all."

Eventually, each of them turned in for sleep. Leo and Shinópu stayed up half the night to make sure the trolls didn't have any second thoughts on attacking them, but they parted ways with smiles and waves after another shared meal in the morning.

They continued their search for Princess Aquamarine by spreading out, using Emer's vine phones when they searched in the misty areas closer to the lake. Entering the city proper, they stopped to make supper, and Jesse pulled Emer aside to an abandoned fabric shop. Once inside, Jesse had Emer try on a dress, freshly altered.

Emer angled a cracked hand-mirror to appreciate Jesse's handiwork. She smiled as she smoothed her hands down the length of the new dress.

"You outdid yourself, Jesse," she said. "It is truly perfect."

In all her time in Somnus, Emer had never seen a dress so lovely and flattering. The dipped neckline showed off the plaited design of her new undershirt. The pink overdress was secured tightly against her waist with a yellow ribbon as thick as her hand, and complementing her blonde hair. It reminded her of the sashes Marin once wore, but this was made from a softer material that shimmered in the sunlight. The sleeves draped below her elbows, and the skirts were loose enough to accommodate riding a horse astride. Emer particularly enjoyed the brown needlework that drew out the green in her eyes.

Its tightness around her stomach reminded her a bit of the clothes from England. Her mind drifted when she thought of her dreams. She had come to accept the people of her dream as real people, but if that was so…*What happened to Caden from England? What could he be doing right now?*

"I have another one," Jesse said, "but I'm still working on it."

"This is perfectly beautiful, Jesse. Thank you."

"Good. Let's hope Prince Seaver agrees."

Emer bit back her smile. Whatever Caden of England was doing, she hoped he was as happy as she was. Caden of Uldra was different, yes, but all the more fitting for her circumstances in Rezhina. He knew the burdens of caring for a kingdom, and she hoped to help him shoulder them.

She also hoped that such dreams weren't foolish. Maybe in this new and flattering outfit, he'd tell her once more how much he loved her.

With that happy thought, she thanked Jesse once more, then skipped from the abandoned shop. She found Thachuma and Mica piling fruits and berries into baskets while Caden and Leo carried in a fox.

"Looks like you had success," she said.

Leo grunted, "I don't waste arrows on missing."

Caden grinned and flashed Emer a wink. He said nothing about her new dress, but his smile seemed wider than usual. They snacked on fruits and jerky meat from previous hunts before separating again to search for Emer's sisters.

This time, Emer was teamed with Jesse and Thachuma as they drove the carriage down the main road. Emer's boots were as worn as her shoes after a midnight masquerade, but she wanted to walk this time. She stayed within hearing range of the carriage but allowed herself to wander the once-familiar streets, imagining her sisters doing the same, wondering where they would have gone for safety.

"Emer!"

She jumped as Caden's voice echoed from the leafy funnel of the plant-phone. Emer picked up the skirts of her dress to dash to the carriage's side of the phone. "Caden? What is it?"

"You'll want to come and see this. I think we found Princess Aquamarine."

Emer followed the vine to guide her to Caden. She found him at the stretched end of the other vine phone, waving her forward.

"Mica and Shinópu are a bit farther out. Come on." He reached back for her to take his hand and pull her forward. It was a small sign of intimacy, but it lightened Emer's heart. She soaked in his warmth, the tenseness of his palm, and the texture of his hand against hers.

As they ran, Emer caught the sound of rushing water, like a giant waterfall. Many things had changed since her last visit to Lithus, but she didn't remember any waterfalls in the city.

She and Caden turned a corner, opening her vision to a great whirlpool that swallowed a quarter acre of the city, swirling with a speed that would drown any swimmers. Yet in the center of the whirlpool rose a little island with a singular thatched-roof house. Emer gasped as she recognized the home of Admiral Ranae's parents.

She almost didn't recognize it without the neighboring houses of the sword master and ship navigator, but the distinctive carving of the Irving family name beside the front door hadn't faded entirely away.

Mica and Shinópu stood a meter away from the water's edge, shifting their heads this way and that for any sign of passing.

Hearing them approach, Mica angled his head back to explain while keeping his eyes on the odd sight before them. "Shinópu said he heard something, so we widened our search. It seemed weird to hear so much water in the middle of the abandoned city."

Emer nodded. "I agree. This classifies as strange phenomena. You think Marin is inside?"

"What else could cause an unnatural whirlpool specifically around the Irving home?" Caden asked.

"True," Emer said. "I suppose if she is awake, we may try to contact her somehow."

"Supposing she's awake," Caden said. "Mica, you said the thorns disappeared the moment Emer awoke, right?"

Mica nodded.

Caden frowned. "Then she's probably still sleeping, and we'll need to figure out how to wake her."

"I'd think," Mica said, "that first we need to figure out how to cross the whirlpool. That's way too fast to swim across."

"Then we go over," Emer said.

"How?" Caden asked.

She didn't have an answer for that. She only knew that now they had found her sister, they needed to rescue her. There was no other option.

"Vines."

Emer turned, surprised by Shinópu's contribution to the conversation.

"That's right," Mica said. "You said you've used them for fishing line. They should hold our weight if we want to swing across."

The image of Caden swinging over the whirlpool like a wild forest child made Emer giggle.

Caden gave her a questioning look before returning his frown to their surroundings. "What would we anchor it against? There aren't any trees nearby to loop the swing."

"Maybe not now," Emer said, "but I can grow one."

"Oh." Caden blinked. "Right."

Emer cleared her throat and shook her hands as if she were about to perform a trick. It was magic after all.

"Trees of strong and sturdy branches who grow as tall as houses, hear my call. Please, I beg you for aid, for one of your kind to sprout before me, beside this great well of water. Sprout and grow. Dig deeply with your roots to climb the air. Fulfill your potential by growing thick and strong."

140

As she spoke, a small sprout broke between her feet and crept upward. Faster than any naturally growing tree, it was nevertheless slow, stretching upward like a waking person.

Caden grunted. "It might take all day to grow a tree large and strong enough to trust with my life."

"Do you have a better option?" she asked, knowing he didn't.

He grunted again and turned away. "I'll grab Leo and the others to let them know we're camping here for the day."

Chapter 12

MARIN

With the sea working with us instead of against us, our boat arrived at a small barren island by the end of the next day. The speck of land was unmarked on every map that should have included it.

"Are you sure this is it?" I asked Ranae.

"Yes," my husband croaked. "This is it. Weigh *croak* anchor, my darling of the sea."

I tried to smile back at the little frog, except my eyes worried. He sounded more and more like a frog lately. I even caught him zipping his tongue out a couple times.

Releasing the anchor from the bow was a nice distraction. I grabbed the tea sieve from the kitchen and studied our destination. There was no beach, only a side of the small island that was less rocky than the rest. With no place to dock, we were left to swim to land. Thankfully, I could ask the water to be gentle with us to keep the waves from smashing us against the rocks. Ranae might have been fine either way. He jumped right into the water and swam effortlessly to the island.

Another tooth came loose as I jumped into the water. I spit it out, feeling the—ninth? tenth?—new hole in my mouth. I lost count as the holes opened into each other. All I could think of was the hunger in my stomach and my desire to return to Somnus.

Crawling up to a flat part of the island, I tried to stand. My vision and body tilted. Was this solid ground? Why did it feel wobblier than the boat?

"*Croak* Marin?"

"Ranae?" I called back, searching for him. My husband hopped up the rocks beside me. "Now what?" I asked. "This was your idea. I have the sieve. We sailed to the end of the world. Where is the well?"

"It should be up here," he said, hopping up the slope, going inland.

I reached my hands out to balance myself. Food. Water. I prayed to the goddesses the well water was fresh. Heavy steps took me upward, following the little frog to a circular stack of stones.

Thank the goddesses, it was there! I almost laughed with joy as I stumbled to the well. I could have dunked my head inside if not for the swirling motion. The well was a small whirlpool.

Ranae jumped to the well's edge and peered down.

"Stay back!" I shouted and stretched my arm in front of him. He could have jumped over, though I feared the worst if he fell.

"Marin," a woman's voice said, jolting my attention across the well.

Garnet stood a couple meters away, wearing a dark red gown and sad frown. How was she there? I would have noticed her approach in her gown that contrasted starkly with the beautiful blue skies and ocean behind her. Was she truly there?

Before I could ask, she said, "I wished to be here with you, though I do not think I am truly here with you. I cannot hear you or influence any part of these dreams. However, it seems you found a way to influence them yourself. This well did not exist until you said it did."

"How?" I asked her. "How is it here then? How are you here? Are our sisters safe?"

Her sad frown morphed into a sad smile. "I always knew you were stronger. I placed you all in these dreams to save you from Tanzi's schemes."

Tanzi? My little sister did this to me and Ranae?

Before I could ask more, Garnet shook her head. "I never found an antidote. However, it seems you created one yourself." She smiled and gestured to the well. "Please, wake up. Tell the others that I am sorry for failing them."

144

Before I could ask her to explain herself, she stepped back until she disappeared down the opposite side of the island. She had said "others," not simply "Emer." Who else was caught in the schemes of… Tanzi? Truly? I needed to wake up to ask Garnet more.

With a new sense of urgency, I handed the tea sieve to my froggy husband. "Do your thing. Take us home."

"Do what *croak* thing?"

"You said we need to drink from the Well of the World's End with a sieve. Sieves have holes. You said that if you coat it with your mucus—" I gagged "—it might stop the water from dripping through. Do it."

The frog tilted its flat head at me. "And you will *croak* drink it?"

"If it takes us home, yes." Surely, this was a testament to my desperation.

Ranae ribbitted, then stepped into the sieve. Some excrement thickened his skin. I had to turn away as he rolled around in the sieve. I loved Ranae, and I had grown less disgusted with the frog version of him, though the sight of those too-long legs wiggling in the air, rocking the tea sieve, preparing it for me to use as a cup…that was too much.

"Is it ready?" I asked with my face still turned away.

A croak answered. I took it as a yes and picked up the sieve. It was coated with liquid like a thick slobber.

If I had anything in my stomach, it would have been relocated to the ground beside me. As it was, I dry heaved and coughed, shutting my eyes.

"You can do this," I said to myself. "You need to do this. You need to wake up. You need to eat food with your teeth again. Ranae needs to be human again. Do it. Do it for Ranae."

"Ranae?" the frog croaked. "I am Ranae, right?"

Goddesses, he was getting worse faster and faster.

I shoved the sieve into the whirlpool and pulled it out. The speed of the whirlpool had cleaned off Ranae's mucus.

"No!" I cried. "It was supposed to work! Water, stop moving! I need you to be caught in this sieve that I may drink you!"

My frustration leaked from my eyes as tears dropped into the whirlpool. It stopped swirling immediately and became as still as a puddle.

"Alright, Ranae, I need you to coat the sieve again."

"Ranae," he croaked back.

"Yes, you are Ranae," I said, reaching for him to hop onto my hand. "You are my husband, and I need you."

"Ranae," he croaked again and hopped onto my hand.

Gently, I placed his sticky body into the sieve. He looked half ready to jump out, so I cupped him in. His little body was so squishy and fragile. Lifting him from the sieve, I kept him close to my chest as I dipped the sieve into the well again. This time, the water held.

"Please," I begged, "let this work. For Ranae's sake. I need him. I love him. Even if he remains as a frog, he is my husband. Even if we can never have children together. I mostly want children as a way to extend his legacy. I love him that much."

A small ribbit echoed from my hand at my chest. I closed my eyes and raised the mucus covered sieve of water to my lips. I tipped it back and let the liquid slip past my gummy mouth and down my throat.

I was incredibly thirsty, and it tasted incredibly fresh—if a little thick. I was also incredibly tired.

With my eyes still closed, I lowered the sieve to the frog in my hand. If he drank from it, I never knew. My head tilted, and the ground rose up to my face. With my cheek against the rocky island, I tried to open my eyes again. I caught one last glimpse of our sailboat and the flat blue horizon. Truly beautiful.

Chapter 13

EMER

The tree beside the whirlpool surrounding the Irving house continued to grow through the night. Emer frequently checked on it while they set camp, complimenting its progress and encouraging it more. She also worked on a vine, asking it to grow long and strong. Both plants needed to be strong enough to hold the weight of a grown adult. Or multiple.

She planned to swing across the whirlpool to find Marin regardless of the dangers. She yearned to see her sister too much to stay behind. Caden also wanted to cross over for the sake of "witnessing history in the making." Emer was unsure if any of the others would want to follow, but the tree and vine would need to hold them for a return trip in case the whirlpool remained.

Emer rested near the growing vine and tree, whispering to them until sleep took her. When she woke, she smiled under the shade of the thick trunk and full branches. The vine was likewise stronger than rope. She asked for permission to cut the vine, allowing it a full meter to grow back at its pleasure. Tying a large knot at one end, Leo climbed the tree to wrap the vine around a thick limb. They had a glorious vine swing prepared by the time breakfast was served.

Emer could almost hear Marin chiding her while she ate with the others.

"Stop bouncing your leg," she'd say. "A princess is supposed to be composed and calming in her demeanor. A nervous princess makes for nervous subjects."

Still, Emer's leg bounced with anticipation. It had literally been a hundred years since she had last seen her sister or anyone from her family. Even if those years had passed in a matter of months for her, Emer was tired of feeling like a stranger in her own homeland. She still felt lost in this new version of Somnus, in her own life plans to help rule a kingdom, and in her feelings for Caden. She missed having an older sister to turn to, to confide in, to ask for guidance.

The berry pancakes were perfectly tart, but she hardly tasted them as she waited for everyone else to finish eating. Caden, likewise, kept glancing in the direction of the whirlpool.

They stood almost in unison when Emer realized he was simply waiting for someone else to stand first. They dropped their plates into the wash bucket, then went toward the whirlpool. Caden checked for his parchment and charcoal to make sure he had enough supplies and that they were secured to him for the swing.

"I'd ask you to stay here," he said, "if I knew you'd listen. As it is, please, let me go first. If the vine and branch hold me, they should have no problem holding you."

"Is anyone else coming?" Emer asked, looking back to the camp. Thachuma and Jesse were busy cleaning up breakfast. Mica approached with his breakfast plate in hand, still working on his pancakes. Leo and Shinópu watched, but seemed content as spectators.

Caden shrugged. "Looks like it's just you and me." He grabbed the vine and lifted himself to stand on the large knot on the bottom. He tested his weight on it, shifting his balance from one foot to the other, then tried a little bounce. The tree groaned and the vine stretched from the weight, but both held strong.

He stepped off, then walked the vine as far inland as it could go.

"Here goes nothing," he said, then started running toward the whirlpool with the vine in hand.

After a few quick steps, he jumped onto the knot and swung over the rushing water. He leaned forward with the momentum and jumped from the vine to fly the last couple meters to the island. He landed on the edge of the plateau, dirt crumbling beneath his feet.

"Caden!" Emer shouted.

He fell forward, crawling inland until he was safe from the ledge. When the ground remained solid beneath him, he turned back to smile at Emer and Mica.

"Well, if not for the possible death by whirlpool, I'd go so far as to say that it was actually fun."

Emer smiled back and grabbed for the vine. "My turn."

"Are you sure?" Caden asked. "I barely made it. I really don't want you to—"

She started running. She lifted herself to stand on the knot, flying forward like a bird taking flight. She remembered a happy memory of Garnet pushing her on a swinging seat made of vines and a wooden plank.

The vine reached its highest point, and Emer jumped.

As soon as her foot left the knot, she knew she was in trouble. She hadn't given herself enough forward motion. She went up, but not over. The edge of the island was too far away.

"Emer!" Caden nearly screamed as he realized it too. He reached for her, too far away, too slow.

There was no "nearly" about Emer's scream. Her frantic and terrified heart screeched from her mouth as her feet slipped past the edge of the island. Her fingertips hit the ledge, but the dirt crumbled in her attempt to grab it.

She scraped against the cliff until the water swirled close enough to yank her away. It pulled her sideways and downward.

Emer closed her eyes against the berating water. It sent her tumbling to the bottom, hitting hard against the ground, then rolling her in the current.

Goddesses, help! As if drowning is too easy a death, I will be beaten until I suffocate!

A voice echoed through her head—or was it the water? It was female and familiar, but Emer couldn't place it. She was too busy trying to survive.

"Water, stop moving!"

The circular force stopped, leaving Emer to drift. The whirlpool became no more than a simple pool. Emer kicked off the ground and scrambled more than swam to the surface. She gasped for air as soon as it was available. Arms reached for her, pulling her onto land.

"Emer!" Caden's voice shouted. She barely heard him, her clogged ears from the pressure change. "Emer, what happened? You alright?"

She could do little more than cough and heave for air. The voices of Jesse, Thachuma, and Leo shouted from behind.

"I am well," she managed to cough out, and an ear popped into clarity. Wiping her eyes dry, she turned back to the whirlpool, now a calm and clear moat around the island. "It stopped?" She turned to Caden with wide eyes. "Does that mean Marin—"

Caden pulled her tightly into his arms. With Emer barely sitting up and Caden on his knees, the hug wasn't exactly comfortable, but Emer didn't complain.

"Devils, I knew you shouldn't have come," he whispered over her shoulder. "That was too close."

Emer swallowed and hugged him back, grateful for his warmth.

"Come on," he said. "You think they'll have a towel inside?"

"Only one way to find out."

Together, they stood and entered the Irving home. Unlike the Somnus castle, the house was untouched by plants and looters. Thick dust covered every surface, but it was otherwise frozen in time. The place smelled like a stale attic. A wooden rocking chair sat before the fireplace, the fibers of a blanket draped over its arm. Dishes were stacked in the kitchen, and a broom rested against the table as if the residents had left in a hurry.

Caden grabbed one of the less-moth-ridden blankets and wrapped it around Emer's shoulders. Smiling in thanks, she took his hand, soaking in the feeling of him, then stepped toward the bedroom in the back of the home.

Again, the furniture all remained, from the hope chest to the small collection of swords and sailing tools. Emer's older sister lay on the bed beside her husband. Where Emer had been changed into her finest gown and tucked under the sheets, Marin and Ranae lay on top of the covers wearing clothes to blend in with the casual dock worker. It seemed that Garnet had been rushed when she put them to sleep to slow their poisoning. She hadn't the help of the castle servants to present them nicely, but they looked peaceful. Almost dead. Emer heard and saw no breath fill their lungs.

"Had I looked as dead as they do?" she asked.

"Dead, yes," Caden said. "But preserved."

Emer stepped forward, unable to contain her emotions. A sob broke from her heart, sending her to her knees beside Marin. Emer buried her face into her hands to catch her tears.

What had become of her sisters? Were Pearl and Garnet the same way? What about the other princesses of Rezhina? How had Tanzi done this? The thought of her other sisters lying as though dead ached within her chest until it cried with pure agony. Caden may have said something, but she missed his words, hidden beneath her sobs and pain.

A hand rested on her head. How pathetic did she look that Caden patted her like a dog? The hand slid down to brush her hair away from her face. Delicate fingers caressed her chin and lifted her head.

Marin sat on the edge of the bed, smiling at her.

"Emer!"

"Marin!"

The sisters embraced and cried together. Emer's tears flowed just as hard as before, but with joy instead. Marin parted only to wrap her arms around her husband instead.

"Human!" she shrieked with joy and squeezed him tightly. "I almost forgot how incredible and life-size you are!"

She gave her husband a dozen kisses all over his face. Emer almost suggested that she and Caden leave the room until Marin launched herself back into a sister hug.

Ranae stood and stretched each of his limbs in every way possible. He groaned with satisfaction and muttered, "Yes, finally. Ahh, that feels good."

The sisters eventually pulled away to study one another's faces, as if to confirm reality.

Marin grinned at her younger sister. "How are you alive? How are you here?"

"I could ask the same about you." Emer grinned back.

"Garnet said you were poisoned, so she put you in a deep sleep. Mother and Father decided it was no longer safe for us in the castle and sent us to Lithus. We were going to take the *Liverthas*, until—" She paused as a sob broke through her words. Ranae's expression slipped into anger. "Oh, Emer, it was awful! Someone sabotaged the *Liverthas*! It started to sink before we even left the docks! That was when it became painfully clear that someone wanted to hurt our family. We grabbed our horses and fled from the city. We thought the cover of night would protect us."

Emer nodded sadly. "Except you took the traitor with you. Tanzi betrayed us all."

"Tanzi?" Marin asked. "Then it is true? I still find it hard to believe. Did you know? Is that why she poisoned you first?"

"No. Garnet told me in my dream, then Caden confirmed it after I awoke."

"You dreamed of Garnet also?" Marin asked.

Emer smirked. "I dreamed of a lot of things, but that is another tale. Tell me more of what happened after you left Somnus."

"We hoped to hide in Lithus with Ranae's parents. We had only planned to wait until word came from Mother and Father to return." Marin shook her head sadly. "After our first day in town, Pearl and Garnet went to the market to stock supplies. Tanzi said she would prepare supper if I fetched water from the well. She threw the water pail at me without warning. The rim hit my mouth." She tenderly touched her lip over her teeth. "That is the last that I remember."

"Me also," Ranae said. "I heard you fall outside and came for you. Not knowing what happened, I grabbed the pail, thinking to retrieve water for your ailment. Then I fell unconscious."

Caden nodded thoughtfully from the side of the room as he jotted down a couple notes. "It was a trap set by Princess Tanzanite. We can assume Princess Garnet found you and saved you by putting you both to sleep as she had with Emer."

Marin frowned. "We can assume. Who are you?"

Emer picked up the introduction, saying, "This is Prince Caden Seaver of Uldra. He is the one who woke me."

Marin's frown turned to Emer. "Then where are Garnet and Pearl?"

Caden pinched his mouth tight. "Princess Pearl is somewhere in the Midnight Forest. No one knows where Princess Garnet is."

"Midnight Forest?" Marin asked. "Where is that?"

"It's a newer name," Caden said, "for the forest between here and the Ezuthithe Caves."

"Then we must find them," Marin said, standing. She wobbled a little from the sudden movement and nearly fell back to the bed.

Emer nodded. "That was the plan. We will head towards the Ezuthithe Caves and find Pearl. Maybe she has more information about where we can find Garnet."

Emer spent the next hour explaining to Marin and Ranae how Caden had found her. Caden picked up the narrative concerning Tanzi's rise to the throne: how she poisoned every other royal in all of the Rezhina Valley, how the people abandoned the cities to live huddled against the mountains instead, and how the lake was cursed with a drowsy mist.

"The lake is cursed?" Marin cried. "I finally learn new methods for cleaning and preserving the lake,

158

and I wake up a hundred years too late! I swear, there is a conspiracy against the environment!"

She collapsed back to the bed while Ranae asked to step outside. Caden joined him to introduce him to his friends across the moat. Emer started explaining to Marin the princes and their situation with the ogres until Marin's downcast face stopped her.

"I know, this is a lot to accept," Emer said somberly. "But you can accept it…after a while."

Marin let out a long breath. "What if I do not want to accept it?"

Emer nodded. "I understand. There are some things I will always miss."

"Only some?" Marin scoffed.

"Caden would clarify that 'some' is a vague word that can mean anything between a couple and many."

Marin's distasteful expression turned into a tease. "He is a funny chap, that prince of yours."

"Yes, he has been one of the highlights in this whole mess."

"I see." Marin smirked. "Tell me, other than all that is normal in the world, what 'some' things do you miss?"

"First," Emer said, leaning back to stare at the thatched ceiling, "I miss our parents. I miss their guidance and strength to handle everything that was thrown at them."

Marin nodded and closed her eyes as if to picture their parents.

"Second," Emer started, then reconsidered the luxuries of servants waiting on her hand and foot. "No, we can do without the second. Third, I miss the masquerades."

Marin grinned to agree and her feet bounced in dancing rhythms. "Oh, I could use a masquerade right now: an excuse to dress up in my finest, hide away from the world, and dance my cares away."

Emer laughed. "You barely touched the dance floor at the masquerades. You only danced with Ranae, then you two loitered around the buffet table like beggars."

"I only loitered there because Ranae would. He was the only one I wanted to dance with anyhow. Either way, I could enjoy a celebration of music. Intriguing as it was to hear music played from a box, the music of England was far too strange for my tastes."

Emer jerked around. "Did you say England?"

Marin blinked. "Yes. Have you heard of the place?"

"Heard of it?" Emer laughed and pulled her sister to her feet and toward the door to share her excitement with Caden. "My dreams were in England also! Did you see the ocean? Please tell me that you saw the ocean."

She spoke as they passed through the home entrance. Caden and Ranae turned their attention away from the moat as they approached.

Ranae scoffed a sort of laugh. "Oh, we saw it alright. We lived on it. And Marin, well, she tamed it."

Marin blushed. "I suppose our dreams reveal our wildest imaginations."

Her husband raised an eyebrow. "You had a wild imagination to turn me into a frog?"

Emer bounced back and forth between their conversation. "Please, tell me everything about your dream."

Chapter 14

EMER

Marin and Ranae were still stiff from their long sleep, so they remained in the Irving home island to discuss the adventures of their dreams. With the whirlpool tamed, the others were able to swim across. Shinópu even laughed as he tried the vine swing and splashed into the moat.

Emer sat with her sister and brother-in-law on the island, amazed and curious how their shared dream was different from hers, despite their same setting in England. She gasped when they explained Marin's discovery of her powers.

"You can command water?"

Marin waved a dismissing hand. "It was only a dream. I know Garnet can control her dreams, though my influence over the water was the only part I had."

Emer shook her head, grinning. "Try commanding the water again."

Her sister frowned. "Emer, it was only a dream."

Emer grinned all the more. "No, it was not. I dreamed of Caden, and he is real. Mica and Jesse were there too. They were real people with pasts and families. England itself had technology and history I never could have imagined."

Marin shuddered. "The black plague is the worst possible outcome of waste. I would hate to see any kingdom of Rezhina fall to such a fate. The boats and preservation operations, however, were developments I would like to implement here."

Emer grinned. "I miss smartphones and their many uses, but I gained the power to influence plants and created a prototype. I can control trees, flowers, and vines by talking to them. My powers have only grown stronger since returning to Somnus. You should try using your magic here."

Marin's frown deepened. "Emer, how could that be possible? Magics were lost decades ago—now centuries. We were poisoned by Tanzi and put to sleep by Garnet. How would that transport us to another world and give us magic?"

"All I know is that the dream was real. Prince Caden had the dreams too, and my magic—" Emer paused at Marin's incredulous face. Squaring her shoulders, Emer pulled her sister closer to the tree and vine across the moat. "You see that tree and vine? I grew them. It took me all night, but it only took me one night."

Marin's bewildered expression remained.

Huffing, Emer called to the large tree. "Great tree, thank you for holding strong and aiding our crossing. Would you please stretch your limbs towards me and prove to my sister that I am sane?"

The sisters stared in silence for a few seconds. Marin opened her mouth to speak, but exchanged it for a gasp.

The great tree moaned and stretched its branches over the pool, growing and reaching for Emer. She reached on her tippy toes to touch the leaf that stretched the farthest.

"I see your struggle," Emer said. "It is well enough. Please, make yourself comfortable."

The tree sighed with a groan and pulled back to rest normally.

Marin stared wide-eyed at the tree. "That was incredible."

"I know!" Emer grinned. "I had no such power before, but I did in my dream, and I do now. You say you controlled the water in your dream? It makes sense. The castle was surrounded by thorns, but they turned to flowers when I woke. This moat was swirling as a whirlpool when we arrived, but now it is calm. Again, try commanding the water."

Ranae stepped closer, his expression wide with wonder. "Go on," he said. "You will never know if you never try."

Blinking, blushing, and stepping up to the moat's edge, Marin stared at the water. "If you can hear me and will obey my words, then create a small whirlpool around my finger."

She dipped her finger into the moat. Immediately, the water rippled with movement and began to spin, her finger pointing at the center.

"Fascinating," Caden said, taking notes. "Between the two of you, our travels should be smoother. Finding fresh water and food will be a cinch."

Marin turned to Emer. "Please tell me you have food. I am hungry enough to eat anything, even meat if it is disguised well enough."

Emer laughed. "Thachuma and Jesse are the best cooks. Come, I think they might have extras from breakfast. Do you still enjoy berry pancakes?"

"As long as they let me keep my teeth." She hummed with satisfaction as her tongue rolled over each of her teeth.

Soon, the whole company had crossed to the Irving home. Thachuma and Jesse enjoyed the chance to work in a preserved kitchen, and the front room had space for everyone.

Ranae sat next to his wife as they ate, wrapping his arm around her shoulders in a sign of affection they rarely made public before. Emer swallowed, happy for them, yet disheartened when Caden sat farther away, writing furiously across his parchment. He would run out again soon, despite his efforts to write smaller.

Their conversation quickly turned back to their dreams as Marin described losing her teeth, and Emer shared her experience of living without touch. Frustrating as their experiences were, they were both glad they'd stayed human as Ranae told his version of the dream.

They continued talking even after they finished eating, packing and setting westward. Ranae and Marin sat on the carriage, still too tired to walk. Emer didn't mind. She was simply happy to talk with her sister as she walked beside them. Emer explained everything else that happened since she woke, including the princes' situations with the ogres and her experience with Charlotte.

Ranae grimaced. "Ogres can be ruthless. That was one reason I joined the navy instead of the army. The ogres never came far enough into the valley to cause problems on the water."

"Still," Emer said, "they caused enough problems in the northern kingdoms. Such is the reason for our haste. We need Garnet's authority to convince our people to help Caden's."

"How?" Marin asked. "We have no idea where Garnet is."

"Hence our search for Pearl," Emer said. Hopefully, Pearl would know what had happened to Garnet. First, to the Midnight Forest. Frustrating as it was to see her future only one step at a time, she had the prickling sensation that they were being followed.

Every time she looked back, she saw no one, and pushed the thought away.

"Wherever you are, Pearl," Emer whispered to herself, "I pray that you are safe. I cannot bear the thought of you feeling as lost as we did."

PART 2

"And thus Snow-drop lay for a long long time, and still
only looked as though she were asleep."
- *Snow-drop*, by Brothers Grimm

Chapter 15

PEARL

I liked apples. They were juicy without squirting, crunchy and chewy at the same time, and you knew how they would taste based on their outsides. Sweet red, sour green, or rotten brown. I never thought of apples as deceptive fruits…

Until one poisoned me.

My eyes opened to a world of noise. A distant rush with moans and horns blurred into a steady hum while church bells rang and heavy footsteps stomped nearby in a morning rush.

I had a strange taste in my mouth that refused to go away, even as I cleared my throat of morning dryness.

No matter. Today was going to be a good day. I said this to myself every morning, and I was usually right by the time night fell.

Someone shouted a word that sounded like my name.

I jolted up, finding my father at the doorway. At least, he looked like my father. He had the same midnight black hair as I did, square face, and penetrating stare from dark brown eyes. However, the King of Somnus would never wear all black like a smithy or shave his full beard to a five millimeter trim only around his mouth.

"Are you still sleeping? Get a move on," he said. "We only have fifteen minutes to get to the castle."

Fifteen minutes? I scrambled out of bed and grabbed the gown draped over a chair before registering the latter part of his words and my surroundings. We needed to be at the castle, meaning we were not already in the castle. Where was I?

The question grew as I slipped on the gown and studied my surroundings. I was in a small room with many trinkets and strange objects.

Father's demands to hurry gave me little time to wonder as I dressed myself in a short-sleeved chemise and red kirtle that was cut open in the front and held together with laces. The vibrant colors and soft fabrics were unlike anything I knew. Whatever was going on, Father seemed to know what to do. As always. Were we…playing pretend? Only Mother played pretend with me. Even then, she had stopped playing pretend with me years ago.

Maybe this was some sort of test to see how well I could follow orders. In that case, I was determined to pass with flying colors.

We stepped out the front door to a cobblestone street. Or maybe an alley, considering how close the other side was. I looked back, confused at the red brick townhome that we vacated, then across the street at the white townhomes with wooden crisscrossing supports. I had never seen a place like this before. Where was I?

"Hurry!" Father called, already several paces down my right. I followed, questions building with every step. The strangest carriages—if I could call them such—lined the side of the road. They were metallic, sleek, and rested on four fat wheels. They had no hitches for horses as far as I could see. The only way I assumed they were carriages were by the fancy seats inside, and I could think of no other use for a contraption so large and enclosed.

I caught up to Father, hoping to ask him about them, but our destination distracted me. The street ended at a wooden gate, bordered by trees. Just behind and above the trees, a large castle lookout tower loomed. I followed Father through the gate.

"Father," I called. "Where are we?"

"What do you mean 'where are we?'" He barely glanced back to confirm my confusion with his own.

"We're at Warwick Castle, the same place I've been working ever since..." His voice drifted. He stopped and stooped to place his hands on my shoulders. "Look, I know this isn't easy, but that's why they call it work. That's why they pay us to do it. It's your first day, so it might be a little overwhelming, but you'll get the hang of it, and if you run into trouble, you know where to find me."

Did I? I knew where to find him at our castle home, but not this place. What had he called it? Warwick? I knew of no such place in all of Rezhina Valley. Was that part of the pretend game we were playing?

I played catch up with his words to put the pieces together. We were playing pretend. We were visiting a foreign castle, pretending to be employees. Alright, I could do that.

But why were we pretending to be employees? Were we secretly spies? That could be fun.

I smiled back to my father and gave him a determined nod. Whatever we were doing there, I would do my best.

Father led me through the gate, where a man in odd clothing met us. He wore a grey shirt tucked into black trousers at his waist. His shirt had pockets over his chest and a metal crest pinned over his right pocket. Father showed him a piece of paper that hung from a cord around his neck.

"Good morn," the stranger said. "They'll have a badge for her after the paper work's done."

Father nodded in thanks and led me upward towards the back of the castle. We entered a small wooden door half hidden by the trees and bushes. What would Emer think of this place, with its variety of trees and flowers?

Father walked ahead of me, hardly glancing back as he spoke. "I already filled out most of the forms. Just do your part and maybe they'll hire you as an actress like you want."

Before I could ask any clarifying questions, he had opened a door and stepped aside to let me through. Another man sat at a desk. He was a well-fed man with spectacles on his round face. His dark hair was dusted with grays and skirted his bald top. He greeted us with a simple wave while looking over the whitest sheets of paper I had ever seen.

"Good luck," Father said. "If you need me for anything, you know where to find me."

Why did he keep saying that when it was false? I panicked a little as the man at the desk beckoned me forward and Father left.

"Come on in."

Nervous, I sat at the chair before the desk, surprised by its cushions. How fancy.

"I know you've spent a lot of time roaming the castle while your daddy works here, but now that you're an official employee, you'll need to fit our standards. With your experience here and your father's referral, you were our most qualified candidate, but slack off and you'll get the same treatment as anyone else. You hear?"

"Yes," I said.

"Good. At least you look comfortable in your uniform. Most new employees fidget like rats in the medieval garb. You go by Pearl, right?"

"That is my name," I said.

My employer rolled his eyes impatiently. "Sure, your nametag can have your nickname, but you need to confirm your legal information for your paychecks."

I frowned. Did he not know who I was? Did that mean that Father and I were truly here as spies? Were we using false names?

I reached for the papers, surprised by their whiteness and concise lettering. How fascinating. How did they make their paper so thin, without any tears or frays?

The birthdate was my own, but that was the only thing I recognized. The address listed as my home was

176

some place unknown, and instead of listing my financials with my name at the Somnus Bank, there were only numbers to HSBC…whatever that meant.

The most confusing part was my name. Instead of Princess Pearl Reo of Somnus, I was listed as Merle Rey. Merle? Father had given me a spy name similar to my real name, but I was grateful to already be "nicknamed" with my real name.

I handed the paper back to my employer. "Yes, all seems to be in order."

"Brilliant. Hans!"

I jumped as he shouted to the hallway. Footsteps came running until a young man about Marin's age bounded into the room. He wore a plain green tunic, laced loosely in his front. His creamy undershirt was rolled up to his elbows and unlaced at the top like the Somnus dock workers. His light brown eyes were bright despite their narrow shape.

"What's up?" he asked.

I tilted my head at the phrase. What…is…up? The ceiling?

My employer answered, "You heard about Reggie's daughter coming to work for us? This is Pearl."

I blinked, surprised by my employer's common use of the king's name. I had only ever heard my mother call him Rezhi. I had no time to question, however, as he continued to speak with Hans about me.

"Teach her the ins and outs as you two dust and polish today. Get it?"

"Got it."

"Good. Go on now," he said, excusing me.

Hans left the room and I followed. He led me to a closet where we grabbed cloths, bottles of liquid with odd tops, and a dusting wand with feathers on the end.

"Let's crack on," Hans said. Before I could try to decipher the unfamiliar phrase, he continued, "I like to start in the Great Hall. It takes the longest, but the rest of the castle goes by quickly once it's done."

"Alright." I followed Hans to a room that smelled of well-kept history. Polished stone of checkered colored squares made up the flooring. The walls were equally smooth and perfectly aligned with cream stones in a brick layout. The large room would serve well for a ball or feasting area. At the moment, however, it was decorated with swords like an armory on display. A full suit of armor even sat atop a horse statue, likewise dressed for war. How fascinating.

Hans walked up to the nearest swords hanging on the wall. "Not much to teach you here," he said. "Even a muppet can do it. Just spritz and dust. They're bolted to the wall, so sometimes you gotta thread it behind. You wanna start on the top and make your way down

178

in case any dust falls to the lower items. Stay here. I'll grab the ladder."

"Alright," I said again. I ran my hand along the flat of a blade. The edges were dulled and the swords were, indeed, harnessed to the wall. They refused to budge despite any force I put on them. The armor on the horse statue, however, was very loose. I nearly knocked the helmet off as I reached up to dust it. Oops.

The whole display amazed me. Did they have no need for these weapons? Why were Father and I spying on them if they were not at war with us?

Hans returned with a ladder unlike any I had ever seen. It was made of metal, like the armor, and reached as tall as a scaffold when he opened it into a triangle.

"You didn't leg it? Good," he said. "You start on the horse display while I do the top stuff. Then you can do the bottom stuff when I'm done."

I nodded and began my labors, analyzing and memorizing the types of weapons to report to Father later. A good spy would do that, right?

It was incredible how quickly the day went when occupied with such simple tasks. When we had finished the great hall armory display, Hans and I went to a hallway with portraits. He led me behind a drooping rope to clean another suit of armor. A man stood at the window, still as a statue… Why did he not blink?

"Pardon me, mister, are you alright?"

Hans laughed. "Pearl, Sir Pomp's not alive."

"Not…alive?" I looked back at the statue-still man and squealed. Hans only laughed harder. "What is he?" I demanded.

"Wax. I call him Sir Pomp, and his friend in the next room is Sir Stan—short for Circumstance. I think they're in league with the mannequins from 'Dr. Who,' but they behave so long as we keep them clothed and feed them souls every full moon."

"Feed them souls?" I cried out and stepped farther away from Sir Pomp. Hans continued to laugh.

"Blimey, bird, you're acting like you've never seen a Tussaud before."

"Tuss-aud?" I asked, testing out the word.

"Madame Tussaud," Hans said, as if waiting for me to catch a hint. "Wax sculptures? Bird, are you knackered? Your pa works here. I know you've seen these dodgy things before."

Without knowing what it meant to be "knackered" or "dodgy," I picked apart the rest of his words. What had he called them? Wax sculptures. I imagined a wax candle carved and painted like a person. Looking back to "Sir Pomp," it was still a

180

surprise. He looked so real. Especially his combed back and receding hair.

Remembering my father's game of pretend, I collected myself and approached the wax man. I gave him a little curtsy.

"Good day to you, Sir Pomp. Please do not eat my soul while I dust you."

Hans laughed and grinned for the rest of our time in that hallway. We moved on to a bedchamber with three more wax men, dressed in long tunics that were cut off in the front at their waists. Again, I marveled at their realistic features.

Hans led me through several similar rooms, each one decorated and arranged as if to tell a story. By reading the plaques, I still only understood half of the tale. Apparently, someone named Winston Churchill had stayed in the room, and that fact alone was enough to make it famous. What especially interested me was that every room depicted a different era. I felt like an alien being introduced to this foreign land by walking through frozen scenes of history.

What a perfect plan for spying. Father must have planned this. Little bursts of joy sparked through me as I considered his trust in me for this mission.

Chapter 16

PEARL

"Alright," Hans said, "time for some nosh. You want a bevvy?"

Did I? Best way to find out was to see it for myself. If I had no need for it, I could always give it to someone else.

He led me back down the stairs to a kitchen built of metal. The room was the greatest marvel I had faced that day and raised too many questions to ask. How did they keep the metal kitchen from overheating? Where were the fires? How did they keep the place so clean? Marin would have been fascinated.

Hans disappeared behind a door, then emerged again with a sly expression. He handed me a brown bag that crinkled in my hands like the thinnest of papers.

"Come on," he said. "Let's go to the grounds to eat. I bet your pa's doing a show right now."

A show?

Curious, I followed him outside to a green grassy courtyard that was maintained well enough to probably impress Emer. We sat and opened our bags. I had an apple, a bottled drink, and a sandwich. I ate the apple first, enjoying its crisp taste. Hans warned me to hide the bottled drink if anyone came too close. Studying the label, I had no idea what was inside, but it tasted like apple juice. When I got to the sandwich, I frowned. It tasted like apples. Apple bread? Apple meat? Maybe it was just the lingering taste from the apple and juice.

"Hey," Hans said around his own apple. "Your pa's show's about to crack on. You wanna watch? You've probably seen it a hundred times, but there's something about the war machine that gets me chuffed, you know?"

War machine? That seemed like an important item of interest for a spy mission. I downed the rest of my drink and followed Hans down the grassy courtyard to the stream. Across a little bridge sat the largest contraption I had ever seen. Two massive wooden triangles reached almost to the tops of the trees. A long lever angled between them, connected to a giant wooden box. Movement caught my eye, and I found Father standing at the base of the machine. Dear heavens, he looked so small beside the contraption. It was easily four times his height.

Another man stood closer to the edge of the stream, speaking to the gathered audience on my side of the stream. Somehow, his voice seemed amplified and echoed close by.

"The trebuchet weight is twenty-two tons. If anything goes wrong, it could be fatal to the worker."

Fatal? Fear clenched my heart as I watched Father grab a metal hat shaped like a straw sunhat.

"And so, for safety," the narrator said, "he puts on a tin hat."

Father put on the hat and the audience laughed.

I frowned. Why was that funny? It only made sense for him to wear head protection. Maybe they also thought the hat looked funny.

"And now," the narrator continued, "he'll step to the back, grab the rope that's attached to the trigger, and take sole responsibility for the launch of the rock. Now, this is war. We need this to go right if we are to succeed in the siege."

War? Siege? Was this foreign kingdom at war with Somnus? Was that why Father and I were here to spy on them? But what siege?

No, if we were at war in a real siege, there would be an army, not a crowd of casual onlookers. We would be at the foot of an enemy castle, not the grounds of their own.

Understanding lit my mind. Hans had called it a "show." A spectacle for entertainment. What kind of kingdom had so much power and peace to create a spectacle of their massive weapons of war?

"Now then," the narrator continued, "our trebuchet master needs our help. So let's give him a countdown from ten. Are you ready to count?"

The audience around me cheered.

"Come on," the narrator urged. "Let's hear it! Are you ready to count?"

The audience cheered louder.

"Alright, let's do it!" The narrator led the audience in a slow count down from ten. At "one," Father yanked the rope to release the weights of the giant machine. The giant box lowered and the long lever lifted. Despite its size and complexity, the trebuchet moved with deadly silence. A small boulder flipped into the air, released at the perfect moment to send it flying as if to reach the sun. The audience cheered louder than ever.

"There she goes," the narrator said, "at a hundred and twenty miles an hour!" How fast was that? I guessed it was very fast as the boulder disappeared behind the line of trees in the distance. "Ladies and gentlemen, boys and girls, I give you the Warwick Castle trebuchet!"

The crowd cheered again. Father waved to the crowd. Or had he seen me? He disappeared behind the machine before I could wave back.

Instead, Hans waved me over to continue our work, dusting room after room, polishing plate after plate, wiping frame after frame.

The sun lowered and I found it difficult to focus. My attention drifted, and too many questions circled my mind.

"Brill," Hans said. "We're done."

"But there are still more rooms," I said. Why did my voice mumble? I had not meant to mumble.

"Blimey, there's always more rooms," Hans scoffed. "Come on, let's grab another bevvy."

I nodded, too tired to argue. Labor was hard, but I hoped to pass Father's test. Whatever it was.

We arrived at the pub with a single person standing in the kitchen area. Stools had been pulled up to the serving counter. A couple large mugs rested on the counter beside a man with hunched shoulders and dark eyes.

Hans grabbed a sandwich and waved goodbye with a simple, "See you next weekend, bird."

I was terribly thirsty. I grabbed the jug and swallowed gulp after gulp. Apple juice again? The smell was off, but the coloring was right. I set the empty jug back on the counter, ready for more.

186

"Um," the man behind the counter stared at me with uncomfortably wide eyes. "That wasn't yours. I don't think you're old enough to drink that."

I scoffed. "Is there an age requirement for juice? I assure you, I have enjoyed these flavors for as long as I can remember."

The man with the dark eyes scooted closer. "I can vouch for her. Give her another."

The barkeep raised an eyebrow, but filled my jug with more apple juice. I immediately took another large swallow, savoring the warm flavor as it rolled down my throat. The dark eyed man watched, an odd smile creeping up his lips.

"Thank you, sir. I promise to repay you."

"Drink up, little girl, and you will. You will."

The man talked idly about his career as I slowly drained a third jug. I understood only half of what he said. All the sun and heat must have really worn me. My head began to ache and my vision tilted. I just wanted to close my eyes.

Somewhere at the edges of my fading consciousness, I heard Father storm into the room. He shouted my name—no, not my name. He shouted my spy name. Merle Rey. He grabbed the man who had paid for my drinks and shoved him away. More shouts, more angry sounds, more darkness at the edges of my sight.

★ ★ ★ ★ ★

I woke with a piercing headache and an angry stomach. It hurt to open my eyes. It hurt to sit up. It hurt to—

I bent over the edge of my bed to regurgitate. A bitter apple taste lingered over my tongue. The rancid smell wafted back up to me, but I was too tired and sore to pull myself back into the bed.

"You're up?" Father said from somewhere nearby. The booming of his voice thundered through my head.

"I feel awful," I said.

"Good. I hope you learned your lesson not to accept drinks from strangers."

"I had no money."

"Doesn't matter! It's a good thing I found you when I did. That man was halfway to taking advantage of you, getting you drunk like that."

"It was only apple juice."

"Apple juice?" his incredulous voice snapped. "Apple juice! Is that what he told you? Young woman, you drank four pints of rum! It's a miracle I didn't find you dead on the floor!"

Rum? But it tasted like apples.

I groaned and buried my face deeper into my pillow. "Forgive me, Father. I do not know what the test was, but I probably failed. Please, take me home."

"Test?" he asked. "Home? What are you talking about? We are home."

I squinted hard to open one eye. The daylight was blinding. "Too bright," I moaned.

The room darkened, as if the sun had heard my complaint and dimmed behind a cloud. Analyzing the darkened room, I found myself still in the strange townhouse near Warwick Castle.

"This is not home," I said. "I mean back to Somnus. Where my sisters and friends are."

Father turned back to me. "What are you—"

"Where Mother is."

Father stopped. I could not see his face, but his stillness spoke for him. Dread crept into my heart. What had happened to Mother?

Slowly, he approached and sat at my feet.

"Merle," he whispered. "Don't you remember? Do we need to go to the hospital to have you checked? Can alcohol cause memory loss?" He pulled something from a back pocket that shone with a bright light.

I buried my face back into my pillow to hide from the brightness. "What memory loss?" I asked. "Where is Mother?"

"Your mother's dead. Don't you remember? She had that car accident three months ago. That's why we moved away, moved here."

What? She was dead? No! It was impossible! Especially if it was three months ago! I remembered seeing her just last fortnight…

I remembered embracing Mother. Tears streamed down her face as Father stood behind her.

"Come with us," I had begged between my own tears.

"I must stay with your father," she said. "We must find out what is happening and who is truly behind this. We will send for your return as soon as we can, but…home is no longer safe for you and your sisters. You must go."

Father had rested a hand on Mother's shoulder while another set of hands had pulled at mine. Garnet. My eldest sister's face was stern and determined as always, but tears glimmered in her eyes too.

"I will keep them safe," Garnet said. "I promise."

Mother nodded and clasped her hand around Father's. Garnet pulled me away. "We need to go, Pearl. They will look after Emer until we find a way to cure her poison. Then we may return and I will wake her. Just as I promised."

Yes, Garnet had promised, and Garnet always kept her promises…until she had failed to keep me safe.

190

I remembered her leaving me at a cottage. I remembered a visit from an elderly woman. I remembered an apple…

With each bite of memory, a piece of truth settled into my mind. Yesterday…the whole day… My mind struggled to grasp the truth. The whole day was no more than a dream!

I looked around myself, surprised to find myself still in the same dream.

I was sleeping, but I could not wake up! The pain in my stomach and head cried for the sweet blissful release of sleep even while I slept. Memories came back to me of fleeing with Garnet. Emer, Marin, and Ranae had been taken by Tanzi's schemes and we were marked as her next victims. Garnet and I made it to the Forest of Denebrae, to a place we thought was safe. Apparently not.

I remembered taking a bite of the most delicious looking apple. Then falling down, falling sick, falling asleep. I dreamed of a place where everything tasted like apples.

Chapter 17

EMER

"Fools!"

Emer jerked awake as Leo stormed through the camp. After two days of traveling with Marin and Ranae, they had reached the fringes of the Sophor Forest surrounding Lithus and Somnus. The grasslands between the Sophor and Midnight Forest usually took three days to cross, so they'd stopped to hunt and rest before the trek westward.

"Wake up!" Leo shouted over Caden's waking form. "I told you this was a waste of time! We were supposed to return to Uldra—our people! We needed that treaty with the ogres!"

Caden shuffled into a sitting position. "What are you talking about?"

Leo pointed eastward. "Ogres are camped in Lithus! I ran into one of the trolls from that pack, and he said they're looking for a new home again. He didn't say who exactly had scared them from their

192

home, but I recognize the terrors of ogres. The smoke, the crying, the songs. All the signs are there. The ogres followed us."

Panic struck Emer's heart. "How do they know where we are? Why would they come this far into Rezhina to follow us?"

Shinópu spoke. "Gother."

Charlotte's most loyal and brutal slave. The one who'd escaped during the mayhem of Charlotte's death.

Caden groaned. "I hoped he'd be lost in the woods."

"Not Gother," Shinópu said. "He may be human, but he is a hunter."

Leo laughed a sort of bark. "Even if he wasn't, I can just as easily imagine the ogres getting fed up with waiting on our return and sending a battalion to collect us. They can hunt too. Ogres are faster and can sniff us out like dogs. We have nowhere to run, nowhere to hide. We're dead! All because you—" he grabbed Caden's collar to raise him several centimeters from the ground "—wanted to chase fairytales."

"He wasn't the only one, Leo," Mica said, standing to defend his friend. "We knew the risks of searching for more allies in Rezhina. We also knew the risks of accepting the ogre treaty. After seeing how Charlotte treated Shinópu and his people, do you really think the ogres would let us live in peace? Knowing how she blackmailed Thachuma and almost ate Jesse and Emer, do you really think a treaty would have solved all our problems?"

"Of course not," Leo growled at Mica, then turned back to Caden. "That's why I joined this suicide mission in the first place. But this—" he threw angry glares at Emer and Marin "—wasn't what I signed up for. This isn't a suicide mission. This is the plan of a coward abandoning his kingdom."

Emer folded her arms. "You would rather risk petitioning my backstabbing little sister for aid than to unite the true rulers of this land? What hope would you have of reaching her in the middle of that sleepy lake? What kind of aid would you expect from a tyrant who gained her authority by subterfuge? What hopes did you have to win her trust when she betrayed everyone who loved her?"

With each question, Leo grew angrier, Mica shuffled uncomfortably, and Caden outright squirmed.

"One of us," Leo said, "was going to create a bond with her. Preferably Caden, as an excuse to sever his bond with Charlotte."

Emer blinked, then gaped at Caden. "You came here hoping to marry Tanzi?"

Caden's squirming intensified. "It was better than marrying Charlotte."

194

While Emer couldn't disagree, the truth of his expedition dropped her heart like a bucket down a well.

"Ah," Marin said. "That actually makes more sense. Expeditions rarely include a small number of servants and three princes—fallen as they might be. You wanted to give Tanzi the option to choose between the three of you. In case she found disfavor with Caden, she could choose her favorite and still create an alliance to the north."

"Why not?" Emer scoffed. "I can see it all too clearly. Each of you falling at her feet, groveling for her alliance, competing to be her champion, wooing my little sister who already schemed her way into ruling three kingdoms. Throw three more at her feet. How could that possibly go wrong?"

"Please note, Emer," Mica pitched in, "Caden persuaded us to search for you instead."

Leo pointed at Mica. "Then you admit it's Caden's fault we were sidetracked."

"Who cares?"

Everyone stopped and turned to Ranae. The navy admiral stood and stared at each of the princes with an expression that demanded attention and obedience.

"No matter whose fault it is, it is done. Pointing fingers at the past only wastes time."

"He is right," Shinópu said quietly. "If the ogres are here, we have no time to argue. Only run."

Caden nodded. "Pack quickly. We need to find a place more secure than the grasslands. We may find refuge in the depths of the Midnight Forest, but that's at least three days away. We should hurry to reach it before they reach us."

Even if the fingers weren't pointing, Leo wasn't done arguing.

"If I must remind you," Leo growled as they packed, "ogres either travel alone or in hordes. I wager they brought their strongest on this mission."

Caden cringed as he wrapped away his sleeping blankets. "I doubt we can fight off more than five. If they scared off the group of trolls, we can bet they outnumber us."

"Fighting would be suicide," Leo agreed. "You and Mica are mostly trained in duels, not warfare. Shinópu and I are the only real fighters—"

"What am I, a herring?" Ranae asked, strapping his cutlass over his shoulder to hang at his left hip.

"Dear," Marin said, "your battles were with cannons on boats."

"I boarded a couple times for sword fights," Ranae defended.

Leo raised an eyebrow. "But did you ever fight on land in the open?"

196

The navy admiral stared straight back. "I practiced."

"Believe me," Leo growled, "ogres don't practice—they kill. Either way, the three of us can't bring down a pack. I say we loop around to give them the slip, then return to Uldra."

"Return?" Mica asked. "Now? After we've come this far?"

"This far to what?" Leo's growl rose to a shout. "We've wasted two months waking up two princesses of times long past. They have no authority, and we have no alliances!"

"But Emer said—"

"Mica," Caden said, his voice calm. "We still don't know exactly where Princess Pearl is."

"The Midnight Forest—"

"Spans hundreds of acres," Caden interrupted again. "Mica, there's a reason it's called the Midnight Forest. No light breaks through, making the forest floor permanently as though it's midnight. Records say its visibility is as bad as the mist on the lake."

Emer shivered, remembering her wanderings on the docks. There, familiar landmarks had helped guide her back to the clear. She would have no such advantage in the blackened forest. Even if she asked the trees to create a pathway to Pearl, how would she tell the path apart from any separation between the trees when surrounded in darkness? How could they find her sister?

Marin folded her arms. "Ranae and I have no reason to go to Uldra. If the rest of you must leave, I bid you farewell. Emer and I will continue our search for our sisters."

Emer frowned. She wanted to stay, but she also wanted to help Caden in Uldra. Marin's assumptions irritated her. She inwardly moaned, remembering why she spent more time with Pearl and idolized Garnet.

"I will stay." Everyone turned to the quiet dwarf prince.

"What?" Leo roared. "Why?"

Shinópu gave no response.

Thachuma stepped forward. "If Prince Shinópu stays, so will I."

"Me too," Jesse said, seconding her husband.

Leo glanced between each person as if they'd gone mad.

Caden chuckled. "Looks like you've been out voted. Ironic that the best hunter among us is the only one who wants to run."

Leo growled. "I am no coward. I simply have an ounce of self-preservation."

"I'm also staying," Mica said. "We came this far. If you turn back, I can't join you."

198

"What about Zubra?" Leo asked.

Mica sighed. "Zubra is lost. Our people have been combined with Uldra's for so long, I don't know if anyone will even return when our lands are freed. But hearing the stories about the sleeping princesses felt like catching clues to a hunt I didn't know I was on. Whenever Caden talked about them, I yearned to learn more about Princess Pearl. The portraits only made me more curious because they all claimed to lack her full beauty. Every time I hear her name, my ears perk up. Even if I don't hear her name, just the conversation, I somehow know it's about her."

Emer mentally scoffed at Mica's hopeless infatuation. She was about to make a snide remark when he asked Caden, "Was it this way with you and Emer?"

Caden grunted. With his face turned away, Emer couldn't tell whether the grunt was affirmative or negative. Her heart clenched at the thought of Caden doubting his affections because they weren't as strong as Mica's.

Mica continued, "I need to see her, Caden. I want to be there when she wakes up. If I don't, I'll regret it for the rest of my life. If I leave now, I'll forever wonder what might have happened. Even if I found love later in life, I'd only love with half of my heart because I'll always wonder: what if?"

Leo grumbled. "If the rest of you loons are staying, it would be foolish for me to return alone. So be it. Everyone on a horse. We need to outpace the ogres."

They packed the carriage and headed out before the sun had finished rising. With limited horses, they paired Marin and Ranae on the largest horse, Thachuma and Jesse on another, and Caden helped Emer to sit behind him on his horse. Leo and Mica drove the carriage while Shinópu chose to stand on the back.

Emer enjoyed the excuse to wrap her arms around Caden's waist, wishing their ride was without the fear of being caught and slaughtered by ogres. What she wouldn't give to have a simple life again, where her biggest concern was how to keep her nerves at bay as she embraced a man she admired.

Riding in front with Marin and Ranae, Emer waved for the admiral's attention.

"Thank you," she said, "for breaking up the argument. You were right."

Caden cleared his throat to add, "Please forgive Leo. As the prince of the former Braeder Kingdom, he lost much and became hard from it. He only wants to protect his people. Our goals are the same, even if our methods are different."

Emer tightened her arms around him and leaned her cheek against his warm back. "He means well, but

I agree. Going back to Uldra now would mean surrendering to the ogres."

Ranae dipped his chin. "Thank you. We aided Ormio and Huiess during their skirmishes. If yours was a war with ships, I would gladly assist and volunteer Somnus's navy pride."

"Thanks," Caden said. "I'm sure your experiences in leading military men will still come in handy."

The men shared nods of respect, and Emer tapped Caden's shoulder.

"Could you slow down a little?" she asked. "I would like to thank Shinópu also."

He spared her an eyebrow raise, but slowed his horse to march beside the back of the carriage until Emer could speak to Shinópu.

"Thank you for your support to move onward."

Either he gave the smallest of nods to acknowledge her comment, or it was a simple result of the bouncing carriage. Emer almost nudged Caden to move ahead when he spoke barely above a whisper. "If Caden had not found you, Charlotte would still be my master."

Understanding lit Emer's eyes. The cause and effects weren't as direct as he implied, but the truth was there. Caden's search for the princesses led to Charlotte's jealousy, leading to her ultimate demise and Shinópu's freedom. "I suppose we both have reasons to thank Caden and to support the mission to wake my sisters."

"First," he said, "we need to escape the ogres."

Usually as calm as a stream, Emer was surprised by the shadows in his eyes. She could only guess it was the smallest hint to the horrors he had faced when his kingdom was destroyed and his parents killed.

What other horrors did he witness as her slave? Remembering Charlotte's demands on her servants, she wondered, what horrors did he *cause* on her behalf?

Some questions were better left unanswered.

Instead, she asked, "Why did you choose to stay with us?"

Shinópu kept his face forward as he replied quietly, "It was the honorable choice."

"Honorable?" Emer asked.

Another subtle nod or possible bounce from the cart.

Emer pondered his words, wondering what was honorable about leading a chase of ogres to the Midnight Forest? Or... "You stayed because you knew Caden and I would stay, and the honorable action is to help us fight off the ogres?"

Another bob of his head. "Yes. I also do not want to return to Uldra."

His eyes, which remained forward during their conversation, turned downward.

"Ah," Emer said with another glimmer of understanding. "Uldra is a place of bad memories?"

Nod.

Growing up in Chafan, Emer guessed he'd never been to Uldra until after becoming a slave to Charlotte.

Emer reached over to place a hand on Shinópu's arm. Finally, his eyes snapped to hers. She gave him a somber smile. "Thank you for joining us, regardless of your reasons."

The faintest hint of a smile lifted a corner of his lips. "I also will fight the ogres."

Was that a desire for revenge? Emer's eyebrows went high, but she couldn't blame him. He'd probably been a child when the ogres had taken over and enslaved him, too young to fight back. Such wasn't the case anymore.

Chapter 18

PEARL

The man who looked like Father stayed home from his labors at the castle to nurture me during my hangover. I asked him about Somnus, but he claimed to know nothing of it.

"What about my sisters?" I asked.

He frowned. "Did you have a drunk dream? You're my only little princess."

No. I could not lose Mother and my sisters. Somnus was not the dream. This place without taste was the dream, despite its vivid and harsh realities.

My questions turned into stories as I recounted memories, hoping to jog Father's. Instead, he listened idly and occasionally laughed as if it was a joke.

Everyone had always called me beautiful, even the most beautiful Reo Princess. Of course, the princesses were the most beautiful people, making me the most beautiful person of all Somnus. I never understood why. Perhaps I was the most beautiful sunflower, but

Garnet was the most beautiful rose, Marin the most beautiful sea coral, Emer the most beautiful evergreen, and Tanzi the most beautiful bud. Why compare between flowers when all were equally beautiful?

However, during my tenth birthday festivities, we had visitors from Huiess and Ormio. Apparently, they agreed about my beauty and I became officially known as the most beautiful woman in all of Rezhina.

Personally, I considered myself rather simple. I rarely cared to wear jewelry or delicate gowns as Marin did. My favorite clothing and accessories were those given to me by those I loved. I could see their craftsmanship and talents in their embroidery and stone settings. It made my heart beam to think they shared such beautiful things with me. Then, whenever someone complimented me, I happily highlighted its maker, hoping to build their business as my thanks for their gifts.

Craftsmen apparently took notice. They gifted me many precious things, asking me to wear them around town and show off their skills. Garnet warned me that they were using me as a walking, talking advertisement. No matter, as long as they were fair with their customers. If I ever found them raising their prices for an item simply because I wore it, I gave mine away to the next person who complimented the item.

I shared all of this with my father's lookalike. He seemed the most concerned when I talked about the multiple attempts on my life. The first time was in my bedchamber with my sisters.

I remembered the autumn of my thirteenth year, when we exchanged gifts to celebrate the end of harvest. I had so many gifts from the townspeople that I ended up sharing most of them with my sisters.

I remembered an especially unique comb. It was beautiful with a dozen teeth, a handle engraved with three flat leaves, and a silver finish.

"Here, Tanzi," I said, handing the gift to her. "This would be perfect for pinning your hair back as you like, would it not?"

Ten-year-old Tanzi's face opened with surprise. "You do not want it? It would be so beautiful in your black hair."

"Perhaps, but I already have my obsidian comb. I do not need a second just because its color is different."

"But this one is nicer," Tanzi argued. "How about you give me your old one, and you can use the new one. The black one will stand out in my hair more anyway with my blonde stripes."

"I suppose you are right," I said, going to my drawer to pull out my obsidian comb. I handed it to my younger sister. "Here."

"Oh, thank you! Ooh, I want to see you wearing the new comb!"

"Good idea," Emer chimed. "Garnet, can you do Pearl's hair?"

At eighteen, Garnet was already a woman to be reckoned with. She was strong and willful, but also loving to the point of spoiling the rest of us. She smiled, took the silver comb, and pulled it through my hair.

Garnet's cry of surprise was the only sound I heard before blacking out. When I woke again, my sisters all huddled around me, concerned. Emer and Marin breathed with relief as I met their eyes.

"Thank goodness, she lives."

"What happened?" I asked.

"We are not sure," Tanzi said. "One moment, Garnet was combing your hair with the new comb, then the next, you collapsed. It was terrifying."

Garnet pinched the silver comb between two careful fingers. "It left some kind of goop on your hair. I almost touched it before you fainted. We had to use rags to clean your hair and the comb before you woke."

"What was it?" I asked.

"I know not," Marin said. "We asked an herbalist to look at the substance. Maybe we will learn more tomorrow."

We did. The comb had been dipped in a highly toxic element. We did not, however, learn who sent the gift or what they meant by it. For the longest time, we simply thought it was someone I had somehow scorned by refusing to wear their unfairly priced accessories. Based on the material, the herbalist supposed that the attacker had meant to paralyze me.

We kept the incident quiet. I refused to believe that anyone could mean me any real harm and begged my sisters not to tell our parents. They would only worry and restrain me from spending more time with our people. Besides, nothing else happened until the next year.

The second time I was poisoned was on my fourteenth birthday. I was finally old enough to begin courting, and I received an anonymous gift. It was a beautiful corset. My sisters jabbered about how flattering and uncomfortable they were. This one was seamless enough to wear on the outside of my dress. Father would have called it a scandal, but the new fashion was all the rage in Huiess and Noz Isle. My sisters encouraged me to try it on immediately, but I was too embarrassed. I decided to wear it for the next midnight ball. Night came, and my sisters helped me dress.

"It needs to be tight enough so your breasts stay still even as you dance," Garnet explained.

Marin smirked. "That might be difficult for Pearl. How are you already as large as I am?"

"You and I take after Father's side in that regard," Emer teased.

Tanzi lay on her bed, kicking her feet. "What are you talking about?"

Marin's smirk deepened. "Just how 'utterly' blessed Pearl and Garnet are."

Garnet responded with a gaping stare, then a blustering laugh. "Why, Marin! You have spent too much time on the docks!"

"Too much time with a certain someone?" Emer teased, making Marin blush.

"Besides," Garnet said, "is it really a blessing if they imbalance me? Pearl, ye be warned of back pain."

"Some future," Emer laughed. She waved her hands before herself, as if looking into a crystal ball, and spoke like a mystic. "Pearl, I see your future… There will be…back pain!"

We all laughed, though my laugh caught in a cough as I struggled to breathe. My sisters grew concerned as my coughing continued.

"The corset must be too tight," Marin said. "Loosen it a little."

"I cannot," Garnet said, tugging the strings on my back. "They only tighten more! How? As if it has a mind of its own!"

My sisters huddled around my back as my coughs became weak. I lost the air to cough.

"Get it off!"

"I cannot!"

"Cut it!"

Garnet dashed to her nightstand where she kept a dagger. Marin and Tanzi had teased her for keeping such a tool in our bedchamber, but I suddenly saw its usefulness.

My vision went dark and my legs crumpled beneath me. My sisters yelped and caught me, lowering me slowly to the floor.

"Hurry!"

"I am!" Garnet said. Her blade pricked my side as she wedged her dagger underneath the corset.

She cut the strings and my lungs swelled with air. I gasped and coughed with heavy gulps. With the corset ripped apart, we all sat on the floor, gathering our breath and thoughts.

"What was that?"

"You almost died!"

"Did someone try to kill Pearl?"

"You think it was on purpose?"

"Who gave you that corset?"

I shook my head. "It was anonymous."

We stayed home from the midnight ball that time. We rarely missed, but we were already exhausted from the struggle and heavy thoughts. Tanzi was the most distraught that night.

I never would have guessed her sorrow had come from her failed plans to kill me.

Then Emer was poisoned.

Mother and Father suspected Ormio spies, but my elder sisters were less inclined to suspect our secret friends.

The memory of saying goodbye to my mother burned through my mind again. I missed her. Would we still be together if we had stayed? If they came with us, would we have lost Marin and Ranae?

Garnet and I had gone to the market, stocking supplies as if we were on holiday to visit our people in Lithus. However, Garnet said she had a bad feeling. We returned to the Irving home with only half of the supplies we had meant to grab. I ached to think what might have happened if we arrived any later.

Marin and Ranae were in the same state as Emer. Mr. and Mrs. Irving had carried them to the bedroom, then run to find a physician. Tanzi was gone, supposedly out to fetch a pail of water for supper. Meanwhile, Garnet made another sleeping potion.

"I can put them both to sleep," she whispered. "Just like Emer. I cannot stop the poison, but I can slow it. It should give us enough time to find the antidote."

"How much time?" I asked.

"I cannot say. It all depends on the poison. If I knew what kind of poison it was, we could learn the antidote. We know so little. I do not know how to save them," she muttered to herself over and over. "I cannot stop this poison. I cannot—I do not know how."

She crumpled to the kitchen floor with the ingredients still in her hands. Her eyes swarmed with terror, worry, and anguish.

I knelt beside her to wrap her in my arms. What else could I give my eldest sister who carried such heavy burdens? I sat and cried with her until her shaking stopped and her breathing slowed.

I helped in what little ways I could to help her finish the potion and administer it to both Marin and Ranae. We had just finished administering it to Ranae when Tanzi entered the room.

"Oh no! What happened to Marin and Ranae?"

"They were poisoned like Emer was."

"What did you give them just now? An antidote?"

Garnet shook her head. "We need to know the poison before we can give the antidote. I gave them sleeping potions to slow the poison. It should give us more time to have a physician look over them and prepare the antidote."

"You...put them to sleep?" Tanzi gaped, slowly coming closer. "That was why Emer refused to die?"

212

"What do you—"

Garnet cut off as Tanzi reached for a shortsword from the wall and, with both hands gripping the handle, smacked it against Garnet.

My little sister had gone mad. I could think of no other reason for her to attack Garnet. Tanzi's face was enraged, eyes flared and mouth snarled. I thanked the goddesses that she was too weak to properly wield the weapon. Garnet bled from her side, but was more bruised than cut.

"You cannot save them this time!" Tanzi snarled. "I will not let you! They need to be out of my way for Sapphire's prophecies to come true! You all need to be gone!"

She raised the sword again at an awkward angle.

"Tanzi!" I cried, confused and terrified. What was this madness? Tanzi had taken Sapphire's odd turn of phrases as prophecies?

Garnet threw herself at our younger sister, grabbing the sword from her. Unfortunately, there were many weapons readily available in the Irving home.

Mr. and Mrs. Irving entered the room as Tanzi reached for a dagger.

Tanzi's wild eyes found the Irvings, and for a moment, I feared for their lives. A bigger fear was yet to be realized.

"They poisoned Marin and Ranae!" Tanzi shouted, pointing at Garnet and me. "I caught them, and they tried to attack me!"

Mr. and Mrs. Irving glared at Garnet, who held the sword and potion bottle. Ranae's mother stepped back while his father took a threatening step forward. "What is the meaning of this? What did you do to my son and your sister?"

"Mr. Irving," Garnet said, her voice calm. "This is not what it seems."

Standing behind Mr. and Mrs. Irving, Tanzi revealed her true face: an expression of victory over one she hated. Why would she do this to us?

Before Mr. Irving could question Garnet, a strange sound began. Running water.

The house shook as sounds of crashing wood and broken dishes added to the increasing water. We ran outside with the Irvings, Tanzi racing ahead. The Irving house stayed strong while their neighbors' houses on both sides collapsed as the ground cracked beneath them. We ran farther, barely outstepping the sudden drop of ground as water poured in from the sides.

Our astonishment stole our focus, allowing Tanzi to escape. I thought it was the last time I would ever see her.

214

Fleeing from the city with little more than the clothes on our backs, I looked to Garnet for guidance.

"Tanzi blamed Marin and Ranae's poisoning on us to create distrust," Garnet said. "She blamed Emer's poisoning on Ormio. She probably wants us to distrust them for some reason. We need to find out why."

My eldest sister gritted her teeth. She was normally so calm and collected during the heat of tension. It was usually afterwards, during lonely hours of over-thinking, that her anxiety attacks struck. "I need to keep you safe. You already had your life threatened with that corset and comb of poi—" A light grew in her eyes. "Oh my. Oh, my word." She combed her fingers through her hair with subconscious pondering.

"What is it?"

"You might have been the first one Tanzi tried to poison. Remember that silver comb with the strange goop that made you faint?"

"Yes," I said, "but I offered it to Tanzi."

"And she rejected it. It is possible that she knew it was poisoned."

The more I thought about it, the more obvious—yet insane—it seemed. Whether or not it was true, I wanted to doubt it.

"What do we do?" I whispered.

"We need to reinforce our alliance with Ormio. You can hide in the Ezuthithe Caves while I head to Othium. I believe the Ormio twins are visiting the city next week. I will return to you after ensuring their trust."

My eyes went wide. How serious was our situation? People were known to spend entire lifetimes trying to find the way out of the Ezuthithe Cave tunnels.

"Alright," I said. Back then, I believed in her plan. I believed she knew exactly what she was doing and exactly how to fix everything. I had no idea she was as lost as I was.

The first hint came when our plans suddenly changed.

We found a cabin in the woods. The door was unlocked, and after days of wandering through the forests, we took refuge inside. The home looked lived-in and abandoned at the same time. Dirty stoneware sprawled across the cooking area. Bits of food and rotten meat lay scattered throughout the living area. Leathers and furs draped across the floor and seats, and a layer of dust covered everything else.

"What a mess," Garnet snipped.

"How about," I suggested, "we clean it? If the home is truly abandoned, we may stay here for the night. If the residents return, they may thank us for our cleaning by allowing us to stay the night."

My sister smiled at me. "You have the sweetest heart. I will start in the kitchen."

We were halfway through our projects when the residents arrived. Apparently, the home belonged to seven dwarf friends, all emigrants from Chafan. To summarize their initial response to finding two young women cleaning their home, they were more than a little surprised. It took a few minutes for Garnet and me to explain our purposes for being there and touching their things. We struck a bargain: allow us to hide in their home for a bit, and we would clean for them.

Garnet stayed for a night to ensure my safety before leaving me alone with them. "You should be safe here. Tanzi already tried hurting you, though maybe I can draw away her attention. Hopefully, she will leave you alone if you stay hidden."

"Are you sure?" I asked. "I cannot care for myself alone—not to mention several others."

Garnet smiled, and for a moment I saw Mother instead. "They will respect you. I made sure of it. They have their future queen to answer to if not. As for you, consider this an opportunity to learn the life of a woodsman instead of a castle princess. If Dot and

Ruby are in Othium as they planned, I should return with them in a fortnight at most."

That was the last time I saw Garnet, and the Ormio twins never came.

Three days passed as I lived with the dwarves. Every day, they left to mine in the caves. They returned at sundown, always filthy and tired, but pleasantly surprised to find their home cleaned and warm with the fireplace lit and soup on the stove. They were kind to me and even began to help me with the chores.

On the thirteenth day, as they were out mining, I received a visitor. An old woman asked for sanctuary. As someone who recently asked for the same, I thought it only fair to share.

"Thank you," the old woman said with a scratchy voice. She wore a long dark cloak with her hood pulled low. She hunched over and kept her head down to hide her face.

"Would you like to remove your cloak and rest at the fireplace?" I asked.

"Yes, that would be nice," she said. "But first, I must thank you for your hospitality. Please, enjoy one of my special apples, grown from my own orchard."

"Thank you," I said, accepting the apple from her basket. The dwarves mostly kept meat in their home. Marin would have been horrified at the amount of

218

meat I had eaten the last three days, but there was little else to fill my stomach. The woman's red apple made me salivate with its beautiful shine.

I raised it to my mouth and closed my eyes as my teeth sank in. My eyes never opened.

Finishing the tale to the man who resembled Father, I waited for his response.

"What a weird dream," he said. "But at least you're catching some sleep. Rest up, Merle. We have work again tomorrow."

Chapter 19

PEARL

When my dream of apple flavors continued, I refused to join Father as a castle laborer.

"I do not feel well," I said, which was mostly true. My head felt ill with depressing thoughts and slight nausea.

"Come on, Merle. You can't quit after one day."

How long would it continue? How long was this dream to last? I wanted to wake up and embrace Mother, to laugh and cry as I told her about this dream where I had lost her. I would spend the whole day with her and my sisters to show my appreciation and love.

Instead, Father grumbled around me. He seemed less and less like the King of Somnus each time we interacted. Was this man truly my father? Every time he called me Merle, I wondered if I was truly his daughter.

I convinced Father to leave me home from work that first day, but he dug in his feet for the next.

"You haven't vomited in over twenty-four hours," he said, "and you sound fine. As long as you're not contagious, you go to work."

"Why must we labor?" I asked, rubbing my stomach that still felt angry. Why did it persist? "I want to go back to the way things were."

"Because that's the way life is. It's hard, but we push through."

I folded my arms. That was something the king would have said.

With that, I went to work, stomach aches and all.

I managed to suppress my internal pain until it flared after mealtimes. Complaining changed nothing, so I kept it to myself.

My first week of dreaming was an ambush of information, culture shocks, and paradigm shifts. The people of this dream claimed not to have magic, though their technology was more powerful than any magic I had imagined. Anyone could access the technology, and it was everywhere. Most fascinating to me was the amount of light in this dream world. I quickly learned that it was mostly created by electricity. They had harnessed the power of lightning and used it for everything. It created lights without fire, and no smoke, oil, or wicks. It was odorless and came in a variety of colors. Even their horseless carriages were adorned with these electric lights with blue, red, tints of yellow, and the purest white. The lights were so commonplace, so effortless, that the people hardly even noticed them. Just a flip of a switch, a press of a button, or a turn of a nob, and they had enough light to continue working through the night.

That was the next biggest surprise for me. These people worked more hours than my servants or even the King of Somnus. I wondered if lights and electricity were very expensive. Why else would everyone work so hard?

The whole concept of Warwick Castle absolutely boggled my mind. They reenacted history and recreated it for the benefit of learning and entertainment. To me, it was like they were playing pretend with Somnus. They wore similar styles of clothing, but the materials were much softer, more flexible, and less durable. A couple of the people acted dirty with smudges and warts on their faces, except they smelled clean like royalty.

Despite the differences, it was where I felt the most at home.

The most bizarre part was their pretend magic. They made items seemingly appear from nowhere, but Father explained that it was all illusions, tricks of the light, smoke and mirrors.

The whole fair was a magic trick. Their dresses and leathers were uniforms. Everyone—from the psychic gypsy to the bird keeper—went home at the end of the night in their simpler clothes and holding their little light boxes of technology.

I labored day in and day out, running with my estranged father into the castle with two seconds to spare, working several hours by dusting, acquainting myself with the castle, and chatting idly with Hans until it was time to sludge back to the townhouse that Father called home. Father would immediately change into a pair of loose trousers and shirt with cut-off sleeves, then stare at a fascinating theater box he called a telly.

When "home," I explored the room that Father claimed to be my own, finding a journal. I studied the words written by a girl named Merle. She sounded exactly like me…if I had grown up in this twisted world. Meaning that she was not me, and I was not she.

There were no clues in the pages about how to return to my real home, and Father's confusion turned into annoyance and anger with each time I mentioned our lives in Somnus.

I often reflected on Mother's words, "If you dislike a situation, change it. If you cannot change it, then change your perspective on it."

There was nothing I could do to change my situation in this strange dream world, leaving my other option to change my perspective.

If this was my new home, then so be it. If nausea, occasional headaches, and chills were a side effect of dreaming, fine. I would make this dream bright and beautiful, regardless.

After my second week of working at Warwick Castle, I expected my manager to hand me a duster and tell me which room to clean. Instead, he said, "Meet with the photographer in the Knight's Village. Your job today is to give him a tour of the grounds and castle."

"Fo-taw-gruffuh?" I asked. I had never heard that term before. Was it another position of work based on their strange technology?

"He's here to take pictures for our adverts and website. He might have some requests for angles and scene set up. His family has connections with lords in London, so aid him in whatever he needs…within reason, of course."

"Oh," I said. "Alright."

I was still familiarizing myself with their strange words and phrases. One of the first that I learned was

224

the phrase to "take a picture." Visitors asked me to do it all the time. I first thought it meant to take a painting off a wall. I quickly learned the error of that assumption. Instead, it involved their strange light boxes, framing their faces in the middle of the viewing frame, then pressing a circle on the screen. Sometimes a magnificent bright light flashed like lightning across the scene. It amused me how surprised everyone was whenever their light boxes did this, as if their own devices had somehow pinched them. Every time, I asked if I did something wrong, but they always laughed and said something along the lines of, "It's fine. I just forgot the flash was on," or "I forgot how bright the flash was."

Strange people and their strange devices.

I was still unsure about the words "adverts" and "website," but thankfully heard them rarely at the castle. The only word I felt truly prepared for was "lord." As a princess of Somnus, I knew lots of lords, and felt confident in at least that area of social manners.

Walking the ten minutes across the castle grounds to the Knight's Village, I expected to find a gentleman in fine clothes aiming the viewing screen of his little light device at various parts of the room. Instead, I found a young man wrapping his arms behind a large barrel.

"Can you help me with this?" he asked, slightly muffled by his face pressing against the wood.

"Of course," I said, dashing to his aid. My arms slid around from the opposite side, lining against his. His shirt was rolled up past his elbows, showing off his strength as he hefted the barrel.

"Where did you want this?" I asked between unfeminine grunts of effort.

"In the corner behind me."

"Alright."

The next ten seconds involved the two of us struggling to move the barrel with grunts and groans. Finally in position, we set down the barrel with a heavy sigh.

My eyes were drawn to the man before me. He looked about Marin's age, or maybe a harvest or two older. I was never good at guessing ages. He had dark hair with a little recession to show off his manhood, and his misshapen nose spoke of adventures. Despite his matured figure, he had a round and friendly face. Like many people in this dream, he wore only a shirt with the sleeves rolled halfway up his muscled arms. An over garment that I had come to know as a "jacket" hung over one of the barstools.

The most disarming part of him was his genuine grin and welcoming eyes. His expression felt like coming home and seeing a friend after a long, long time.

"Thanks," the man said. "I'm Honorable Wright, by the way. Mica Wright."

Was his name Honorable or Mica? Why did that second name strike me with familiarity? Was he a worker around the castle?

I smiled back, and introduced myself as Pearl.

"Thanks, Pearl," he said. "Want to help me with the next one?"

"'Want' might be a strong word for this case," I laughed. "Maybe we can slide it over?"

His responding laugh was contagious. "Maybe."

We braced side by side against the next barrel. "Push on three?" he asked, then counted.

After a few hard shoves, we managed to move it next to the other.

"Phew," Honorable/Mica sighed. "I've got to say, I'm impressed. I expected empty props, but you have real liquids in there."

I tilted my head, confused. "You do not work here?"

"I'm currently hired to take some photos, but no. I usually work in London."

Take photos…London. "Oh! You are the lord from London!" I dropped into a little curtsy.

"Please, I'm just the lord's Honorable son." He waved as if to shoo away formalities. "Here, I'm simply Mica the photographer."

"Then why were we moving the barrels?"

"Staging," he said, as if that explained everything. "In fact, would you mind posing for a couple photos? You look like you were born to stand in front of a camera."

"I do not mind."

"Brilliant, you're the picture of perfection. Could you sit on the front barrel?" He pulled a cheesy grin and batted his masculine eyelashes. "Please?"

I laughed and jumped onto the barrel.

His camera flashed a couple times. Sometimes he asked me to change my pose in minor ways, or he snapped a picture without warning.

"Pictures don't do you justice," he muttered. "Do you mind if I do a video?"

"Video?" I asked, only vaguely familiar with the term. I knew it had something to do with their cameras and the telly, but that was about all.

"Yeah," he said. "You don't need to do anything fancy. Just sing a little song or give your usual speech when greeting someone to the castle."

I had no speech for greeting people, but I had plenty of songs. However, the thought of singing in front of Mica made my insides squirm. Thankfully,

228

these past couple of dreaming weeks made me proficient at ignoring my uncomfortable stomach.

"I am out of practice for singing," I said.

He raised his eyebrows. "That means you practice. Oh, please, now I have to hear you."

My cheeks heated. "I suddenly feel far too shy."

"Please?" he pleaded. "It could be anything—it could even be 'Mary Had a Little Lamb.' I won't judge you. Treat me like a friend, or pretend I'm not here."

Why was it all too easy to imagine Mica as one of my closest friends?

Relenting, I closed my eyes. I began with a hum and rocked my foot against the side of my barrel seat for rhythm.

> Here, Imazhin's shores
> Have much to teach me.
> Goddess of the lake
> Is she who greets me.

> Here, Imazhin's shores
> Remind me where to put perspective's North.
> Minds become as clear
> As waves that pull in and out, rolling forth.

> I was once a fool
> Who thought the world was at my feet and palm,

But I never once
Could tell Imazhin's waters to be calm.

Only she alone
Commands the sea to rise or fall with pride.
Only she alone
Can humble every man who sails her tide.

Here, Imazhin's shores
Transform the troubled mind to higher planes.
Woes are left behind
On solid ground while I ascend domains.

Here, Imazhin's shores
Have much to teach me.
Goddess of the lake
Is she who greets me.

The room echoed with the last notes of my song. Then silence.

"Are you still here?" I asked, opening my eyes. Mica stood at the back of the room.

"Yeah," he said quietly, stepping closer on light feet, as if afraid that his footsteps would break the magic of the music. "I did a zoom-out effect to show off the scenery. You have a beautiful voice, and that was a beautiful song. I've never heard it before. I can't wait to review the recording. It might be one of my best works. To think, you did that without any rehearsals or second takes. You're amazing, you know that?"

My cheeks flamed under his praise, and his camera clicked again with another picture.

"That should be plenty for this location," he said, adjusting a camera nob. "If you have other duties to attend to, I don't want to take too much of your time."

I shrugged. "My duty today is to aid you in your task."

"Brilliant." He grinned. "Because I lied about not wanting to take too much of your time. I'd love a tour of the castle and grounds. Also, I heard you have the world's largest trebuchet. I'd love to catch some pictures of that."

"Of course," I said, directing him outside. "Right this way, Honorable Mica."

I guided him down the path of the Riverside Arena, oddly embarrassed as my father did his usual skit with the massive machine. Mica took several pictures from multiple angles, but there was something in his attitude that separated him from everyone else who watched and snapped pictures.

This notion increased as I guided him around the castle, courtyard, and gardens. After two full weeks of working, I felt confident enough in my knowledge about the oddly refurbished castle. The sun was high in the sky by the time we finished in the Peacock Garden. It was the time of year for roses, as they bloomed most abundantly. I wanted to smell every variety, and Mica was more than eager to catch more pictures of me between the flowers.

I tilted my head at him. "You take pictures differently than other people. I once saw a woman take a photo of every angle with every five steps. You seem more…careful with your pictures."

Mica smirked. "That's because I'm not taking pictures for online maps, and I actually want my pictures to look good."

I pondered on that. Were some pictures better than others? Comparing them to small paintings, yes, some paintings displayed more skill than others. That was when it all clicked. "You are an artist."

"Yeah," Mica said, raising his camera to his face again.

Of course. Everyone could draw, but few took the time to draw as carefully as Mica took his pictures. Few took the time to make their paintings as realistic as possible. In this world with its technology, the most realistic pictures were created with a snap of a camera, so of course everyone created them, probably for the same reason most people drew pictures in Somnus: to describe events, to record memories, and to share stories.

"Do you tell stories with your pictures?" I asked.

"A picture might be worth a thousand words, but they're still snapshots of life. Great photographers can tell stories with a single snapshot. My best friend was a novelist who created characters to laugh and cry with, places to fascinate the mind, and adventures to keep you up at night, wondering what happened next. Photographers can do that too, but instead of spending hours writing words, we research subjects, strategize angles, and manipulate lighting to create our stories." He turned his camera around in his hands.

Most of what he said made sense except, "Manipulate lighting?"

"Sure," he said. "Depending on the shutter speed or aperture, I can add brightness or make it darker. Then, using a computer, I can add a filter to emphasize certain colors or adjust the contrast."

"How fascinating," I said, understanding only the concept of his words. "I would very much like to see some of your works, especially if they tell stories as you described."

"Photography like that is hard to come by, especially these days when everyone has their own camera with easy filters. Since anyone and everyone takes pictures these days, fewer people understand the art of photography. Fewer people respect it as an actual career."

His voice lowered and his eyes saddened as he looked down on his bulky camera.

"I wonder," I asked, "can you teach me how to photograph?"

Mica's face twisted into confused humor. "Wha— are you not English?"

I bit my lips inward. "No. I was born and raised far away from here."

He laughed. "Oh, you fooled me. Your accent's as clean as the Queen's English. I never would have guessed without your 'how to photograph.'"

"Did I say it incorrectly?"

He quirked a smile, as if this was a conversation he never imagined having. I could say the same.

"You know, now that you mention it, I realize it is a funny phrase." He chuckled. "Curious. I know there's a right way to say it, but at the moment, all I can think of is your turn of the question. What was it again?"

"Can you teach me how to photograph?" I repeated.

"Ah, right," he laughed as his eyes lit with en- lightenment and humor. "The phrase is 'can you teach me photography?'"

"Either way, the question still stands. Can you?"

"I can, but I'll need to check with my valet about my schedule. I should also check in with your manager to let him know I'm done for today."

"How lovely," I said. "I also need to clock my hours for the day. I may guide you there."

"Or," he said, extending his elbow to me, "I may escort you instead."

I grinned and happily took the gentleman's arm. We parted temporarily as he called upon his valet and I went to the office. Clocking out was quick work, but I lingered, hoping to say goodbye to my friend before heading home. Besides, my father worked later, so I could stay and wait for him.

Mica stepped out of the office with another man. He was taller and had the face of a stone: hardened, expressionless, and weathered enough to make his age unknowable. If I had to make a guess, I would have said early thirties. Again, I was awful at guessing ages.

"Honorable Wright," I said, giving a little curtsy. "If you are waiting for a carriage, perhaps you should wait inside. It looks like it might rain."

"As usual. You're really not from here, are you."

His words were more of a statement than a question, allowing me to ask, "Who accompanies you?"

Mica thumbed at the man behind him. "Miles Knightly. He's my adopted valet."

"Adopted?" I echoed.

"It's a long story." Mica smirked.

I buckled down with my biggest eyes, full of curiosity.

Mica laughed. "I'm no good at telling stories. That was Caden's job. Do you want to tell it, Miles?"

The valet's shoulders slumped slightly. Not from a burden, but from sadness. Was it a tragic tale?

"My former duty was to the Honorable Caden Seaver. As Honorable Wright mentioned, Seaver was a storyteller, an author, but one lacking inspiration. To strike his imagination, Honorables Seaver and Wright went backpacking along the western coastline. There, they found a peculiar young maid who claimed to be a princess from another world."

That last sentence harnessed my attention.

"A princess? From another world?" I asked. "What was her name?"

"Rio?" Mr. Knightly guessed, looking to Mica for confirmation.

"Reo," Mica corrected. "We all called her Emer though—"

"Emerald!" I burst, then clapped my hands over my mouth. It was improper for a princess to shout, but how could I stay quiet when my sister had found a way into my dream?

Mica and Knightly responded as expected to my sudden interruption. They stared with surprised eyes. Mica also looked puzzled, which confused me.

"Did you know her?" he asked.

Not trusting myself to speak without shouting, I kept my hands over my mouth and nodded.

"How?" Mica asked. "She claimed to be from another world and had never come this far north."

I slowly lowered my hands and prayed to the goddesses that these men would understand. "Princess Emerald Reo of Somnus," I said, earning an extra surprise from the men—apparently, they had heard of Somnus, "is my sister."

Chapter 20

PEARL

"They disappeared?" I asked. We had moved our conversation to the Conservatory Tea House as Mica and Mr. Knightly recounted the story about Honorable Seaver's attempts to return Emer to Somnus. The kitchen was busy as they prepared for afternoon tea, but the seating was closed to the public. We snagged two two-seater tables next to the large arching windows for our conversation. I was grateful to have some place private, but even more, I was grateful to finally have someone who knew about my sisters and Somnus.

Knightly shook his head slowly. "No one knows what happened to Honorable Seaver and the woman known as Emer."

"We know," Mica argued. "Emer returned to Somnus, and she took Caden with her."

Knightly's sad frown remained. "There's no proof. No one else was there. As far as the world's concerned,

Honorable Seaver took Emer to Merlin's Cave and they were lost in the storm or abducted."

"But there is proof!" Mica pointed at me. "Pearl knows Emer!"

Knightly shook his head again. "She could be from the same acting group as Amber Princeton."

"Pearl," Mica asked, "did you see Caden in Somnus? Is he alright?"

I shook my head. "Unfortunately, I know of no Cadens or Honorable Seavers. But I have been asleep for the past couple weeks, so it is possible that he and Emer are in Somnus now without my knowledge."

Mica drummed his hands on the table with excitement. "You're sleeping too? Do you have hypoesthesia too?"

He reached across the table and grabbed my hand. There was no way I could have prepared myself for such physical contact. I froze even as his warm hand enveloped mine.

What just happened? Why did he look at me with such anticipation?

"I…what?"

"Hypoesthesia," he said, as if that confusing word should explain everything. "Can you feel me? Emer said she felt nothing but wool."

"Oh," I said, trying to make sense of his words. How could anyone think when such warm hands touched them? No gloves. Just…warmth. "I, eh…you are very warm, Mica." Maybe as warm as my face.

Mica looked down at our hands and drew his back. "Oh. Then, how do you know you're dreaming?"

I gestured to the glass of water in front of Mica. "Everything that I eat tastes like apples."

"Apples?" Mica repeated.

I nodded. "All drinks are apple juice, and all food is applesauce or apple crisps. It put me in trouble when I drank four pints of rum during my first day here." I paid for it ever since with my constant nausea and aches.

Mica's eyes went wide. "You don't look old enough to drink legally. I'm barely legal."

I shrugged. "According to your laws, I am not. Regardless, the point is I am dreaming and cannot wake up as you said Emer was. Exactly how did she wake? What was the place where Emer returned to Somnus?"

"Merlin's Cave," Mica said. "It's in Tintagel. Miles, how long of a drive would that be?"

Mr. Knightly fiddled with his phone, its light casting a peculiar glow across his face. "It's almost three hundred and fifty kilometers away. A drive would take at least three and a half hours."

My jaw dropped. "You can go so far so quickly? May we start now?"

Mica turned to his valet, eager anticipation lighting his eyes. Knightly sighed and flipped his wrist to glance at a leather—bracelet? Right, I had seen people wearing those before. They called them "watches." An appropriate name for how often the people "watched" them.

"We would arrive around supper time. Are your obligations in Warwick complete?"

Mica grinned and cupped his bulky photo machine. "With Pearl's tour and photogenic poses, I have more than enough to showcase their Knight's Village."

Knightly cleared his throat. "Pearl is underage. We would need her guardian's permission."

"Oh, yeah." Mica chuckled nervously. "Thanks, Miles. I don't know what I'd do without you."

The valet suppressed a smirk. "Accidentally commit a dozen felonies to serve a score of unfinished projects."

Mica laughed and nudged his valet playfully on his shoulder. Despite the younger man's playfulness, the older man became more stiff.

I thought of my guardian—the man who looked like the king of Somnus, but acted like a tired laborer. Considering how protective he became of me after my drinking mishap, I doubted he would allow me to go to Tintagel, especially if it was to leave this dream altogether.

"I have no guardian," I said.

Mica shrugged as if that was expected. "Emer didn't either, but she was given payment from her employer. Do you have any loose ends to tie before we try to wake you?"

I thought about Hans. No, if this was only a dream, he would not miss me. And since it was a dream, perhaps I could return to it another night. "No. I am eager to return home."

Still, the men refused to take me until after I had spoken to the castle manager. I left him a note to pass to my father while Mica confirmed my manager had his card of contact information.

Mica and Knightly escorted me to the parking lot where we boarded one of those strange carriages that constantly occupied the streets. Knightly sat up front behind a wheel like a great ship's. Mica helped me into the low seats behind. They were furbished in leather and cushioned like my father's throne.

Our drive began quietly as I took in the experience of my first ride in an automobile. I asked Mica questions about how it worked. Despite his assurances that he knew only the basics of car mechanics, his descriptions went over my head.

"If you asked me about cameras," he said, "that would be another story."

"I enjoy stories. What can you tell me?"

He started to explain the various buttons and purposes of his bulky device, leaning against my shoulder to show me. Similar to the moment he had grabbed my hand, I had to catch my breath and settle my stomach again from his touch. Never before had I sat so close to a young and charming man.

We quickly became distracted by the small viewing screen displaying his recent photos. I gaped in amazement at the tiny version of me sitting on the barrel. It was a frozen image of the past, clearer than a polished mirror. He played the recording of my song and said nothing as we both listened. The more I learned about what cameras could do, the more they amazed me. Not only could they capture images, but also sound, like preserving an echo.

When my song finished, Mica said, "That's gold, you know? You're an amazing singer. Is that a song from your home world?"

I began to talk of Somnus and its music, but the topic quickly shifted back to Mica's pictures when he showed me a picture of Emer. It seemed impossible, but there she was. Mica told me about Emer, Caden, and the places they went together. It was extra peculiar to see pictures of Emer in fashions of this land, standing at stone castle balconies, sitting before cold fireplaces, or walking beside the man named Caden. I had seen Emer accompany men before, but never with such interest in her eyes.

With every photo, our conversation shifted. We discussed so many things with the eagerness of strangers, yet the casualness of best friends. Talking with Mica came as easily as talking with one of my sisters. He laughed a lot and seemed as genuine as gems. I hardly noticed the time passing until my stomach growled for supper.

"Excuse me," I cringed. "I may have skipped lunch." That happened more frequently lately, as my nausea gave me little appetite.

Mica's eyes became worried for me. "Well, that won't do. We can stop for supper before reaching Tintagel. Miles," he called to our driver, "what city is ahead?"

"We are about fifteen kilometers out of Exeter."

"Brilliant," Mica said, then turned to me. "What are you in the mood for?"

I shrugged. "It matters not what I eat. It all tastes like apples."

"Oh, right." He pursed his lips and hummed in thought. "Everything tastes like apples. Care to test that?"

"How?" I asked.

Instead of answering me, he turned back to our driver.

"Hey, Miles. Can you stop at Nando's?"

"You assume Nando's is as popular everywhere as it is in London. I'll need to pull aside to search their locations."

"Oh, right." Mica blushed. "Sorry."

His reddened round cheeks and sheepish smile brought out my own smile. His willingness to accept fault was another token of adoration. How could a grown man be so adorable?

"You're in luck, Honorable Wright," Mr. Knightly said. "Nando's is in Exeter. We can be there in twenty minutes."

"Brilliant," Mica said. "Actually, I remember Emer saying that one of her sisters was vegetarian. Was that you? Nando's is known for their chicken, but they have vegetarian courses if I remember right."

"Vegetarian?" I asked.

"Someone who doesn't eat meat."

"Oh, that would be Marin," I said.

"Brilliant, because it's their peri-peri we want to test."

"Peri—what?" I asked. "Is it going to make me intoxicated?"

Mica laughed. "No, but if you have any tastebuds at all, you'll taste it."

I raised my brows at him, but he said no more.

Nando's turned out to be a restaurant. The concept of restaurants still boggled my mind a little. The people of this dream world paid other people to make food for them. The best thing I could compare it to from Somnus was our inns, where travelers without their own homes to cook were provided breakfast or supper. Except these restaurants worked all day and served locals as much as travelers.

Once, when I had slipped a complaint to Father about working at the castle, he suggested I go work for one of these restaurants instead. That concept was even more bizarre. Restaurants here were not home kitchens of Ma and Pa's cooking turned into additional income. They were companies with kitchens spread across the kingdom and strangers working their recipes. Such a peculiar world.

Our carriage parked, then Knightly came around to open Mica's door. Mica offered his hand to help me exit. I appreciated his help. These seats were far too low and the carriage was too close to the ground. I grabbed his hand firmly to stand from the carriage, mildly embarrassed by how much I enjoyed the feel of Mica's hand in mine.

He led me inside to wait in line where we could choose our meal.

"Pick a type of chicken from the peri-peri menu," Mica said. "Then choose the hotness level."

"Hot?" I asked. I was fairly certain I could recognize temperatures in my mouth. Simply not flavors. Considering the menu and my skipped lunch, I chose five chicken wings.

When requesting my order, Mica added a request to have each chicken wing served in different spices, ranging from lemon and herb to extra hot. He also requested milk on the side. Knightly stood at the register to pay and wait for our order while Mica took me to the seating area. We made ourselves comfortable at a booth, returning to our conversations from the vehicle until Knightly joined us with two platters of food. He set a plate of sweet potato wedges and a pita wrap in front of Mica, a sandwich known as a burger for himself, and five bread-covered chicken wings for me.

The smell alone singed my nasal hairs.

"What is that?"

Mica sheepishly pushed the concoction of spices closer to me. "Your taste test."

"You expect me to eat that?" I cried. "What is in it to make it smell so…pungent?"

"Er, good question," Mica said, looking back on the menu. "I think it's the peri-peri, whatever that is. A pepper?"

"Pepper?" I asked. "Such as black pepper?"

He laughed. "Oh, so much more than that. Just take a small bite. Here, start with this one. It should be the least spicy."

I took a bite of the breaded chicken and tasted sour apple on more sour apple.

To Mica's surprise, I shrugged.

"Alright," he said, gesturing to another piece, "try this one. It's the spiciest."

He also opened the milk carton as if he expected me to need it immediately.

I swallowed my nerves and picked up the crispy chicken. The texture was firm and flakey, more than the breaded cheese rolls from Huiess. I closed my eyes and took a bite into the crispy chicken. Based on the smell alone, I expected it to explode in my mouth. The texture made the experience unique. It was crunchy and juicy all at once.

But it was still apples. I took another bite to be sure, then shook my head.

"I taste apples."

Mica's face shifted back and forth between disappointment and amazement. "But you can smell it?"

"I currently smell nothing else."

"And you see the chicken. I've heard of experiments with food coloring that can change people's perceptions on what they're eating."

I focused my eyes on the chicken and inhaled the spicy aroma. A regular-sized bite confirmed the taste of apples. I shrugged.

"Here, try dipping it in this." He pushed a small cup of sauce across the table.

I expected nothing different as I dunked the piece of chicken into the small dish and chewed it. Unfortunately, I was correct. More apples. Mica gaped at me.

"Is something wrong?"

"Your tastebuds, apparently," he said. "I believe you. You either have an insanely high tolerance for spices, or you have no tastebuds."

I pouted. "You doubted me before?"

He shrugged. "Your sister had no sense of feeling, so I expected something similar, but…taste seems like an odd thing to lose."

I pointed at him with my second piece of chicken. "Is it? Have you ever tasted food while dreaming?"

"I suppose not."

Our conversation shifted back to the topics discussed in the motorized vehicle, all the while Mica and Knightly failed not to stare in wonder at my continued eating.

With our stomachs filled (mine aching a bit more than usual), we returned to the vehicle to drive another hour to the town of Tintagel. Knightly parked us at the edge of a cove. The grey water rushed angrily into the small bay, and what looked like mountains in the far distance might have been a line of clouds. It was hard to tell, and I wondered how far the water went.

"This is where Emer returned to Somnus?"

Mica shrugged. "We suppose. I didn't see exactly what happened. It was storming and a bunch of branches barricaded the rest of us away while Emer and Caden went to the cave."

"What do you remember?" I asked. "Tell me everything."

He took a deep breath. "Let's see, when Caden and I arrived at this spot, we found Emer standing up there, in the middle of the bridge." He pointed high up to our left at the incredible bridge that spanned between the mainland and the almost-island.

"Up there?" I pointed to confirm.

"Yep. Caden ran up to her, but as he did, thorny branches grew from the fence to block his path. He scraped by, but it was too thick for Miles and me to pass. Next thing I saw, Caden was up on the bridge with Emer. They both came down and went to the cave below. That was the last anyone saw of them."

I mulled over his story, wishing to know more. "Maybe we should retrace her footsteps. Can we go up there?"

"Sure, why not?" Mica shrugged and started down the path to the left. It branched off to stairs, some leading to the beach below and some to the ruins above. We took the stairs upward as they wound between rocks of the steep cliffside.

We walked into what looked like the foundation for a castle, as low stone walls outlined rooms. It reminded me of when I used to build my own little castles for my dolls, using little stones that would tumble before I could stack them too high, leaving me to pretend the walls were finished.

Mica led me to the middle of a metal bridge, saying, "Emer was standing here when we found her. Caden joined her, then they went back this way." He pointed back the way we came. We returned down the steps, then continued onto the rocky beach.

Reaching the shore, I closed my eyes and spread my arms before the misty waves.

"To think, Emer stood here. I may be worlds away from home, but my sister was here too. It almost helps me feel at home. If only the sun shone a little more."

The area around us brightened, as if the clouds had broken to create a ray of light for us.

"Er," Mica slurred. "Did that just happen?"

I opened my eyes, expecting to see a bright ray of sunlight peeping between the clouds. No, it was still covered. Yet the area around us was as bright as a summer day.

Mica's attention spun around us. "Where's that light coming from?"

I shrugged. There were many things about light that made little sense to me. For instance, how fire created it and how mirrors could intensify it. Were light and heat connected? If so, then how could some of our most chilly winter days be completely cloudless? I disliked those days. They were deceptive.

"Is this the cave?" I asked, walking towards the gaping hole at the bottom of the mount.

"Yep," Mica said, following me, still glancing around for the answer to unknown questions.

I stood at the edge of the mouth, peering into the darkness. "It is too dark. Can we light the inside?" I asked, thinking of those phones that flashed brilliantly.

Before Mica could pull out his phone or some other lighting device, the cave lit up with a bright white light.

Mica turned to me and jumped. "Holy crap!"

I followed his eyes to the source of the light: my chest. Or perhaps my heart.

"Oh! What is that?" I asked.

Mica nearly shrieked, "You don't know?"

"It does not seem to hurt." Unless I stared at its brightness for too long. "What are you? And may you get off of me?"

The little ball of light fell to land at my feet. At least it listened and had a pleasant nature. Mica, however, stepped back, all the more terrified.

"Little ball of light," I said, squatting beside it, "can you dim yourself that we may study you closer?"

The light dimmed, but revealed nothing within itself. It seemed to be pure light.

"Holy crap," Mica cursed again. "Emer could control plants. You can control light?"

Could I? "This little ball of light seems to do my bidding. I cannot say that I control all or any light. Also, what is this curse you keep using? I have heard Hans use it, though he never called it holy. I thought that curse word meant poop. Do you believe in holy poop?"

Mica's shocked face twitched with humor until it morphed entirely into laughter. He continued until he required a deep breath to finish.

"No," he said between chuckles. "It's only an expression. Because, holy crap, *you can control light*. Caden almost wrote off Emer's magic as parlor tricks, but whatever you just did was something else. What else can you do? I think you did something outside the cave too as it got brighter, but the sun was still behind the clouds."

I raised my hands, confused. "All I did was ask, and it happened."

"Then ask something else," he urged.

Unsure of anything, I crouched beside the light again. "Little light, can you wake me? Can you take me back to Somnus?"

The light pulsed several times, slowly, then quickly.

I shook my head. "What does that mean? I do not speak…light. Can you speak or write it for me?"

To my astonishment, the light grew, stretching itself across the ground in a cursive sentence.

Mica read the words aloud. "Light alone cannot wake you."

The sentence pulsed before shrinking back into a single ball.

"Wait," I asked. "What do you mean 'light alone?' You can help me, but you need help too?"

The light stretched into another sentence.

"Light is truth. Truth is light."

Mica scratched his head. "What's that supposed to mean?"

The light pulsed and stretched again.

"One is incomplete without the other," I read.

I pouted my lips, feeling like a student before a priestess as she read scriptures about the creation of Rezhina Valley. I tried hard to pay attention and understand our religious history, but why did they always speak in riddles?

The sentence pulsed, but remained for us to ponder its words.

"I think," Mica said, "it means you need a light and a truth to wake up. Caden and I had a theory that Emer could use her magic to take her home. At first, we thought it was literal, that she could grow a tree to carry her home. Then, we tried to simply activate her magic in places with magical legends, such as this cave."

I stared at the sentence of light and our cavern surroundings. "It seems that I need to find a truth. Whatever truth Emer might have found here, I have a feeling that my truth will be found elsewhere."

"Where?"

I shook my head. "I cannot say, because I do not know."

Chapter 21

PEARL

"I don't know what Caden and Emer did differently," Mica said as we rejoined Mr. Knightly at the black vehicle and populated area of the ruins. "I don't know exactly how Emer returned to Somnus and took Caden with her."

A growl so low I almost missed it came from Knightly. "Because they didn't 'return.'"

Mica's eyebrows lowered and his mouth tightened. It was the closest expression to a frown I had seen on him.

"They did return," Mica said firmly. "Maybe I'm telling myself a fairytale, but considering the more realistic possibilities, I choose to believe the fairytale."

Knightly scoffed. "That's what fairytales are for, right? To either hide ugly truths or warn children about them."

"What do you mean?" I asked.

256

"Take the tale of the *Pied Piper*," Knightly said. "A town with a rat problem paid a piper to draw them out. He did, but the town refused to pay him his full dues. For revenge, the piper drew out their children and sealed them in a cave."

"How horrible," I said. "You tell this story to your children?"

Knightly scoffed again. "To teach them to pay their debts. It's a more pleasant story than the possible realities. Some theories say all the kids died of a sickness, but why were only the children affected? Another theory says the town was so starved that they sold their own children for money to gypsies or colonists. At least in the fairytale, they lost their children by mistake."

I gaped at Mica. "Is that true?"

He gave one of his sheepish shrugs. "All that's actually known for certain is that hundreds of children in a single town suddenly disappeared."

Two different stories to explain the same tragedy. Or was it a tragedy? "Maybe they woke up, like Emer did."

Mica blinked at me as his lips edged up into a delightful smile. "That's a better fairytale."

Knightly turned away to hide his grumbles. Mica, on the other hand, raised his camera to snap a picture of the water's edge.

I pointed at Mica's camera. "Can you teach me more about how to use that? This is a lovely area, and maybe if I have an image of this place, I may use it to ponder Emer's disappearance after we leave."

"Sure," Mica said, guiding me back to the edge of the small bay for a better view. He pulled the thick strap over his head then lifted it over mine, hanging the bulky device like a millstone around my neck. He rotated to stand beside me, close enough to graze elbows as he reached for the camera.

"Hold it like this," he said, emphasizing his grips around the device. "The lens is most of the weight, so use your left hand to hold it. Your right hand is a little trickier as you want your thumb loose to adjust any digital features and your index free to reach the capture button."

"Alright," I said, taking the camera as he suggested. He made a few adjustments, playing with my fingers. Never in my fifteen years had any man touched my hands in such an intimate yet playful manner. He made my insides warm while my skin shivered.

"Good," he said. "First thing first, you need to take off the lens cap. Then press this little button on the lens to rotate it out. Digital cameras will scream at you if you don't."

"Scream?"

He laughed. "Not verbally, but—" He flipped a switch to light up the square screen on the back. A sign covered most of the options, saying, "Before taking photos, rotate the zoom ring to extend the lens."

"What a mild scream."

He laughed again, harder. "Alright, next put your eye up to that tiny window at the top."

"Like this?" I asked. "How marvelous! It truly is a tiny window! Except everything is blurry."

"You need to focus on your subject." His hand wrapped around my left on the lens. "Find your subject, or the object you want to take a picture of, then rotate the lens slowly, like this, until it becomes clear."

His hands cupped mine, rotating the lens, causing my view in the little window to wave in and out of focus. I focused on the image in my tiny window as the image came into focus. White lines became crisp and bubbly waves became defined. A bird flew by in clear definition, and I picked out the form of a great ship in the distance.

I pressed down my finger on the button he indicated. The camera responded with a satisfying *shh–click*.

"Now," Mica said, gently pushing my hands and camera away from my face, "you can press this button to see the photo you took in the larger viewing screen. See?"

The image I recently viewed through the tiny window became replicated on the back of the camera. "How wonderful! How does it work?"

"The camera? It's actually a crazy trick of capturing light."

"Capturing light?"

"Yeah. The trick is to capture just the right amount of light. It's all about the shutter. When you click this button," he gestured to the one that initiated the picture, "a shutter opens and closes between the lenses. The speed of its opening and closing determines how precise the moment is that you want to catch." He flipped his camera and pointed it at the water. "See, a quick shutter speed catches an exact moment in time." He took a picture, then showed it on the screen. The water was so crisp and clear that I could count the bubbles between the waves. "Having a longer shutter speed lets the image blur a little." He made a couple adjustments on the camera, then took another picture of the same spot of water. This time, the waves looked feathery and soft. My heart melted a little at the serenity of it.

"How interesting," I said. "May I try?"

"Ah, not yet, because the shutter speed is only half of it. The second part is the aperture."

"Aperture?" I asked.

"The size of the hole the shutter makes when it opens. A large hole lets in more light than a smaller hole. If you have a slow shutter speed on a bright day, you need a smaller hole to control how much light comes through."

"Alright, I think I understand. May I try now?"

He laughed, reset some settings, then handed the camera over. "Digital cameras can be conveniently set on automatic, but professionals know how to work the settings manually, manipulating the light to their advantage."

"Manipulating the light," I echoed. "Because you cannot ask."

He smirked. "No, only you can do that. Actually, can we show my valet? Maybe the show of magic will convince him we're not crazy."

I shrugged. "We can try."

Mica waved for Knightly to join us before I asked for a ball of light to appear.

The light appeared again, just as I asked, like a tiny sun floating above my palm.

Knightly went through a couple phases of doubt, confusion, and even anger before accepting my magic. Meanwhile, I bounced the ball of light between my hands, learning that it would not do anything unless I asked it verbally.

"Lucy," I said. "Yes, I think I will name it Lucy."

Knightly frowned. He liked to do that. "It's an element, not a pet."

"I think she likes it," I said. "Do you, Lucy? Bob up and down for yes, or shake back and forth for no."

The light bobbed up and down and sideways then stopped.

"Huh." Mica's wide eyes studied the little light. "Looks like she can't make up her mind."

"Or," Knightly grumbled, "it has no mind to make its own choice."

Mica waved a playful hand at his valet. "Oh, quiet you. Only you could take the fun out of magic. That's what it is, you know? Magic!"

He grinned at me so wide and joyfully, that I knew Lucy, my little ball of light, was a good thing. We continued to talk about my light magic and the magic of cameras as the sun lowered to the blue horizon. That sight was a magic of its own.

"Is there no land on the other side?" I asked, watching as the sun dipped directly into the water. No mountains blocked its light. The shapes I thought were mountains before were merely clouds, crawling like caterpillars across the horizon. No, caterpillars was the wrong description. Caterpillars could not filter the sunlight and make it change to the most beautiful shades of pink and yellow.

"There's land," Mica said, "but it's too far for us to see. I think Emer was amazed by the ocean too, saying something about your homeland being surrounded by mountains."

I nodded. Hearing about Emer and Somnus burned my heart a little. How I longed to see them both again.

Mr. Knightly cleared his throat and tapped at the leather watch on his wrist.

Mica laughed. "Here we are, staring at the sun, and I didn't even notice the time passing. Miles, could you arrange a place for the three of us to lodge for the night?"

"Of course." He gave a little bow, then began fiddling with his phone.

Turning back to me, Mica said, "I'm sorry we weren't able to return you to your homeland, but I'm not sorry for the chance to spend more time together."

I smiled. "Me too."

Knightly drove us back into town to a two-leveled cottage. A post hung at the front, featuring four stars and "B&B." Whatever those meant. It was luxurious, with temperature-controlled rooms and cushioned mattresses, though Mica fondly called it "quaint."

I explored my room, enjoying the front window view that faced the beautiful shoreline, then joined

Mica and Knightly on the main level common area to chat.

We were halfway through a review of the pictures Mica took at the cave when my lower stomach burned with more vengeance than usual. I groaned and clutched my stomach as if it only needed a hug to feel better. "Oh, what did I eat?"

"Nando's?" Mica guessed. Somewhere in there must have been the answer as his eyes lit with fear. "Oh, bugger. I forgot about the other end."

"What other end?"

He cringed. "I'm sorry. I didn't realize it would still affect you even if you couldn't taste it, especially if you're not used to spices."

"How will it affect me?" I cried. Why did it hurt so much? My constant nausea had gained a partner in crime as my body burned from the inside.

Mica's cringe deepened with his confession. "Spicy food hurts just as much coming out as it does going in."

"Coming…" It dawned on me. "I suppose this is an appropriate situation to curse with 'crap.'"

Mica laughed. Hard. He bent over and slapped his hand to his knee. "Oh, Pearl, I'm sorry you're in pain, but you slay me. What did I ever do without you?"

Pleased as I was to make Mica laugh, the pain urged me back upstairs to my room.

264

All etiquette went out the window as I moaned and groaned on the toilet. If Mica said it burned this much going in, perhaps I was grateful that I had not tasted it. Or perhaps that was the problem. I would not have eaten so much if I knew how much it would burn.

I remained on the toilet until my legs became stiff. Standing hurt, and a red ring imprinted my bottom. I closed the door behind me as I vacated the water closet. It smelled downright awful, yet I anticipated returning within the hour.

"I may never forgive you, Mica," I moaned alone. Still, I reflected on our time together and smiled.

Chapter 22

PEARL

Apparently, B&B stood for Bed and Breakfast as toast and oatmeal waited for me in the morning. Before taking a bite, I asked Mica, "Is this spicy?"

Mica laughed and shook his head. "This is as tame as it gets."

"Good," I muttered, still queasy from my constant nausea and lingering effects from the diarrhea. I shoved a spoonful of oatmeal into my mouth. It tasted like chunky applesauce. "It seems that I am collecting a list of things not to eat: nothing fermented or spicy. Is there anything else I should add?"

"Poisonous?" Mica shrugged.

"Too late," I mumbled around my food. This whole dream was a result of poison.

A cheerful tune stole our attention as Mica retrieved his phone. He apologized to me for the interruption before pressing a button and holding it up to his face.

"Hello? . . . Your daughter?" Mica glanced at me. "Yes, Pearl's right here—she's—" He paused as a masculine voice shouted through his phone. "I understand you want her home right now, but seeing as we're in Tintagel, the fastest we can do is three hours—" More shouting.

With a relenting little grunt, Mica held the phone to me. "A man claiming to be your father wants to talk to you."

Blinking, I took the phone. I had never spoken on one before and was unsure if I held it right as I put it to my cheek.

"Hello?" I asked.

"Merle Rey!" the voice of my father raged and swore at me. "Where are you?"

"Tintagel."

"What the bleeding blazes are you doing there?"

The skin above my cheeks grew hot and tears began to form. I had hoped to be awake and back in Somnus with my real father before this strange impersonator discovered my disappearance. Even if he was an imitation, his voice sounded the same. I hated disappointing him. I hated making him scared and angry over me.

"Forgive me, Father," I cried. "I wanted to go home. They said they could take me home."

"They kidnapped you?" he roared.

"No! No, nothing like that. They are helping me return to Somnus. They knew about Somnus and Emer and—"

"Stop it!" he shouted. "You need to stop this Somis craziness! This is exactly the worst kind of trouble it could get you in!"

A sob broke from me. Father had never shouted at me this way before. I hated being in trouble, but even more, I hated that he knew nothing of our true home, even saying its name wrong.

"Do you need me to call the police?" he asked. "Tell me exactly where you are—I'll come get you."

"No, there is no need. Mica can bring me back—"

"I don't want you to spend another minute with that man! Get away, as fast as you can. Run to the police, and I'll come get you."

Another tear rolled down my cheek as my sobs turned into flowing cries. "Father, please do not be angry with me, but I do not want to leave Mica and Knightly. They have been good to me, like the best of friends."

"Merle, I won't say it again—"

"My name is not Merle!" I burst. "And you are not my father!"

Too distraught to hear or say more, I shoved the phone at Mica and ran up to my room, slamming my door behind me.

Throwing myself onto my bed, I buried my face into my pillow to muffle my cries and catch my tears. My fever returned, heating my already warm face and shivering my body. I burrowed under the blankets and barely heard the soft knock on my door several minutes later.

"Who is it?" I asked.

"It's me," Mica said, muffled behind the door. "Can we talk?"

Talking. I wanted to talk to my sisters or, better yet, to my mother. She could always dry my tears. The mere thought of her pained my heart.

"Pearl?"

His worried voice made it easy to imagine him on the other side, waiting for my response. He was a good friend, and I needed a friend.

"Come in," I said, emerging from under the blankets and wiping my eyes clear of tears.

The door creaked open and Mica stepped inside. He stood there like a scolded puppy with hunched shoulders and looking at me with his chin tucked down.

"Er," he started, "Miles is ready to take you back to your father as soon as you're ready."

"The man on the phone is not my father. He sounds like him, looks like him, and even acts like him in some ways, but..." I sniffled and shook my head.

Mica's eyebrows raised. "Yes, he sure acts like a man worried about his only daughter who never came home last night. Why didn't you mention him as your guardian?"

"He may be my guardian, but he is not my father. My father is the King of Somnus. This man…he is wrong. He claims my mother is dead and that I have no sisters. I know I have sisters. *You* know I have sisters."

Mica's eyebrows drew together and he nodded. "Emer had someone claim to know her too. Her mum. But she called her Amber, and Emer said she wasn't really her mum."

"Emer found our mother in this world?" I sat up eagerly.

"Someone like your mother," Mica clarified carefully. "Amber didn't have any sisters. That woman wouldn't know you."

My heart sank.

"Er…" Mica shuffled. "So, what's next? We can run around the country with the bobbies on our tails as we try to find your way home…but it might kill my reputation. And Mr. Knightley's. And my father's, and his position in Parliament depends on his reputation, so a bad one would put him out of a job and make my family destitute…I'm sorry, Pearl. As much as I want to go gallivanting across the country

270

on another magical adventure, I need to return you to your father."

I bowed my head to hide the oncoming tears. "I understand."

With nothing to pack or prepare, I joined Mica back down the stairs and to the vehicle. Beginning the drive back to Warwick, I struggled to keep my tears from forming. The effort added a headache on top of my nausea, hints of fever and diarrhea.

Mica placed his hand on mine. "I wish there was more I could do to help."

I shook my head. "Your friendship and belief in Somnus are more than I would ask of anyone. Thank you."

He pouted his lips in thought until one seemed to strike him. "Hey, how would you like to go shopping before heading back to your father? Hey, Miles, doesn't Warwick have a large shopping centre?"

"I believe it does," Mr. Knightly said. "The Royal Priors should have anything you need."

"Brilliant." Mica grinned. "We'll return you to your father in style, so he'll know we meant no disrespect to you or him."

I shrugged. "So long as those are the rules of this world, and it causes no burden to you. If I may, I would like to use this time to look over your pictures and study them for any clues."

"Good idea," Mica said, pulling out his camera. We spent most of the drive looking over his pictures of Merlin's Cave and discussing the various topics inspired by his pictures. We also discussed a bit more about the art of photography and Mica's favorite locations to take photos. I loved to watch his eyes widen and smile grow while he talked about Kew Gardens and Hyde Park. His eyes turned wistful as he mentioned places he wished to photograph, like the insides of Westminster Abbey and St. Paul's Cathedral. Apparently, they had places "too sacred" for photography. How interesting. How was a photograph any different from a painting or drawing of a place other than its speed of creation?

Before I knew it, the vehicle slowed as Knightly parked us on the side of a street. Mica offered his hand to help me out and into the Royal Priors Shopping Centre of Warwick.

Pausing at the first clothing shop, Mica suggested we go inside.

"What if the next shop has something better?" I grabbed his hand and pulled him along. Yes, I was procrastinating the moment Mica would return me to the man claiming to be my father, but I also truly enjoyed shopping. I loved seeing the beautiful creations of others, and this shopping centre made it so easy to glance through the large windows at the products of each store. In Somnus, our markets often displayed their goods outside to invite people in, but as soon as it started raining, it was a race to pull the products back inside.

With England as cloudy as it was, I assumed they had the same problem. Thankfully, they had glass like it grew on trees. I was fascinated to discover the street itself was covered by a glass roof, as if we were both indoors and outdoors at the same time.

After walking around the entire shopping area, I pulled Mica into some of my favorites. Knightly shadowed us as I asked for Mica's opinion on this dress or that hat or this bag. He seemed to enjoy the phrases, "It looks great on you. Do you want it?"

I wanted it all, but I had no need for any of it. Eventually, I found a dress that made Mica smile widest. Reaching down to my ankles and wrists, the off-white fabric was patterned with light pink and blue swirls. Never in my life had I felt such a soft material. In the fitting room, I found that the stretchy fabric emphasized my figure. Maybe too much?

Considering the other styles from the windows, I doubted if I could find anything less promiscuous. I wished my sisters were there to give their commentary.

Rolling my shoulders back, I decided to go with it. The dress was beautiful, and I liked it, and it was—

Goodness, was that the price? It cost as much as a day of work at the castle!

I shuffled out and gently hung it back on its hanger.

Stepping from the fitting room, Mica was nowhere to be seen, but Knightly stood at the edge of an aisle. Seeing me, he waved down the aisle until Mica joined him. The younger man's eyebrows wrinkled at the sight of me.

"It didn't fit?"

"It fit, I suppose," I said.

"Then why do you look sad?"

"Because the money would be better spent elsewhere."

Mica stepped forward and gestured for me to pass over the dress. "How much is it? This isn't Harrods or even Westfield. That bit of change bothers you? Pearl, I thought you were a princess?"

"I am," I said, "and if my people cannot afford such apparel, then neither should I."

Mica tilted his head, and Knightly frowned.

"Did I say something wrong?" I asked, sheepishly.

"No," Mica said, "just different. I hope you know these are the more affordable brand name dresses. Here, do you think this necklace will go with it?"

He held up a necklace to the dress. It was a singular pearl pendant at the end of a silver chain.

"How lovely," I said. "Are you sure? This is too much."

Mica waved a hand of dismissal. "I need to show your father you were treated nicely. Come on, let's ring it up."

I thanked Mica repeatedly as he bought the outfit, then went back to the fitting room to change. Biting my lip and hunching my shoulders, I emerged. Mica did a double take.

"Well! Aren't you the picture of perfection?"

He took me by the hand and pulled me into a spin.

Knightly cleared his throat. "I'm having a sense of déjà vu. M'lord, we don't have time for a photo shoot. We don't want to keep Pearl's father waiting."

"Are you sure?" Mica sighed. "But we still need to stop for lunch. Isn't there a place nearby with a bunch of restaurants? We can invite her father to join us and hopefully clear up the misunderstandings over a meal."

"That's not a half-bad idea," Knightly said, pulling out his phone. "I believe the place you were thinking of was Livery Street. They have a Nando's."

"No," I said, a little too quickly.

The corner of Knightly's mouth twitched. Was that a smile?

Before I could accuse him of such a tease, he raised his phone to his face and began speaking slowly and clearly.

"Mr. Rey? Yes, your daughter is well and we have brought her back to Warwick. We would like to join you for lunch on Livery Street. May we expect you there in fifteen minutes? Five? Excellent. Your daughter will be there."

He pushed his thumb to his phone and nodded to Mica. "We should be on our way."

Mica smiled. "I think you handled that well. I'm pretty sure if I'd been the one talking, I would have made it sound like we were trading her for a ransom. Like, 'We have your daughter. She is whole and in one piece. Meet us for lunch if you want to see her.'"

Knightly smirked. "And this is why I make your business calls."

I grinned, thinking of Princess Sapphire from Huiess and the funny way she phrased things sometimes.

Then my eyes caught an elderly man sitting against a building, wearing dirty rags and looking like he missed smiling.

"Just a moment," I said, stepping away from Mica and Knightly. I knelt beside the man on the street, discovering that he was homeless and was younger than I thought. But he did miss smiling.

276

I removed my necklace and handed it to him, wishing him well before catching up to Mica as he started across the street.

"You gave him something?" Mica asked.

"I gave him my necklace."

He stopped walking. I was fairly certain that was a dangerous thing to do in the middle of roads, but he gaped. "You mean the one I just bought for you? Why?"

"He needs it more."

"What's he going to do with a necklace?"

"Sell it, of course," I said, urging Mica to finish crossing the street. "Then he will use the money to feed his family. As I said, he needs it more than I do."

"But…it was a gift," Mica said, finally stepping onward, his voice a little broken. As soon as we reached the other side of the road, I paused to explain.

"Forgive me, Mica. Did you not give it to me?"

"Yes, for you."

"You gave it to me to do whatever I wished with it."

"And you wished to give it away? Did you not like it?" Goodness, he looked heartbroken.

"No, I liked it very much," I said in a hurry. "It made me very happy, but the greatest happiness I can have is from making others happy. Thank you, Mica, for giving me something to make others happy too."

He stared at me with those wide eyes of wonder, then released a breathy laugh. "Someday I'll give you something you can't give away."

"The gift I enjoy the most is an expression of true gratitude. I only get that by giving. The look in their eyes and tender smiles are gifts I can keep and cherish forever."

"Then I'll find you a gift of true gratitude that you can cherish forever. But first, let's go convince your father not to draw and quarter me over lunch."

Chapter 23

EMER

Fear clenched Emer's heart as she stared across the grasslands until they ended at the Midnight Forest. She could pick out the first scattering of trees in the distance, but the trees behind quickly faded into shadow as the density grew and her sister's curse blackened the area.

Marin and Ranae's horse pulled up beside hers and Caden's.

"Oh," Marin said. "I see why they renamed it to Midnight Forest."

Caden grunted. "I suppose we can expect something different for every sleeping princess. Thorns around Emer, the whirlpool around you, and darkness around Pearl."

"Poor Pearl," Emer whispered. "She must be terrified in there."

"If she's awake," Caden said. "You had no idea you were surrounded by terrors."

Yet we must brave the terrors to wake my sisters. Emer shivered.

"I think the horses need rest," she found herself saying.

"Again?" Caden asked. "We've barely made any headway since pausing for lunch."

"But they carry more people than usual. They need rest and water. Marin? Would you pull some water from the soil to create a place for the horses to drink?"

Her older sister raised her eyebrows, but began to call the water up from the ground.

The carriage pulled up beside them, and Leo frowned. "Why are we stopping? The forest is finally in sight. We should push ahead."

"The horses need to rest," Caden said, dismounting. He raised a hand to help Emer down, but kept his eyes on the forest.

"Thank you," Emer said, hoping to earn his attention as her feet touched the ground.

He spared her a glance, then mumbled, "I need to write this down." With a blushing neck, he released her hand to grab his parchment and charcoal. Emer huffed. Was he embarrassed by her?

"Perhaps," Marin suggested, "we may rearrange ourselves to burden the animals less."

Ranae smiled and graced his wife with a kiss on the top of her head. "Always thinking of the animals. The four horses pulling the carriage look to be the strongest, but rearranging a team is rarely a good idea. Maybe we can make room for one or two of us to sit inside."

"I can do that," Jesse said, hopping into the carriage.

Emer nodded. "True. When Charlotte first arrived, it carried all her luggage, the ogress, Shinópu, and Gother. The carriage horses may be strong enough to pull five of us."

They discussed a change of seating while the horses rested, then everyone mounted. Emer had hoped the rearrangements would allow her and Caden to remain together, but Marin asked her to join her inside the carriage, leaving Caden to ride alone.

Emer's dissatisfaction and desire to return to their former arrangements increased as Marin peppered her with questions about the types of plants she grew with her magics—asking if they were good for the growth of the ecosystem as a whole. Growing a giant tree outside the Irving home had been useful, but what would happen to it? Did it have the nutrients available to grow there naturally? Would it wither and die without them?

"For that reason," Marin explained, "I had the collected water return to the ground. The plants and animals that naturally inhabit that area need it too. If I left it there, who knows what kind of effects it could have?"

Emer pulled the carriage window shades back to lean her head outside. "Are we there yet?"

Leo chuckled from behind. "I've been asking myself that all day. We should reach the edge of the forest in a couple hours."

"Emer," Marin said, "we have the power to change the world around us. We cannot ignore the consequences of our actions."

Emer internally grumbled and pulled herself back inside. The next couple hours were the longest of her day. She missed the horseless carriages of England that drove at blurring speeds over smooth roads.

Marin prattled on about her past plans to ban butchers from the city limits, then added her new discoveries about aquariums and adding a river to the ocean to cycle the water. She pondered over the possibilities of piping waste out of cities and increasing wages for a civil cleaning force.

"Perfect," Emer muttered. "Our cities are already abandoned, letting us make whatever changes we want."

Marin scowled, but went on to explain the good that could come from their valley's mini apocalypse. Ignoring Marin's comments only led Emer to worry about Pearl's situation and Caden's situation and the possible situation between Pearl and Caden.

Hadn't they reached the forest yet?

She poked her head out of the window again. Nope. She found Caden talking to an attentive Mica about…Pearl. Her mood soured as she waited inside the carriage, trying to ignore the conversations around her and inside her head. Maybe she could shut them out if she fell asleep…

The carriage slowed, and Emer jerked awake. Pulling back the curtains, she saw that they were nearly to the black edge of the forest.

"Perfect," Emer said, opening the door and letting herself out. "I need to relieve myself."

Leo groaned loudly, calling the others to stop.

Caden trotted over with his face toward the forest. "If you can hold it long enough to enter the forest, the darkness of the woods will hide you without causing a scene."

Emer gave him a downward stare, despite his higher position on his horse. "Maybe a man can relieve himself that easily, but I would rather squat behind a carriage where I can see what plants and bugs are beneath me."

Jesse laughed. "Thanks for that image, but I'll back your opinion."

"Fine," Caden said, his neck reddening from Emer's candor. "We pause here. We can gather sticks to create torches before entering the forest."

Everyone dismounted and began to look for debris while Emer stepped away to relieve herself. Coming back, she spotted everyone scattered around the grasslands except Marin and Ranae.

She paused outside the carriage as a hushed conversation caught her ear.

"Are you sure?" Marin's voice asked.

"Yes," Ranae's low voice replied. "I made you wait long enough. I could imagine Scott as our own, and then I wanted one of our own."

"Oh, Ranae."

Emer waited after a couple seconds of silence to make sure their conversation was done before knocking and opening the door.

She found Marin and her husband flustering to hide evidence of a recent passionate embrace. No amount of smoothing her hands down her dress would disguise the redness of Ranae's mouth and Marin's tangled hair.

"Sorry." Emer blushed. "Did I interrupt something?"

Ranae growled. "As a matter of fact—"

"Did you need something?" Marin asked.

Emer cleared her throat, but kept her eyes averted. "Usually, we all help to gather supplies."

"Oh," Marin said, disappointed. "Ranae, hold that thought. I will not let you forget, or regret, this conversation."

Embarrassed for them and herself, Emer stepped away from the carriage, then put a small hill between herself and the others as she searched for loose sticks.

"Emer?" Marin called. "Where are you? Are you alright?"

Emer sniffled back her worries before calling back, "Over here."

Her older sister walked over the hill to her. "What are you doing over here?"

"Collecting kindle."

"Are you not excited to see Pearl?"

"I am," Emer said, confused. "How did I imply otherwise?"

Marin gave her a doubtful look. "You keep trying to delay our journey."

Emer distracted herself by reaching for another loose stick. "The Midnight Forest is foreboding."

"Is that all?"

"No," she mumbled.

Marin folded her arms to demonstrate her stubbornness. "What is wrong?"

Emer sniffled again and refused to meet her sister's eyes. "Everyone knows Pearl is the most beautiful among us."

"As Mica is eager to mention, yes. Does that make you jealous?"

"No," Emer said. "Maybe a little. Maybe a lot. See, we are physical opposites. She has the black hair, dark brown eyes, and youthful face that makes everyone adore her. I have blonde hair, green eyes, and I could probably disguise myself as a man with my figure. I never minded that Pearl was more beautiful, but… what if Caden loses interest in me when he sees her?"

Marin's eyebrows went high. "Do you honestly think that he would do that?"

"No," Emer said again. "Maybe?"

To Emer's dismay, her older sister laughed. "Dear Emer, you have nothing to worry about. Pearl would put your desires before her own and encourage him your way if you have your sights set on him."

"As if I could be satisfied as his second choice?" Emer asked. "Why does he ignore me?"

Marin paused and pinched her lips together. "Only he can answer that."

Emer didn't like that answer. She prodded, "How do you know that Ranae loves you?"

"Other than the fact that he tells me every day?"

Emer grimaced. "Yes, because Caden has only said it once."

Marin released a long breath. "You need to remember, Ranae and I are married. Your relationship with Prince Caden is still young and growing."

"Then how did you know that Ranae loved you in the beginning?"

"In the beginning? It was little things: the way he smiled at me, or encouraged me in my pursuits, or listened to my troubles. When we began courting, it was how he found any excuse to hold my hand and spoil me with gifts, or the way he kissed me. Now that we are married, he reminds me with hundreds of small daily things. He makes promises to me and keeps them."

As she spoke, Emer reflected on Caden's smile and how his eyes softened when she had worn the new dress. Surely, he supported Emer's pursuits to find her sisters and listened to her complaints. Then she remembered how he held her after pulling her from the whirlpool, how gentle and deeply satisfying it was to feel his arms around her.

They hadn't kissed since leaving her father's castle, but Emer remembered the distinct pressure of his lips against hers. It was hard to forget after feeling nothing but wool while she dreamt. The mere memory of his kisses shivered happiness through her.

"Marin?" Ranae's voice called over the hill. "Emer?"

"Come on," Marin said. "We should return to the others."

Emer nodded, only half satisfied with their discussion. Marin was right. Only Caden could answer her questions. She wanted to ask him right away, but he was already in the middle of the group, arranging sticks into bundles.

Emer added her collection and helped bind them together with the long blades of grass.

"Emer," Mica asked, "can you ask the trees to make a path for us?"

"A path to what?" she asked. "Paths need an ending destination, and we do not know where she is. Even if I part the trees, the darkness remains. We will be left groping from tree to tree and easily lost in any small opening. Without markers, we will be lost."

Mica hummed with thought, then picked up one end of Emer's phone vines to walk into the forest with a lighted torch. Within a few steps, he faded into the darkness of the forest. The vine wasn't even half unrolled before the forest swallowed his torch light.

"How unnatural," Marin gasped.

Caden frowned as he scribbled down notes.

"Mica!" Leo shouted into the forest. "Come back! We can't see you!"

"But I'm only—"

288

"Come back!" Leo roared, despite Mica's voice proving his short distance.

"How are we supposed to find her?" Marin asked. "It is pitch black in there."

Caden grumbled. "I don't know. The only way I broke through Emer's thorns was she subconsciously let us through. Then the whirlpool stilled when you asked it to stop in your dream."

Leo growled. "What are you saying, Caden? We have to sit out here and wait?"

"Or you can sit out here and die."

Everyone turned towards the new voice. Except it wasn't new at all.

Gother marched over a little hill at the head of a dozen ogres. They were each armed with swords fit for their oversized bodies and snarled maliciously at Emer and her friends.

Chapter 24

PEARL

The British version of my father burst into the restaurant like a madman. When his eyes found me at a table with Mica and Mr. Knightly, he burst into tears. That was unsettling. He looked like the King of Somnus in every way, except I had never seen my father cry.

I barely had the chance to acknowledge his presence before he had his arms around me.

"Merle! There you are! What the blazes were you thinking, running off like that? You had me scared to death!"

His voice was the exact same as the one I knew and loved, even if it rasped with background tears. I took no pleasure in making him worry over me and found myself crying too.

"Forgive me," I said. "I meant no ill-will upon you."

290

"There you go again," he chuckled in my ear, "talking like a lost princess."

Mica cleared his throat. "That's because she is, Mr. Rey."

Father pulled back from our embrace to let his attention slip to the men beside me. Glaring eyes, jutted jaw, and flaring nostrils were expressions I recognized. Uh, oh. The last time I saw that look was when he found me drunk on my first day. In Somnus, he made that face whenever a lesser noble attempted to woo my sisters or me.

He cradled me closer even as he stood and angled himself between me and Mica. "Who exactly are you, and why did you take my daughter away from me?"

"Father, do not be mad at them—"

"Stay out of this, Merle," he growled at me while keeping his eyes on Mica. "How old are you? Did you know my daughter's only fifteen?"

Mica cleared his throat. "I know my hair suggests otherwise, but I'm only eighteen, Mr. Rey. I can assure you that all my time with your daughter was accompanied by Mr. Knightly."

"I could still make claims against you both for kidnapping and pedophilia."

As much as I feared Father's anger and the possibility of making him cry again, I refused to stand aside for Mica and Knightly to take the blame.

"No," I said. "That is wrong. If you think I was kidnapped or abducted, I cannot allow such falsehoods to hold. I ran away."

Father's anger at Mica turned into surprise at me. "What? Why?"

I squared my shoulders, knowing he would mock my words. "I needed to return to Somnus. You refused to help me, so I convinced these men to take me to Tintagel, where someone was known to return to Somnus."

I prayed Mica and Knightly would secure my slanted truth. Father needed to trust them if I hoped to ever see them again. The king look-alike glanced at my companions, but his worried expression landed on me.

"I know something changed for you the day you started working at the castle with me, but running away like that was foolish. If something bothered you, why didn't you come to me?"

"I tried to," I said, "but you disbelieve in Somnus. You have forgotten it, or—as Mica believes—I have replaced your Merle. I am the one who does not belong."

"How could you say that?" he asked, tears re-forming.

Because it was the truth. If only he would believe me. Instead, he would forbid me from any excursions ever again. I needed to obey and earn his trust again.

Bowing my head, I said, "I will return home. All I ask is that you do not punish Mica or Mr. Knightly. They are kind, understanding, and good men, undeserving of your anger."

Father scowled at my companions. "I'll be the judge of that."

"Please, Father." I waited until his attention was back on me before continuing. "I am fifteen now. I wish not to go against your wishes, but I will if you restrain Mica from me. He is my best friend. Please. Just stay for lunch with us before taking me home."

"Please," Mica added. "Order whatever you want. I'll pay."

Father grumbled and crossed his arms for most of the meal, but I had hope that by the time we took the bus home, Father would not hate Honorable Wright. Mica was the kind of man who had never met a stranger—he made friends with everyone.

Father's glowering eventually softened as we sat and ate. Mica bowed with a kiss to my hand as we said goodbye.

"Will you visit?" I asked.

"Of course," he said. "So long as our parents permit. You called me your best friend, right? What kind of friend would I be if I left you all alone in this mad world?"

I smiled back, enjoying the warmth in my core. It was far more pleasant than the constant queasiness that flared with every meal.

Before I could worry that I may never see Mica again, I spotted him the next day at the castle while dusting the armory. He was back with his camera, snapping photos while my employer gave him a tour. He flashed me a wink before following the tour into the next room.

Every day, I hoped to find Mica around the corner. I fondly recalled our conversations, and I thought of new things to ask him. The list grew when Father gave me my own smartphone, equipped with GPS locating for him to always know where I was.

Whether he meant to or not, Father gave me a better way to contact Mica. We shared messages daily, developing our friendship as days turned into weeks.

During this time, I also gained a friend in Hans. Without revealing specifics, I explained that I needed help with some technological things because I came from "far away." He showed me how to use my new phone to take pictures, communicate with messages, and research online. Thankfully, after my first experience in the pub, he also understood my questions if any of the pub food was alcoholic or spicy.

We found ourselves paired together for many tasks, particularly when performing cleaning services at the Knight's Village. We set up a system where he would take care of the bedrooms with the bunkbeds and double beds as long as I cleaned the wet rooms. I accepted the arrangement because I learned something new about the fascinating toilets and showers every time I worked around them. The only difficult part was sometimes the stench increased my constant nausea.

We were preparing one of the larger lodges with an upstairs double bed when a friendly voice greeted me from the wooden doorway.

"Have you seen Lucy lately?"

I jumped around and nearly dropped my sanitation spray bottle.

"Mica!" I ran and threw my arms around his shoulders. I had only ever embraced my sisters and fellow princesses before coming to this world, but I found a growing fondness for the gesture—especially when Mica chuckled in my ear and held me with strong yet gentle arms.

"Lucy," I said, referring to my magical ball of light, "prefers to perform without spectators. My friend and fellow employee, Hans, is upstairs." Indeed, in my privacy, I asked Lucy multiple questions to learn more about her, but I found her written responses limited to "Truth is light" and "Find truth."

Despite her lack of information, she could accurately perform any task I asked of her, whether it was to appear from nowhere, grow larger, multiply herself, or even change colors.

To Mica, I said, "My shift ends in a couple of hours. Will you be around then? Lucy shines brightest after the sun goes down."

Mica smiled. "Sure. My parents enjoyed my photos so much they decided to visit. They're checking in tonight, but I asked to come a little early."

"How wonderful! How long will you be staying?"

"Two days," a deep voice said as Knightly entered the lodge. I greeted him with a smile, which he acknowledged with a straight face.

Two days was normal for most visitors, but it felt too short for Mica.

"Who's this?" Hans asked, coming down the stairs.

"Hans," I said, gesturing to Mica, "please meet my dear friends, Honorable Wright and his valet, Mr. Knightly."

Hans' pierced eyebrow went high. "Blimey, these are the guys who abducted you?"

Goodness, burn that gossip. Knightly coughed into his clenched fist. I had done my best to explain what had happened, but Hans seemed only half convinced of their innocence.

I continued to speak in Mica's favor after bidding him a temporary farewell and moving to the next lodge for cleaning. Once it was prepared for its next guests, we took the grounds cart back to the castle office to complete our work shift.

Thinking of Mica and the way he made me feel, I wondered what the normal protocol was for beginning a courtship in this dream world.

"Hans," I asked as he drove the cart, "what do you do when you like someone?"

Hans blinked at me with wide eyes. "Like, *like* like?"

"Please, forgive me for misunderstanding what you mean when you say the same word three times."

"When you say you 'like someone,' do you mean you like him like a friend, or you like him, like, you wanna kiss him?"

"That was a lot of 'likes.'"

Hans laughed. "You didn't answer my question, but based on your blush, I think it means you *like* like him."

Still slightly confused by his phrasings, I clarified, "I enjoy his presence. He understands me better than anyone else, and he treats me…like a princess."

Hans gave me a doubtful pout. "Blimey, you like that lovey-dovey stuff? Does your pa know?"

I blushed. "Love" was a bit extreme, but I clamped my mouth shut on my confession. No, Father did not know, and I dared not to tell him. I wished to tell my sisters, but Hans would do. "No one knows. What if my affections are unwanted?"

"Bird, there's only two reasons a bloke would friend-zone you, you ready? One, they ain't interested in girls, because that's seriously the only reason any-one wouldn't be bonkers about you."

Blushing, I asked, "And two?"

"Two, he also thinks he's in the friend-zone, and is in the same rut because he doesn't wanna jeopardize your friendship by asking for more."

"You say he might think the same about me? How would I know? How do we get out of the 'friend-zone' then?"

"Kiss him."

My slight blush flared into a full burn.

"Blimey, why do you look gobsmacked?"

"I have never kissed anyone before."

"Say again? You're fifteen and you never kissed nobody?"

My eyebrows puckered as I sorted out his double-negatives. "I have never kissed...anybody."

"Poor bird, say no more. I'll teach you everything."

298

"Everything?" I asked, curious and terrified at the same time.

"Sure thing. There's only three things you need to know about kissing. I learned this from another bird, so it should be easy enough. You ready?"

"Uh-huh?"

He raised a finger: "Peaches." Finger two: "Pears." Finger three: "Plums."

Fruit? "I do not understand."

"I'm gonna say 'em again. Watch my mouth, bird, you ready? Peaches," he said, pursing his lips. "Pears," he said with an exaggerated open mouth. "And plums," he finished, sticking his tongue out for an emphasized "L."

I felt a part of my innocence shatter. "I may never look at fruit the same way again."

He laughed. "Just wait until you get some watermelons and alfa-alfa."

"Ew!" I covered my eyes as if to block the mental image.

"Look, just a peach should be enough to tell him you're interested, but make sure it's on the mouth. Cheek peaches don't mean nothing, especially in France or Italy. Better yet, turn it into a prune by holding it longer than a second. That'll show him you're serious."

"Prune?" I asked, testing the movement of my mouth. "Just how many types of fruit—I mean kisses are there?"

"I'll let you figure out the rest. That's half the fun."

I cringed and covered my eyes again. Thankfully, we had reached the main castle for our conversation to be diverted by parking and clocking out.

Hans waved me closer before we left the small office. "You wanna practice on me?"

"Practice what?"

"Peaches, pears, and plums."

I blinked, utterly confused. "You want me to practice kissing…on you?"

"Yeah." He smiled bashfully. "I kinda *like* like you, bird."

He started to move closer and close his eyes.

"Hans!" I backed away, embarrassed and confused. "I was asking about Honorable Wright."

He frowned at me. "That balding prat? I thought it was all hypothetical to tell me how you felt. You're always so nice to me."

I shook my head. "I do not think of you that way. Forgive me if I misled you, as you are one of my dearest friends."

"Friends," he spat. "I see it in your eyes. You think I'm a nutter. Go on and tell Lord Wright how you feel. Then you can know how it feels to be pied off."

300

He spun on his heel and marched away before I could say more.

What just happened?

Father was still working, leaving me to wonder and wander around the castle and grounds. I sorted through the events and Hans' slang, but found myself at a loss for understanding and a loss of friendship. He felt for me the way I felt for Mica. Rejecting him had burned our friendship. Would the same happen if I confessed my feelings to Mica?

My wandering took me back to the Knight's Village. I arrived as the sun began to lower and the automatic lights switched on. One of the lanterns next to the door of Mica's lodge was burnt out.

Stepping up to it, I asked, "Lucy, can you duplicate yourself and sit in the lantern for the night?"

A tiny ball of light appeared in the fire-less lantern. "Is that Lucy?"

For the second time that day, I jumped to find Mica standing behind me.

"Sorry," I said. "I was just lighting a lantern for your lodge. It gets rather dark out here after sunset, so I wanted to be sure you could find your way."

He stepped closer until the glow lightened his soft smile.

"Thank you," he said. "It's very kind of you. And Lucy. It's nice to think of someone leaving a light on for me to find my way home."

He grinned and suddenly I felt like I was on my way home too. He was so sweet, so dear to me. I felt like I had known Mica all my life.

"Come on," he said, reaching for my hand. "I found the perfect spot to teach you a bit more about photography, but we need to hurry."

I took his hand, my nerves easing within his soft touch. If I held his hand a bit longer than necessary, would that be enough to express my feelings? Maybe in Somnus, but this world seemed more complicated.

Mica directed me southward to the grassy field used for extra parking when the castle had large events. He walked me over to the river's bank of trees and bushes, putting the greatest distance between us, the trees to the west, and a glorious sunset filtering through the clouds.

"Oh good," he said. "We made it in time." He snapped a couple photos, then showed them to me as we stood shoulder to shoulder, bending our heads close to the small viewing screen.

Hans' words about fruit rushed through my mind, rushing blood to my cheeks.

Clearing my throat and thoughts, I gestured to Mica's camera and asked, "May I try?"

"Sure."

He raised the camera strap over my head and measured its balance and equilibrium. Gently, he scooped my hair from under the strap to let it rest against my neck. I failed to ignore the tenderness of his touch.

I pointed the camera at him and was greeted with an up-close view of his teeth.

"Why, hello there."

Mica laughed. I was half tempted to snap a photo to capture his smile forever. "You're zoomed in. You're supposed to point it towards the sunset."

"What if I want a picture of you?"

"Point it at the sun, or I'll take it back."

I guarded the camera away from him. "Why can I not take a picture of you?"

"I actually don't mind pictures of me—really, I don't," he said to my pouting look. "I just prefer to be behind the camera. Every time I look through the lens, I'm reminded to look at life through the lenses of a camera."

"Please explain. You mean to hide?" I asked. "You like to see everything without being seen?"

He shrugged. "Yeah, I guess that too. But I meant it metaphorically. There's a saying—I'm probably going to slaughter it—but it goes something like, 'Live through the lenses of a camera; focus on what's important, capture the good times, develop from the negative, and if it doesn't work out, take another shot.'"

"Why, Mica, that was almost poetic."

He chuckled. "My friend, Caden, said stuff like that all the time. Maybe he rubbed off on me."

"Remind me, how do I take a picture?"

"You press the button on the top."

"Which button?" There were at least four on top, not including the buttons on the front and lens.

Mica's right hand cupped around mine. "Right here, between the nob." His left arm wrapped around my shoulders for his left hand to reach mine beneath the camera.

His warm arms cradled me, held me—practically embraced me!

"You got it," he whispered near my ear. "Now, capture the moment."

I closed my eyes and made a mental capture of his embrace.

"Pearl?" he whispered.

"Yes?"

"Do you, er…" His voice drifted as his heartbeat throbbed harder behind me.

"Yes, Mica?" Dear goodness, was this my moment? Hans suggested a prune, but even the thought of a peck on the cheek intimidated the life out of me.

What was the difference between a peach and a prune again?

Meanwhile, Mica fumbled over his words.

"Would you, er, ever consider some, er…" His heart hammered, and he let out a little huff. "Actually, do you need help finding the button again?"

"Oh." I blinked back to the camera in my hands. "No, I think I have it." To prove my words, I snapped a photo of the sun over the trees. Mica's arms lowered, and he stepped back. I took a couple more with different angles.

Removing the strap from around my neck, I handed the camera back to my friend. He looked somehow defeated. I mirrored the feeling as my nerves got the best of me. We chatted idly as we walked back to his lodge. Lucy shone brightly for us in the broken lantern like a little star.

Before I could say any more than "Goodbye," my phone rang. It was Father, asking where I was.

"On my way," I said. Covering the speaking part, I asked Mica, "Will I see you tomorrow?"

He shrugged but gave me a pointed look. "If you come visit. I'll be here."

I grinned while waving goodbye, then skipped to Father at the castle's main tower.

That night, I dreamed of Somnus as usual…but I also dreamed of Mica. My memories flashed and his face slipped into them. He was there, like a fish out of water, sitting beside me during tutoring, complaining about reading, splashing with my sisters in the lake, teasing me at our midnight dances.

My younger sister's voice whispered like a narration to my thoughts. "He was with you all your life…like a friend. Only a friend. He is closer to you than a casual friend—as close to you as one of your sisters. He is like a brother to you. Do you really want to ruin that bond with your silly infatuation?"

Terror clenched my heart. No. I could not tell Mica of my feelings. It would ruin our friendship. I needed his listening ear and relieving jokes. I was determined not to lose him.

Chapter 25

PEARL

I spent most of the day with Mica while he stayed at the castle. I met his parents, who were positively lovely, and Knightly shadowed us everywhere we went. But it was Mica who made the day delightful. He asked me to guide his parents through the castle tour, though he added enough comments from his previous experiences to make the highlights two times longer. Thankfully, we made it in time for the birds of prey show and the trebuchet launch. Mica took just as many pictures as usual, but more frequently shared them with me, telling me why each picture was better than the first.

Mica's parents knew little of our excursion to Tintagel, but their influence and presence encouraged Father to forgive Mica. At least enough to let me join the Wrights for dinner and to linger around the castle with them after Father went home from work. Mica and I went to the field to photograph the sunset again, inspired by the fresh beauty of another wonderful day. We found a place to sit on the grass with Knightly leaning against a tree, close enough to watch but far enough to give us privacy.

I sat back on my elbows, wishing the ever-persistent clouds would move and reveal the star lights. I asked Lucy to appear, multiply, and arrange herself above me into the patterns of the Somnus sky. That began a fascinating discussion of myths and fantasies as Mica and I shared stories about our constellations.

"The Huiessians," I said, "believe that when we die, the light of our souls joins the stars. Instead of the goddesses, they believe in the unknown gods of the stars. They pray to the starlights, asking for guidance. I wonder if there is truth to that. My brother-in-law, Admiral of the Somnus Navy, says he sails by the guiding light of the stars."

Mica tilted his head at me. "It always amazes me how similar yet different our worlds are. We have the technology to know what stars are, but we also use them to navigate our way home."

"Yes," I said, "pieces are the same. Is it because some things hold true no matter where you are? Lucy said light is truth, but there are pieces of truth everywhere. How am I to know which piece is correct, or where to find the whole truth?"

Mica chortled. "An age-old question only theologists claim to answer."

I sat up to face him directly. "Even with all of your technology, your people still rely on faith for answers?"

He shrugged. "Fewer choose to rely on faith than others, but yeah, we can't prove everything."

"How fascinating," I said, staring back at Lucy's stars. "Then the unknown is a universal truth."

Mica chuckled. "That's a boggling thought. Oh, Pearl, what did I ever do before I met you?"

I frowned, suddenly curious.

"Mica, how long have we been friends?"

He leaned back on his arms to stare at the cloudy sky. "Seems like forever. Why stop now, right?" He grinned at me, but I pouted.

"Truly. How long have we known each other?"

His grin wavered as he turned back to the sky in thought. "Oh, I don't know, I guess it's been…"

I held my breath. What would he say? Since we were children?

"About three weeks," he finished.

"Three weeks?" I asked. "Is that all?"

He grinned. "I know, it feels longer. I feel like I've known you all my life."

I gasped. Then what was true? "Have you?"

Mica smirked. "No. At least, I don't think so. Naw, I would have remembered someone like you. Unless you used to be blonde and wore color-changing contacts. Hmm, nope, even then. Pearl, you're one of a kind, and you're simply too perfect to forget."

He was too perfect and too kind. Of course, I had met the man of my dreams in my dreams, where I could do nothing to make him or my feelings real.

The clouds started to drizzle, encouraging us to stand and end the night. Mica walked me home with Knightly two steps behind, then bid me goodnight with a gracious bow over my hand.

As much as I desired to increase our friendship as Hans had suggested, my nerves and my sister's warning stopped me. I could not destroy this friendship as I had with Hans. It mattered too much to me. Mica mattered too much to me.

I discovered just how much he mattered when I woke up the next morning.

"Today is going to be a great day," I mumbled to myself, despite the aches in my stomach.

Memories of the night before filled me with happiness until I realized today was their checkout day. Mica and his family had left the castle.

Was today going to be a great day? My best days happened with Mica. Could I have great days without him? When would I see him again? Would I ever?

Father and I had the day off from work, leaving me with no plans, nothing to look forward to…

My digestive system eventually complained enough to force me out of my bed. First, I puked. Then I groaned, curled in a fetal position until it hurt to stand.

Today was turning out to be an awful day. I returned to bed, hoping to start it over.

"Do you want to go out for lunch?" Father asked after I denied breakfast. I was tired of apples. I was tired of feeling sick to my stomach. I was just… so…tired.

"Come on," Father said, sitting on the edge of my bed. "You can't stay in bed forever."

I could beg to differ. If I dreamt for an entire month already, what was a few more? Or a year? Or a hundred?

"Merle," Father urged. "Did he hurt you?"

"No," I mumbled. "I only miss him."

"Oh." He sounded disappointed. He hoped Mica had hurt me? Perhaps that would give him a legitimate reason to punish Mica.

I rotated my back towards Father and grabbed the nearest book on my nightstand. He sighed and left me alone. Only then did I start to actually read the words. It was a story about a girl falling in love for the first time. Did it always hurt this much? If so, why did we keep doing this to ourselves?

Time slipped away as I read. By the early evening, my stomach grumbled. With hunger this time.

Groaning, I sat up. I smelled like pond water, and my head spun from standing. Using the wall for support, I shuffled to the kitchen. A plate of chicken and salad sat on the table, but Father was nowhere to be seen. It was placed on a tray, as if he had meant to bring it to me in bed. I sat down and stirred the salad before stabbing a clump with my fork.

I had very little desire to eat anything that tasted like apples. My stomach grumbled, and I relented. Bite after bite, I tasted apples, apples, and more wretched apples.

I ate for the sake of eating. The joy of savoring and exploring favorite flavors was lost. After force-feeding myself until the plate was emptied, I took the dishes to the sink. My phone sang to me as I started shuffling back to my room.

"Hello?"

"Pearl?"

My heart lit within me as if struck by lightning. "Mica?"

"Yeah. Where are you? My parents went back to London, but I stayed an extra day. Did you have the day off?"

"Yes," I said, clutching my phone to my face, unwilling to miss a single word. I glanced over my sleeping attire, suddenly embarrassed. I needed to change clothes and wash up. "Can I meet you at the parking field in a half hour?"

"Sure thing. See you soon."

I hung up and dashed back to my room, ignoring the splitting headache and dizziness. It was probably from the quick movements after lying in bed all morning and afternoon. I stripped from my sleeping gown to quickly rinse my body, then slipped into the dress given to me by Mica and shoved on some shoes. The headache increased and my neck grew sore, but I was out the door in record time. My head spun, threatening my balance, but I kept going, leaning against the street wall for aid.

The sun was fully set by the time I reached the parking field. Mica stood near the center, with Mr. Knightly leaning against his usual tree.

My knees wobbled at the sight of Mica's grin. Or maybe it was a partner in crime with the headache. Either way, I found my balance in Mica's arms.

"I thought I would never see you again," I said, nearly weeping.

He chuckled softly in my ear. "What a silly thing to say. I see you every night in my dreams."

I returned his laugh. "Every day is a dream to me, but you make it bright."

"Pearl, are you alright? If you keep sagging like that, you'll pull us both to the ground."

Oops. Where was my strength to stand?

My phone jingled again. Fumbling for it, I found Father calling me.

"Father?"

"Merle, where are you?"

"At the castle." Habits wanted to add that I was with Mica, but instincts told me to leave out that information unless Father asked for it.

"Oh? I'm glad you made it out of your room. Did you want to go out for supper?"

"No, thank you. I ate the supper you left for me."

"The…supper? Blast, did you eat that chicken?"

"Yes?" I said, wondering why he seemed upset. It had not smelled alcoholic or spicy.

"Didn't it taste funny to you?"

I sighed impatiently, my best impersonation of Tanzi yet.

"Merle, I meant to throw away that chicken and salad. I got it out for lunch, but you said you weren't hungry."

"Oh." I cringed, suddenly anxious about what sickness would strike me for eating the meal. As if my stomach could handle one more issue. Despite Mica's arms around me, my body shivered and my face began to sweat. I started towards the castle, but the

314

movement pulsed through my brain, causing me to teeter sideways. I sank to the ground and vomited.

"Pearl!"

"Who was that?" Father asked in response to Mica's shout.

My head and stomach felt slightly better with the release, but I remained on the cool ground, yearning to rest and balance my overheating face.

"Blast," Father cursed. "You probably have food poisoning. Come home, right this instant."

Food poisoning? Father spoke of the chicken and salad, but my mind went to a poisoned apple. Yes, the stomach aches and nausea I experienced ever since starting this dream…it was food poisoning. Which meant this new addition only made it worse.

Chapter 26

EMER

Emer's heart raced as Gother and a dozen ogres glared hatred at her.

"Run?" she asked.

"Where?" Mica asked back, standing at the edge of the Midnight Forest, holding his torch and one end of Emer's vine phone. He was right. They could run into the forest, but quickly become lost. Also, the ogres could smell them and hunt them in the dark. They'd have to fight and defend blindly.

Caden grumbled. "This was why we needed to hurry."

Before anyone could argue, one of the ogres bellowed and charged down the hill at them, raising his massive blade.

Leo shouted, "For Braeder!" and released an arrow before grabbing his broadsword. Shinópu and Ranae quickly followed, bearing their swords.

"Ranae!" Marin cried.

"Stay back!" he shouted in return.

Emer felt her sister's fear when Caden unsheathed his sword and put himself between her and the oncoming ogres. She had to help.

"Wild grass," she called, "wrap your strands around the ogres' ankles even as they try to trample you! Hold them in place!"

One, then two ogres tripped as the wild grass obeyed Emer's command. Leo and Ranae fought two ogres each while Shinópu was caught in a blurring duel with Gother. One more ogre became wrapped in Emer's grass while Leo struck down another. Four ogres still slipped through, charging at Emer, Marin, Jesse, Thachuma, Mica, and Caden. Only Caden and Mica had swords. Thachuma and Jesse wielded cast iron pans while Emer and Marin wielded nothing but…

Emer hissed at her sister, "Use your magic!"

"How?" she panicked.

Watch and learn, elder sister. "Blades of grass, stiffen your spines and stand as needles between us and the ogres! Do not let them reach us!"

The grass in front of them stood stiff and strong, pointing their tips to half a meter high. Three of the four ogres paused. Ranae finished off a second ogre and came running at the hesitating three. Shinópu and Gother continued to fight at impossible speeds while

Leo checked on the incapacitated ogres to make sure they stayed that way. The fourth and largest ogre jumped right over the needle-like blades of grass.

Marin screamed and stumbled in her hurry to back away. The ogre landed within arm's length, shaking the ground with its mass. It snarled at them with gaping holes between its yellow teeth, eyes black as the dream where Emer had endlessly fallen toward needles. It stood twice as tall as Caden and carried a massive cleaver, appropriate for its size.

Emer managed to keep her feet beneath her when the ogre's landing shook the ground, but Marin was down on her backside, engulfed by its shadow. It raised its giant knife.

"Save me!" Marin screamed.

Caden and Mica rushed forward, but wobbled. The ground rumbled as they moved closer to the ogre.

The ogre swung his cleaver down, right over Marin's head. She screamed again, and Emer turned away. She winced with the sound of a sickening crack.

"What the devils?" Caden swore.

Emer turned back, terrified of what she might see, but needing to know. The ogre's knife hovered a meter above the ground, right above Marin's face. It was stuck in a thick layer of ice that formed around Marin.

Mica and Caden swung their longswords that had seemed much larger until compared to the ogre's massive cleaver. They both scored hits, but only Caden's drew a thin line of blood into the ogre's side. They were like papercuts to its thick skin.

The ogre kicked Mica away like he was no more than an abused pup who deserved better parenting. Caden thrust his sword at the ogre, but fumbled as the ogre blocked. The ogre grabbed Caden by the arm, then lifted him from the ground, shaking him like a rattle until he dropped his sword.

A frying pan flipped through the air, but landed short before hitting the ogre.

"I'm sorry," Jesse shouted. "I was aiming for its face!"

"You missed," the great ogre chuckled, a hideous grin spreading its already wide mouth.

"And you are stuck," Emer said, grinning back. As soon as she'd turned back to see Marin safe from harm and the giant knife stuck in the ice, she had an idea. She whispered to the long wildgrass, asking it to wrap around the ogre's feet and legs. One foot came free for a moment when it kicked Mica, but became trapped again when it stood still to shake Caden.

"I see a light!" Mica shouted, pointing into the forest.

"A light?" Emer asked. She mimicked Mica's movements, trying to spot the hope in the darkness. "Where?"

Mica ran forward, trailing behind one end of the phone vine. "It's far away, but it's right there."

Marin scrambled from her ice cave to join Emer out of the ogre's reach. Jesse and Thachuma had taken cover on the far side of the carriage, either hiding or looking for more pans. No one else confirmed the light in the forest.

Caden grabbed a small dagger from his belt and punched it into the ogre's arm that held him. The ogre shouted and released him instinctually.

Caden picked up a part of the vine. "Take the lead, Mica!"

Mica jogged into the darkness, tugging Caden along. The ogre roared and bent over to rip at the wildgrass holding him. Emer and Marin grabbed onto the vine's end to follow. Right before Caden was swallowed into the darkness, he looked back at Emer.

"Stay close," he said. "I don't want to lose you in here."

Emer's cheeks warmed at his intense stare and sentiment.

A few more steps, and Emer had lost sight of Caden's silhouette. The darkness enveloped them until she no longer saw her own hand holding the vine. There was no clear pathway, and walking directly straight through the forest had them tripping over ferns and bushes.

Emer stumbled a second time over a bush and almost lost her hold on the vine. She huffed. "Hold on, Mica. Forests are not grown for straight paths." She raised her voice. "Flourishing plants of the Midnight Forest," she said. "Please, pull away from before our path. We do not wish to harm you or trample you. Pull away from before Mica's feet and bloom all the more fully in the surrounding areas."

The darkness became alive with sound. Leaves rustled and trees creaked. The sound was more than slightly unsettling in the darkness.

"Emer?" Marin asked nervously. "How can we know they will follow your command?"

Mica spoke from somewhere up ahead. "It actually worked. There are still trees ahead, but it feels like walking on a path."

"Perfect," Emer said as she noticed the change beneath her feet too. "The ground is still uneven—nothing I can do about that—but our pathway should be clear now."

An angry ogre roar reached their ears, closer than expected.

"He escaped," Emer said, vocalizing her lesser worry. Worst yet, he was following them into the forest.

"Run, Mica!" Caden hissed.

They dashed forward as the forest darkness became tangible, cold, and moist. Even without the foliage in the way, they stumbled and nearly tripped in the dark.

"Not so fast," Marin puffed behind.

"Hold on to each other," Caden said.

Emer felt his hand reaching for her, and she gladly took it. She slid her other hand down the vine until it touched Marin's. Emer only hoped Caden and Mica made a connection as they scurried farther into the forest, stealing her sight of the end of their chain.

They jogged in silence, only the sound of their hurried footsteps to confirm their presence. As much as Emer wanted to call ahead to Mica, fear clenched her heart at the thought. What if the ogre heard them? Who else could be hiding in the darkness, waiting to catch them?

After several more seconds of huffing away, Emer dared to hope that they lost the ogre.

Caden muttered somewhere ahead of her, "Thanks for clearing the path, but you shouldn't have come."

She scoffed, "You will not leave me behind again, Caden."

At the same time, Marin said, "Our sister is in here. She needs familiar faces when she wakes to this polluted version of Somnus."

Emer caught a hint of disappointment and relief in her voice. Relief to escape the battle? Disappointment that she was unable to help more?

Instead, Emer asked, "What about Ranae, Leo, and the others?"

Marin chuckled nervously. "He knows better than to die on me now. He has a promise to keep."

"I'm worried about Shinópu," Caden said. "If he can't beat Gother, we're all in trouble, but at least Gother won't be able to find us in this forest. Unlike the ogre that might be chasing us. They're safer out there than we are in here."

Marin huffed, "Where exactly are we going?"

"To the light in the middle of the forest," Mica said.

Caden grunted. "We're supposing it's Princess Pearl and not some trap."

"It's not a trap," Mica said, quiet but determined.

Emer swallowed, wishing she had an ounce of his faith. Instead, she walked onward through the darkness, struggling to keep pace with the men's brisk jog over the uneven terrain.

"Pearl," she muttered aloud. "Where are you?"

Chapter 27

PEARL

The dirt of the Warwick Castle parking field was less than comfortable, but I was too drained to move. I closed my eyes, my phone slipping from my hand. The voice of my father kept calling my name. Between the blurriness of my mind, I could pretend he was the King of Somnus, calling me by my princess name.

"Pearl, what's happening?" Mica shouted, kneeling beside me. "Miles! Call for a doctor! Run for anyone or anything to help!"

Miles' heavy footsteps ran away, and Mica slid his legs under my back to cradle my head in his arms.

My neck was stiff, and I needed to think through my day until I remembered why I laid on the ground.

"Pearl, what's wrong?"

"Food poisoning," I managed to say before the convulsions started. My face found the dirt again, and I gagged on digested apples.

Mica was at my side again, rubbing my back even as my body shook from the tension. "Pearl, are you sure it's food poisoning? This seems more serious. We should get you to a hospital."

"It is no use," a woman's voice said.

My eyes snapped open and found my eldest sister, Garnet, standing in the dark. Mica's head jerked to the side as he also noticed her there.

"Who are you?" he asked.

"Garnet," I rasped. I cared little about how she came to see me or why. All that mattered to me were the tears streaming down her face.

"Forgive me," she cried. "I meant none of this to happen. You were poisoned before this dream started, and now your body succumbs to it despite all my efforts. Please, forgive me. I could not save you."

"There is no blame," I said, hoping to ease her tears. It was no use. She continued to cry and step back, fading into the shadows of the night.

"No, please!" I called to my sister. "Do not leave me!"

Mica held me tighter, cradling me in his lap and arms. "She is gone. Who was she?"

My body hurt too much to answer. I had no answers to explain Garnet's sudden appearance and disappearance. Instead of dwelling on confusion, I thought of Mica's arms around me. "Please, do not leave me too."

He took my hand and pulled me into a sitting position beside him, letting me lean heavily across his chest.

The clouds drifted like a miracle, opening a window to the light of the stars beyond. My eyes widened at their beauty. Their arrangements were different from those I knew. I remembered Mica talking about them the day before. Had it truly only been yesterday when we lay in this spot, talking pleasantly about stars and faith?

"Mica, what will happen to me if my body dies in Somnus? Will this dream end? I do not wish to leave you."

"You won't leave me," he said, "and I won't leave you. I'm right here."

His words blurred through my mind. Had he truly said them, or had I simply imagined them?

"The stars," I gasped. "They burn so brightly. Are they…could they be…Do you think someone left the light on for me to find my way home?"

Mica's gaze turned upward to the stars. "Maybe. Sailors say the stars lead us home. I've always thought they talked about using the North Star for navigation. But maybe you're right. The stars lead us home…to the heavens. Pearl, if anyone deserves Heaven, it's

326

you." His words caught on a sob. With a throat-clearing cough, he continued, but his voice remained scratchy. "They say it's peaceful. That you won't feel pain. Pearl, I don't want you to leave me, but I don't want you to hurt anymore. Please," he sobbed, "I need you to be happy, even if it's not with me."

"I am happy. Especially with you. You make me happy, Mica. I like you."

"I like you too, Pearl."

I groaned and tried the phrase from Hans. "I mean to say that I *like* like you. I like you more than as a friend or a brother." He went still, but I had to keep speaking while I had the courage and strength. "I was too scared to tell you. I feared my emotions would ruin our friendship if you felt differently. If this is the end, though, I cannot hide the truth any longer. I have feelings for you, Mica."

His eyes watered and his smile was sad. Goodness, he was going to break my heart. He was sad because he knew this would hurt me and he was a good man. My big mouth had ruined everything.

"I have feelings for you too, Pearl."

My quick intake of breath turned into an un-feminine cough as my fever flared. Mica stroked my hair back, shushing my worries with calming words. "Breathe. Let out the bad air, then take in deep breaths of good air. I'm here. I'm not leaving you."

He held me until my coughing subsided. This sickness made me ready to return home, and when I nestled back into Mica's arms, I felt peaceful enough to call it home. Anywhere was home, as long as it was the arms of this man who felt a mutual admiration for me.

"Pearl," he said, "you love the gratitude of others, right? Can I thank you for the adventure and hope you've given me? I have a gift for you that you can't give away, something for you and you alone."

His eyes dropped to my lips and I understood. A kiss. He wanted to give me a kiss—a gesture of more than friendship. Something for me, and me alone. Something I could not give away, but a gesture of gratitude and love for me to keep and cherish forever.

"Is it alright?" he asked, tipping my chin upward with the tip of his finger. "Will you accept my gift and not give it away this time?"

"Never before have I wanted to be so selfish."

Mica slowly lowered himself until his lips met mine. He gave me a peach that was almost long enough to call a prune. He tasted like apples.

Chapter 28

EMER

"Really," Mica asked in the darkness of the Midnight Forest, "none of you can see this? We're almost there."

"No," Caden grumbled, "and I'm growing impatient with that ques—tion!"

Caden's final syllable was accompanied by an ogre's roar that was far too close for comfort and the jolt of his hand being yanked from the vine.

"Caden!" Emer cried, looking about, but seeing the same blackness everywhere. She only heard Caden scuffle and the ogre grunt.

The vine in her hand pulled her forward as Mica increased his pace.

"Hold on, Mica," Emer called. "Caden lost the vine!"

"He—" Mica groaned. "But the light is right here! I'm standing in it! How can you not see it?"

"See what?" Marin shouted.

In two more steps, Emer saw what Mica saw. Blinking hard to adjust her eyes, she found herself in a bubble of daylight where the trees broke open, revealing a small glade with a cottage house, a vegetable garden, and a young dwarf filling a bucket at the crossing stream. As quickly as he spotted the newcomers in the glade, he brandished a large hunting knife.

Marin followed her into the glade and yelped at the sight.

"Who are you?" the dwarf demanded with a slurred Chafan accent.

Mica stammered. Emer made a quick decision about what scared her more: the approaching dwarf with the hunting knife or Caden's scuffle in the dark.

She turned back toward the darkness of the forest, saying, "Trees! Please, help Caden to escape from the ogre."

Leaves rustled and wood cracked as the plants moved. Emer watched the darkness for any sign of movement while Marin raised calming hands to the dwarf.

"Please," she said, "we mean you no harm. We are—"

Emer blocked out her sister's words as she listened more carefully for Caden's movements between the trees.

330

"Voices! This way—oh!" Caden stumbled into the light of the glade. Emer reached for him, half to help stabilize him and half to reassure herself that he was well. He had a severe cut down his left arm and a bleeding nose. The skin around his right eye was red, turning into a massive bruise.

Any other examinations had to wait as the ogre crashed into the light.

Caden had barely managed to grab his dagger again before the ogre caught him by the shoulder, lifting him as if to break his arm. Before his feet left the ground entirely, Caden jumped, pushing both of them back into the darkness.

Emer's shout for him was drowned by an ogre's great howl.

Then all was silent.

"Caden!" Emer called again.

In the darkness, she heard a sigh, then a small chuckle. "Keep talking," he said. "I can follow your voice back to the light."

"Sure," Emer said, relieved that he still lived. "Though you should be the one to keep talking, since we both know I am safer in the light than you are."

"Now you know how I felt when you went onto that misty dock by yourself. I'm half tempted to stand here a moment longer just to make you sweat."

"Caden!" Emer complained, and he stepped forward into the light. Ogre blood splattered his face. With that danger resolved, Emer pivoted back to the strange dwarf. Marin was speaking with him, trying to convince him that they were friendly and equally confused about what was happening.

The dwarf crouched in a defensive position that could quickly turn deadly. He stared at each of them with suspicious and dangerous eyes. "Tell me why I should not kill you."

Still holding his dagger, Caden raised his blood-covered hands. "Er, we come in peace."

With a second thought, he wiped his hands and dagger on his trousers, spreading the blood more than cleaning himself from it. Sheathing his weapon, he raised his hands again and smiled innocently.

The dwarf's dangerous expression remained.

"Is Princess Pearl here?" Mica asked. The young dwarf's guarded eyes grew wide. Mica gestured back to Emer and Marin. "Her sisters, Princesses Aquamarine and Emerald, want to see her."

The dwarf dropped his mouth and knife, then followed the knife to the ground as he bowed with his knees, elbows, and palms to the dirt.

"The day has come," he whispered. "I, Hanzo Horichaha, swore an oath on my honor to protect the princess until her sisters came to wake her." He raised his face slightly to ask, "That is why you came, right?"

"It is." Emer stepped forward and bid the young dwarf to rise. "How long have you been protecting our sister?"

Hanzo brushed himself off, subconsciously bringing attention to the fact that he wore trousers, leathers, and furs like a hunter. "One hundred summers ago, Princess Pearl and her eldest sister came here for sanctuary. The families of my father and mother, my grandparents and great-grandparents, have watched over her since she fell asleep. I was born in this glade of light, where the darkness surrounds but never enters. Just as my parents were born here and their parents before them."

Caden hastily scrambled for his writing tools and recorded his words.

Marin stepped forward, concerned. "Have you never ventured beyond the glade?"

Hanzo snorted like a brute. "Leave? How? No one leaves but by death. No one comes but by birth. There was an awful sickness carried in by a rodent who made it into the glade. It killed many and convinced my uncles and their families to leave. I do not know if they survived. I am the last to remain, and you are the first to arrive. How did you come through the darkness?"

"I saw the light of the glade," Mica said. "Where is the princess?"

"Over here." Hanzo dashed behind the cottage, leaving Emer and the others to chase after him. Rounding the cottage, they found a brightly shining platform.

Pearl lay on top in a glass coffin. Emer, Caden, and Mica all stopped short, though for different reasons. While Emer was surprised and joyous to find her younger sister, Mica whispered, "she's beautiful," and Caden blurted, "That's bizarre."

Mica back-handed Caden on the arm. "Respect?"

"She's sleeping in a coffin. *Who* makes a *clear coffin?*"

Hanzo replied, "We could not bury her. She does not look dead, only sleeping. And she does not age. We wanted to preserve and protect her, but she is too beautiful to put in a box."

"I'll agree with that," Mica said. He stepped toward the younger princess, mesmerized.

"Er, Mica?" Caden asked. "You alright?"

Mica took another heavy step without removing his eyes from the sleeping princess. "Have you ever seen…anyone…so beautiful?"

Caden glanced at Emer. "Yes?"

"What?" Emer blinked.

Marin likewise leaned forward to give Caden a wide-eyed stare of wonder. "I thought you said you had researched our family? Then you would know Pearl was declared the most beautiful among all the princesses of Rezhina."

Caden shrugged. *Shrugged.* Emer gaped. "Sure, she's pretty, but she's not—" He made vague gestures, some pointing at Emer, floundering with his words.

"Are you not a wordsmith?" Marin asked.

"Yes, which means I know better than anyone that words are hard," he said, looking around for a distracting subject. He didn't need to look far. "Mica, what are you doing?"

Mica had found his way to Pearl's glass coffin and slid his hands over it as if giving her a bubbled hug. With a little heave, he pushed off the glass lid.

"Mica!"

"What are you doing?"

"Get away from her!" Hanzo shouted.

Like a moth to the flame, Mica was hypnotized by Pearl's light. He lowered his mouth to hers for a brief second before Hanzo plowed him to the side. He quickly wrestled the prince until the dwarf sat on top of him.

"You dishonorable man! You cannot disrespect my princess! I will kill you!" A flash of metal showed the dwarf's plans as he angled his knife at Mica's throat.

"Hanzo!" Emer shouted.

Hanzo paid her no heed, but he paused as something else caught his gaze. Emer's attention jerked as she noticed it too. The darkness surrounding the glade disappeared. The trees remained, but the "Midnight" of the Midnight Forest was gone.

"Where am I?" a small voice asked from the platform. Princess Pearl sat up, rubbing her eyes awake.

"Pearl!" Emer and Marin shouted while Hanzo yelped, "My princess!"

The hunter scrambled off Mica to prostrate himself before the young princess. Mica simply stared in awe.

Pearl's blinking eyes found her sisters, and her face lit up with a glorious smile.

"Marin! Emer! You are awake!"

Pearl reached for her sisters as if to leap from her coffin and embrace them. Emer and Marin knew from experience how exhausted her body would be after a hundred years of sleep, sending them rushing to her aid. They each took an arm for a three-person hug.

"Did Garnet find your cure?" Pearl asked, leaning back from their embrace to look around. "Where is she?"

"We hoped you could tell us," Marin said.

Pearl didn't hear, as her attention was stolen by Mica behind them. Emer thought her sister's smile couldn't get any brighter. She was wrong.

Pearl literally glowed with light when she spotted Mica.

"Whoa!" Marin stepped back, as if her glow could catch her on fire. Mica, on the other hand, grinned wider and came closer.

"Mica," Pearl whispered and stumbled in her eagerness to reach him. Mica dashed to her aid, catching her by the hand. "You came to Somnus with me?"

"I came to Somnus for you," he emphasized.

Caden stepped forward to bow humbly. "Princess Pearl, if we may introduce ourselves, my name is Caden Seavers, Prince of—"

"Caden!" Pearl grinned brightly, and Emer panicked.

How does she know him?

"You came to Somnus after all!" Pearl continued, touching his shoulder, bidding him to rise. "Just as Mica said! How I wish Mr. Knightly could see how well you are."

"Miles?" Caden asked, rubbing the back of his head. "How do you know Mica, Miles, and me? I have many British memories of them, but none with you."

"You and Emer were gone before I met Mica and Mr. Knightly. I mostly know of you through them." She squeezed Mica's hand and shared a tender smile. "It truly was more than a dream."

"Truly," Emer agreed. "I want to hear all about it, but first, what can you tell us about Garnet's fate?"

"Very little." Pearl's smile dampened slightly. "She was gone when Tanzi found me, though she must have come back to put me to sleep as she did to you two. She told me to wait here, in this little cottage with the Chafan refugees. She left to warn the Ormio princesses and planned to bring the twins back to me. Except Tanzi found me first—or, at least, I believe it was Tanzi. She appeared to me as an old hag and sold me an apple. I was so hungry for some sweet fruit. The kind dwarf families only ate meat and potatoes."

"So," Caden said, "you said the Ormio twins were coming here?"

Hoping to gain Caden's attention again, Emer asked, "Do we have time to search for the Ormio twins, Ruby and Dot? They may know if Garnet made it to Veriae, but the ogres have obviously lost their patience."

"Obviously," he agreed. "We should return to see if our warrior friends need our help."

Marin spun towards the front of the cottage. "Ranae!"

EMER

Emer heard hurried voices as she rounded the cottage with the others. Five figures stepped through the wild path she had created through the forest. She breathed with relief to recognize the figures as human.

Leo jogged, with Ranae limping behind. Shinópu leaned heavily on Thachuma and Jesse.

"There you are," Leo shouted. "You cowards, running away like that!"

Caden groaned. "We didn't run *from* the fight, we ran *to* Princess Pearl."

"Same direction," Leo grumbled. "You're lucky we managed to win. It took two of us to take down Gother."

"Thank the goddesses," Marin whispered and ran to her husband. "Forgive me for leaving. I just—"

"I wanted you nowhere near the fight," Ranae said, taking her into his arms. "I would have been distracted, worrying about you. Besides, you had your sister to save. Hello, Pearl."

Pearl curtsied to the group of warriors. "Thank you for fighting so bravely, even if I do not understand why. Regardless, it pleases me to see my sisters united with their friends. Please, tell me all that happened while I slept."

Caden, Mica, Emer, Marin, and Ranae sat with Pearl to review Tanzi's rise to power and the ogres terrorizing the north.

Meanwhile, Hanzo and Jesse worked together to help the wounded. Shinópu was the most injured but complained the least. He had cuts across his arms and a jabbed hole in his side. Jesse analyzed it and—much to Thachuma and Hanzo's relief—found it had missed the major organs. Still, she anticipated a couple of weeks before Shinópu could fight again. He nodded mutely as Jesse gave him strict instructions to help his healing process.

Of course, Caden took the lead in the history review for Pearl. Emer scolded her jealousy each time he piped up with enthusiasm.

He spoke just as eagerly to Marin after she woke, she reminded herself. Yet it bothered her, and then it bothered her that it bothered her.

While the princes discussed their situation with the ogres, Emer excused herself. She wandered into

340

the forest that now looked like any other. She found a hint of happiness at a fern that soaked in the newfound light.

Footsteps crunched the leaves behind her.

"Emer, you alright?" Caden asked.

"How is Pearl?" she asked, struggling to hold back the bitterness. She kept her face stoic and toward the fern.

"She seems fine," he said. "She's not the one I'm asking about."

Emer swallowed back her emotions. "What exactly did you mean when you said you have seen someone as beautiful as Pearl?"

Caden scrambled with frustration. "Look, I'm sorry if I offended you or your sisters. I really didn't mean it that way."

Emer bit the inside of her lip, and Caden slid a nervous hand through his hair.

"It's not like it's a secret. I think you're gorgeous."

"More than Pearl?" Emer prodded.

"Is there a ranked competition or something? Why does this surprise you?"

"I was never more of anything among my sisters."

Caden's frustrations slipped off his shoulders. He reached for her hands. "How could you even say that? You're more of everything to me. Why does it matter?"

"I am the middle child. Garnet is the best leader, the best judge between justice and mercy, and the best at making hard decisions. Marin is the best fisher, sailor, swimmer, and environmentalist. Pearl is the most beautiful, the most innocent and charming. Fortunately innocent, because she could murder someone and people would call it cute. Then Tanzi was the most open to new ideas. At least, everyone thought she was. She was always thinking of others and how to be more involved in their activities.

"Then there was me," she finished, "the middle child, who was average at everything."

Caden didn't say anything at first. Then, with a little shrug, he said, "You're first in my books. Before I even knew you, back when I was researching all of the sleeping princesses, I admired you the most. Garnet had too much responsibility as future queen, and I knew I couldn't help her shoulder all of that. I can barely shoulder my own kingdom. Even if Marin wasn't married, I'm not into all that water stuff. I prefer my feet solidly on the land. Pearl is pretty and naïve, sure, but…is there such a thing as too innocent? I don't think I could joke around with her like I can with you. Of course, Queen Tanzi scares the devils out of me, so she was only an option in comparison to Charlotte."

He smirked in an obvious attempt to lighten his nerves. "But I didn't pick you out of a process of elimination. I picked you first. Princess Emerald was more than beautiful to me. She captured my every waking thought. When you awoke, you were my every dream come true. You drive me crazy sometimes, I'll admit, but I can debate policies with you, and you open my mind to thoughts and concepts that enlighten and enchant me."

"Then why have you ignored me these past few days?" she asked.

"Ignored you?" He frowned. "I couldn't stop thinking about you. I could hardly get any research done—you were too distracting. You thought I was ignoring you?"

She shuffled. "It surely seemed that way."

"I found it hard to think of anything else. I mean, I partnered you with Shinópu because I couldn't focus on finding your sisters like I needed to for the sake of our kingdoms, but the last thing I wanted to do was push you away. Emer," he paused to cup her cheek in his palm. "Princess Emerald, I love you."

She breathed with sweet relief. "I love you too, Caden."

"Really?"

Emer sighed and grabbed him by the collar. "Stop questioning everything I say and kiss me."

His chuckle cut off as Emer pressed her lips to his.

He kissed her back, softly, tenderly. His touch was as gentle as a lamb, but Emer had enough of wool. One hand grabbed his tunic while her other slipped behind his neck, both hands pulling him closer. Caden's lips laughed against hers as he wrapped his arms around her, tightening their embrace.

"Oh!"

Emer and Caden broke apart to find Pearl and Mica standing nearby, holding hands. Pearl's cheeks were more rosy than usual.

Caden smiled at Emer. "See what I mean about you being distracting? I didn't even notice someone approaching us."

Emer bit back her own smile as her face increased in temperature. "Yes, Pearl?"

"First of all," her sister said, "when did you learn to make fruit pies?"

"What?"

"Sorry, inside joke," Pearl said, waving her hand and suppressing giggles. "One from my dream, which apparently, was more than a dream."

Mica gave Caden a knowing, teasing look.

"Oh, shove off, Mica," Caden said. To Mica's confused expression, Caden explained, "It's a phrase from England. Have fun sleeping tonight. I bet you'll be bombarded with memories that aren't your own that'll

344

only make you more amazed at the woman in your arms." He finished with a grin at Emer.

Mica laughed. "If you two lovebirds are done kissing in the trees, we wanted to discuss with everyone how we plan to find the other sleeping princesses."

"Come on," Emer said, tugging Caden back into the glade. "I can distract you another time."

* * * * *

TANZI

On Noz Isle, within a stone castle in the middle of a misty lake, Queen Tanzanite woke with a sudden jolt, sweating and panting for breath. She had never known a restful night ever since she became queen, but she could never remember the nightmares that plagued her.

Sapphire had predicted as much.

That beshrewed little Huiess princess had predicted many things—all of which had come true, including Tanzanite's rise to the throne. No matter. She was dead like all the others. Tanzanite didn't need Sapphire anymore.

It was another perfect day in her perfect world. Bad things happened every day, but not to Tanzanite. She took a bath with clematis flower scents and sipped on her favorite rum. After powdering her face and applying her dyed face paints, she picked up her brush and asked her looking glass for her usual daily affirmation. "Am I the most beautiful woman in all of Rezhina?"

"Nay, my queen."

Tanzanite's brush dropped. Every day for the past hundred harvests, the mirror had answered the same, "Yay, my queen. Thou art the most beautiful woman in all of Rezhina." She must have heard it wrong.

"What was that, Mirror?" she asked again.

"Nay, my queen. Princess Pearl Reo is the most beautiful woman in all of Rezhina."

The queen's hand trembled. Pearl? Her older sister?

With a near growl, Queen Tanzanite grabbed her mirror by its frame and demanded, "Show her to me."

The vision of the mirror swirled, then solidified on a picture of her dastardly perfect older sister, smiling and most definitely not dead. She looked as young and beautiful as the day Tanzanite had killed her. Pearl's perfectly punchable face turned side to side, showing off her natural beauty and undeserved happiness. Her mouth moved, speaking to someone beyond the mirror's image.

"Who is she talking to?" Tanzanite demanded. "Widen your vision!"

"Yay, my queen."

The mirror stepped back to view the irritating princess holding hands with a young man. He was so far beneath Pearl's beauty that Tanzanite actually laughed. Then the image widened more to reveal a few inconsequential strangers, plus Emerald and Aquamarine.

"No!" Tanzanite slammed her fist against the stone wall. Blood leaked from her knuckles, but she didn't feel the pain. She only felt hate.

Garnet's sleeping spell had worked? How? Putting the princesses to sleep shouldn't have stopped Tanzanite's poison. Either way, it didn't matter. They were awake, they were alive, and they were together. Three sisters. Three disasters.

At least Garnet wasn't there. Tanzanite smiled at that minor relief. All the same, she asked her mirror to confirm. Yes, Garnet slept like the dead.

At least the worst disaster was still contained. As for the others…

Queen Tanzanite whipped out a piece of parchment and a pen of snake venom ink. It was time to call in a favor. She had a job for her hunters.

End of Book Two

Acknowledgements

I'd like to thank the folklorists who collected, recorded, and distributed various tales on "The Frog Prince" and "Snow-drop." I enjoyed finding so many versions of "The Frog Prince." Many of these tales involved the princess sleeping with the frog (inspiring the marriage situation between Marin and Ranae) and/or collecting water with a sieve from the Well of the World's End. Only the most modern tales involve a kiss—in fact, one version has her chop off his head to turn him back into a prince! (Aren't you glad I didn't use that version?)

Julie Carpenter gets a megaphone shout out for going the extra mile by reading "Dreaming Beauty" before providing solid feedback on this book's developmental stage. Karie from CookieLynn Publishing helped again to put those pesky little commas in their rightful places.

Thank you, Robyn Cheatham for Alpha Reading and for being Mica's #1 fan. I'm sorry you're grossed out by the "fruits" concept, but I'm honestly confused that you've never heard me reference it before. Also, I'll give shout out thanks to Beta Readers Abby Smith, "my favorite fairytale genre lover" Bettilee Hunt, Colleen Dowda, Jenny Roemmich, and especially Jim Doran for leaving constructive feedback.

Lovers of the cover can look up Arcane Covers for more incredible artwork.

As always, I can't thank my husband enough. Michael, thank you for *not* giving me Marin and Ranae's argument, but for loving and supporting me in all my craziness.

Last, but not least, God deserves my thanks and more. As Pearl says, "The unknown is a universal truth," because "even with all of [our] technology, [we] still rely on faith for answers." I can't prove anything, but His inspiration and guidance make these books possible.

About the Author

C Rae D'Arc has been involved in every stage of a book's life. As a writer, editor, retailer, reader, and reviewer, she has worked four part-time jobs at once. Thankfully, one of them actually paid her. She received her Bachelors in English from Brigham Young University, where she studied British and American literature, folklore, Shakespeare, and West European fairy tales. She now lives in the Tri-Cities of Washington with her husband and Aussie dog.

PS. To save you from hiccups, D'Arc only has one syllable.

www.craedarc.com
www.facebook.com/c.rae.darc
www.instagram.com/craedarc

Fall in love with a
D'Arc Romantic Comedy